MARK PAWLOSKY

HACK

— A —
NIK BYRON
INVESTIGATION

GIRL FRIDAY BOOKS

 GIRL FRIDAY BOOKS

Published by Girl Friday Books™, Seattle
www.girlfridaybooks.com

Produced by Girl Friday Productions

Production editorial: Bethany Davis
Project management: Sara Spees Addicott
Cover design: Emily Weigel

Image credits: cover © Shutterstock/Orhan Cam, Shutterstock/Motortion Films

ISBN (paperback): 978-1-954854-60-4
ISBN (e-book): 978-1-954854-61-1

Library of Congress Control Number: 2022903955

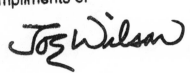
HACK

*To Jen, Ben, and Will—my love and
devotion, forever and a day*

AUTHOR'S NOTE

Hack is set in Washington, DC, where I once lived and worked and which I still remember fondly. The city and its environs have changed considerably since my days there, and, out of a sense of nostalgia, I've resurrected several long-shuttered establishments for the telling of this story. I have attempted to remain true to the more iconic landmarks, but, for my purposes, I have altered some locations and conjured up whole entities—the Northern Virginia County Sheriff's Department, among them—where none exist.

CHAPTER 1

December 15, 2018, Interstate 270, Maryland

The rattletrap panel van was pushing sixty-eight miles an hour, headed north on Interstate 270 just south of the Pennsylvania state line as darkness descended. The road noise in the cab was deafening, and Cooley had to shout to be heard.

"You see that fireball, Nuky? I bet that sucker rattled the fuckin' china cabinet in the fuckin' White House," wailed Cooley, highballing on a combination of adrenaline and meth.

Cooley's companion, a towhead named Nukowski with a stringy mullet and eyes as red as cayenne peppers, let go a long blue cloud of vape as he stared out the passenger window at the vanishing countryside and muttered under his breath.

"Whaaaat?" Cooley said at the top of his lungs. "I told you I can't hear you with you mumblin' all the time."

"I seen it," Nukowski said, thinking, *The bomb was supposed to go off in the morning when people were at work, not Sunday night when no one was around.* "Lucky we didn't get blowed up ourselves, and would have, too, if that security guard hadn't spooked us. You screwed the pooch, Cooley."

"Uh-uh. No way. I didn't set that detonator. Hawk did. And he told me he double-checked it and all I had to do was flip the switch. Something musta triggered it." Cooley defended himself.

"It didn't look like no fuckin' FBI building, either," Nukowski said.

"Hawk never said FBI office," Cooley replied, hunched over the steering wheel, one hand obsessively clawing at his rubbery, loon-like neck while he stared out at the highway through slitted eyes. "He said FBI had top-secret operations there." Cooley slapped the steering wheel and let out another high-pitched war whoop.

"I signed on to kill government agents, not blow up fuckin' shopping centers," Nukowski said, glaring at his addled accomplice and wondering how Cooley had ever survived two tours of duty in Afghanistan.

"That weren't no shoppin' center. It was an office park," Cooley corrected.

"Same difference," Nukowski replied.

"No it ain't neither, and besides," Cooley assured him, "Hawk said we'll have plenty more opportunities. You're just tired, s'all. Why don't you try to catch some shut-eye whilst I drive. We got a long road ahead of us before we get back to Michigan. I got this."

Nukowski muttered under his breath again, and Cooley, nerves frayed and jangled by the meth, and seemingly exasperated by his companion's sourpuss attitude, taunted in a braying voice, "Twat you say? Cunt hear you. Bare ass me again."

Nukowski seethed and contemplated plunging the tip of his vape stick deep into Cooley's right eye socket, then thought better of it. Instead, he said, "Can't sleep in this fuckin' washtub. Tell me again about Hawk's plans."

Cooley whipped his bullet-shaped head around to face Nukowski and flashed him a set of mossy teeth. "Well, now, Nuky, that right there's the beauty part."

CHAPTER 2

December 15, Washington, DC

It was a dreary gray mid-December evening and, as he had been every weekend for the past three months, reporter Nik Byron sat alone in *Newshound*'s Washington, DC, office, single-handedly manning the phones, knocking out mundane news stories, monitoring social media feeds, and keeping one ear tuned to the police scanner while drinking bitter coffee from a mug inscribed with the phrase "World's Greatest Reporter." The irony was as cruel and comical as it was inescapable.

Months earlier, Nik had landed in Washington at the peak of summer to strangling humidity, swarms of cicadas, and the devastating news that he had been demoted and would no longer be *Newshound*'s DC chief editor, a promotion he had been promised after uncovering a massive banking scandal in the Midwest for the feisty online news operation.

Instead of sitting atop *Newshound*'s food chain when he arrived in Washington, Nik was now a bottom-feeder, the casualty of a hastily hatched media merger. He was relegated to weekend duty, the drudgery of the graveyard shift, and assignments no one else wanted. He had been given the title chief deputy editor, as if that carried any weight at all.

Nik's only "scoop" since arriving in DC was a story on King Kobe, a packaged food mogul, who, it turned out, was adulterating the ultra-premium beef with horseflesh from some stables he owned outside The Plains, Virginia, and selling it to high-end restaurants in and around the nation's capital for top dollar.

The story had resulted in two utterly predictable outcomes: health officials declaring themselves shocked and launching an investigation, and Nik's officemates seizing on the story and knighting him the Galloping Gourmet. They had even chipped in and bought him a stick pony that made galloping sounds when you rode it around the office. The good-natured ribbing only helped to underscore the demoralizing turn of events Nik's career had taken.

As he switched off the office lights and headed for the door, Nik was grateful it had been a relatively quiet weekend. He planned to meet with two colleagues after work, and he was looking forward to an evening on the town. His erratic work schedule and complicated personal life made for a meager social existence.

In his late thirties with a thick tassel of golden hair, a perpetual three-day stubble, aquiline nose, and easy manner, Nik seldom wanted for companionship, but before relocating, he had committed to a long-distance relationship with his girlfriend, Haley Patterson, a budding entrepreneur who had launched a successful online cosmetics company in Kansas City.

The cross-country courtship, emotionally intense, sexually adventurous, and all-consuming at first, had flagged by month three and cratered in month five, just before Thanksgiving. Nik had remained faithful to Haley during the trial run and spent most nights at home by himself with his dog, Gyp, a high-strung vizsla, in his Georgetown apartment, but now, single again, he was eager to socialize with friends and drown his sorrows in what his colleagues had dubbed "boozehounders," nights of hard drinking, gossip swapping, and scheming to undermine Li'l Dick Whetstone, their tyrannical boss.

Nik was standing in the hallway absentmindedly locking up and musing about the night ahead when the police scanner in the office burped to life. The scanner was tuned to filter out routine calls and only monitor critical developments.

Nik pressed his ear to the door to listen and silently cursed his luck. Two more minutes, and he would have been riding the elevator down to the parking garage, home free.

The scanner crackled with nonstop chatter, though Nik had a hard time deciphering what was being said through the closed door, and he couldn't make heads or tails of the shorthand codes that were being broadcast.

"Damn it," he cursed aloud and pushed back through the doorway, dropping his bag on the carpet and stumbling across the darkened office to where the scanner sat next to a bank of television monitors and the light panel. He toggled on the lights just as a voice spilled over the speaker: "Injuries reported, extent unknown, medics dispatched to Trident Office Park, Homeland Security alerted, code Z as in zebra." There was a brief pause, and then: "Switching to secure channel." The squawking ceased and the monitor fell silent.

Nik didn't know what code Z was, but Trident Park rang a bell. It was a southeast office complex where a number of high-tech companies, including OmniSoft Corporation, were located.

When Nik had first joined *Newshound*'s DC operation, he had been saddled with the OmniSoft saga—a hair ball of a story so convoluted and vexing that the other reporters in the office had run screaming from it.

The owner of OmniSoft, Cal Walker, claimed the government had forced him into bankruptcy in order to gain control of his proprietary surveillance monitoring software—named POOF. When Walker decided to fight back and sue the US government in federal court for $100 million, every attorney in town he approached refused to represent him on the grounds that they thought he was delusional, a conspiracy kook, and, moreover, penniless. Washington lawyers were greedy, but they weren't stupid.

Walker had no choice but to represent himself, and Nik, as the new guy on the beat, had inherited the long-running case just as it was headed to trial, along with thousands of pages of court filings, government documents, and constant chirping in his ear from Walker.

Walker explained that POOF—which stood for Phantom Omniscient Ocular Functionality—was developed to be an encryption-cracking, data-mining, and software surveillance program all rolled into one that, when fully operational, would throw a digital net over an individual's activities and capture their every move, transaction, and interaction in real time.

One arm of the program allowed operators to build comprehensive databases on targeted suspects, their families, and associates beginning with just the tiniest piece of digital information, such as an email address. Another aspect identified all computer and communications devices the individual had access to, and a third component was capable of invisibly infiltrating those devices to secretly monitor and track activity.

Walker first started developing the technology after 9/11 to target terrorist organizations and had funded the start-up company out of his own pocket in the early years. It was only later that he received some government funding and grants to continue his research and keep his small company afloat. He promised his government handlers he could develop POOF for a few million dollars and have it up and running in no time. In reality, it would take Walker years and tens of millions to build the software framework.

Walker told Nik that POOF's code was capable of penetrating computer networks, government mainframes, server farms, laptops, and any and all mobile devices and apps, and it worked by mimicking the host operating system.

"Think of it as a needle," he had once confided to Nik over morning coffee, "in a haystack of needles. With one hack, we're in. Then we burrow like a tick."

Nik wasn't a technology expert, but Walker, a former CIA and National Security Agency analyst with a doctorate in computer science from MIT, had a brilliant, if somewhat rogue, reputation among software developers, coders, and hackers and was nothing if not persistent. Colleagues took to calling Walker Sir Veil for his genius in creating tracking software.

Nik found himself grudgingly admiring Walker's grit, and when he heard Trident's address broadcast over the scanner, it flashed through his mind that the cash-strapped Walker might have staged an explosion to collect an insurance payout.

Nik quickly searched *Newshound*'s office for the bureau's operating manual, known as The Brains. It contained the contact information for every meaningful government agency and their department heads in the metropolitan area.

After rooting through desks and cabinets, he found The Brains in a stall in the men's john. Nik bypassed all the federal agency listings and skipped to the directory for district offices and dialed the number for the police precinct nearest Trident Office Park.

He reached a bored female desk sergeant and was immediately stonewalled. He hung up and scanned social media channels. He found reports of a bright flash followed by a thunderous clap, but nothing else. Not surprising. The office park was in a remote area and likely near-deserted on weekends, especially around the holidays. He then dialed Walker's cell phone, and the call immediately went to voice mail. He left a message. His next call was to a nearby fire station. The dispatcher told him units were on the way but didn't have any further information on injuries.

"Can't verify it, but heard it was a gas-line leak," the dispatcher said.

That, at least, was somewhat comforting. If it was a garden-variety disaster, Nik could ignore it and let local TV news— whose unofficial slogan was "If it bleeds, it leads"—deal with it while still rendezvousing with his friends on time, but the mention of Homeland Security nagged at him. Nik was trying to decide what to do next when his mobile phone lit up with a text message. Call me. IMPT.

It was from Jake Korum, a former Army Ranger and FBI agent who was now a sheriff in Northern Virginia.

Nik had been introduced to Korum by Rebecca Isaac, a security specialist and ex–Israel Defense Forces operative who had saved Nik's life one night when she pulled him from the path of an oncoming SUV that was bearing down on him. In Isaac's world, there were black hats and white hats. Korum's was a white hat.

"What's up?" Nik said when Korum answered his phone.

"You hear about the explosion over at Trident?" the sheriff asked.

"Yeah, I was just leaving work when it happened. Trying to run it down now," Nik said. "Know anything?"

"Official word is it was caused by a gas leak," Korum offered.

"Good. I heard that, too," Nik said a little too buoyantly, relieved to know his night wasn't going to be ruined after all. He checked his watch. He still had plenty of time to keep the date with his friends. "Well, I mean, not good, but it could have been something worse, I suppose," he added quickly.

"It don't make sense, Nik," Korum said laconically.

Nik envisioned Korum in his office, dressed in his nut-brown uniform, brass buttons as shiny as stars, polished cowboy boots propped up on his desk, Stetson hat tilted back on his head, toothpick dangling from his lips. Korum liked to play the role of the good ol' boy, but the West Point graduate and Rhodes Scholar was as sharp and hard as an ice ax.

"That whole complex was developed to mainly run on alternative energy—wind, solar, hydro—and be self-sufficient," the sheriff continued. "They got their own power plant, massive storage batteries, redundancy. They feed the grid their excess capacity."

"Soooooo . . ." Nik interjected.

"So I'm bettin' it weren't no simple gas-line explosion," Korum said. "You know they handle a lot of classified work over there for the intelligence apparatus—NSA, FBI, CIA, US Cyber Command."

"I'm familiar with companies in Trident," Nik said, sounding a little defensive. "They have government contracts, but what of it? So does every high-tech firm inside the Beltway with two employees, a coffeepot, and a receptionist."

"Not like this. They're into super-spook shit over there. Cyber weapons, domestic spying software, metadata harvesting, quantum computing," Korum said, and Nik was reminded that the office park was rather controversial and had been the target of protests by privacy rights groups in the past.

It occurred to Nik to call Dick Whetstone, his boss, and palm the story off on him, but then he recalled Whetstone was out of town speaking at a media conference and wouldn't be back for a week or more. Just as well. There was bad blood between the two of them. That had as much to do with their differences in news judgment as it did with Nik's belief that Whetstone was out to sabotage his career.

"They mentioned code Z," Nik said to Korum. "Ever hear of it?"

"Yeah. Fed speak. Shorthand for 'lock it down.' Shit 'bout to hit the fan."

"Hmmm," Nik responded noncommittally.

"I'm telling you, Nik, it don't pass the sniff test. I'd send my folks, but I don't have jurisdiction. You should go nose around. See what turns up," the sheriff prodded.

Nik tried to tune Korum out. The last thing he wanted to do on a Sunday night was drive across the Anacostia River to an office park in southeast Washington, but he had to admit Korum's hunches had proved prescient in the past. He waffled. "Awright," he said finally, "I'll look into it."

"Good, and I'll let you know if Sami hears anything," Korum said, referring to his spokesperson and lead investigator, Samantha Whyte, a former star reporter for the *Washington Post*, who, without warning, had walked away from her job one day never to return.

Nik knew Whyte but was still undecided about her. Professional but emotionally distant and at times somber, she was always available to answer Nik's questions, but rarely, if ever, volunteered any useful information unbidden. On the few occasions when she did loosen up and drop her guard, Nik found her funny, charming, even.

Then there was the *Washington Post* connection. Though he couldn't prove it, Nik suspected Whyte had tipped off her old employer to a bid-rigging investigation he had been working on for weeks. He'd have to watch what he shared with Korum.

As if reading Nik's mind, Korum said, "Be careful who you trust. You know what NSA stands for, right?"

"National Security Agency," Nik said. "Everybody knows that."

"Un-uh," Korum said. "No Such Agency."

Nik disconnected from the sheriff and punched in Patrick "Mo" Morgan's number. Nik could hear a din in the background when he reached Morgan and fellow colleague Mia

Landry at the Third Edition, their new favorite watering hole. Nik broke the news to his colleagues.

"Too bad for you," Mo said. "We'll hoist a cold one in your honor."

"Make it quick," Nik said. "I need you and Mia to tag team this one."

"Aw, fuck, I knew I shouldn't have answered the phone," Mo groused.

"Cheer up," Nik said. "With any luck, we'll be back at the Third Edition before last call."

As it turned out, it would be the new year, and under different circumstances, before the trio reconvened for a boozehounder.

CHAPTER 3

December 15, Washington, DC

Nik slammed into the roadblock three miles from the Trident Office Park. Two patrol cars were wedged nose to nose in the center of the road, lit up by flashing light bars and flares running along the shoulders, giving the street the appearance of an airport runway.

Nik coasted to a stop, and a cop in a wide-brimmed Smokey hat and raincoat walked in a cautious arc toward his vehicle. A steady, cold rain had begun, and Nik cracked the window of his ancient Land Cruiser and nodded when the officer drew near.

The cop stood behind and off to the side of the driver's door and shined a light into the interior of the vehicle and then directly into Nik's eyes, temporarily blinding him. "Where you headed, sir?"

Nik squeezed his eyes shut and looked straight ahead. Black dots the size of hockey pucks danced in front of him when he tried to refocus.

"Trident, there's been an explosion. I'm a reporter with

Newshound," Nik said and fished his credentials and driver's license out of the vehicle's console and handed them to the cop through the window. The officer took them and walked to the back of Nik's car, keyed the microphone mounted on his shoulder, and read out Nik's driver's license and license plate numbers.

He reappeared at Nik's window a couple minutes later and returned the identification.

"There's another roadblock 'bout a mile up. It's manned by Homeland Security. I don't expect you'll get through, but I've been instructed to let you pass," the cop said, waving to the other trooper to clear a path in the roadway for Nik.

Nik thanked the officer, started pulling away, and then braked. "Any other media come through this checkpoint?" he asked, his breath stacking up outside his window like a tiny rain cloud. The cop paused before answering. "You're the only vehicle we've seen so far," he said.

"And why Homeland Security?" Nik queried.

"You'll have to ask them that. You need to move along now, sir," the officer said in a determined voice.

Nik maneuvered his vehicle around the police cruisers, punched the accelerator, and squirted through the roadblock. Within a matter of minutes, he rounded a curve and saw more flares and orange pylons in the distance, but no cars. The second checkpoint appeared abandoned.

Nik arrived at the entrance to Trident Office Park a few minutes later, just in time to witness a mob surging toward him as he stood outside his parked vehicle.

"What's going on?" he yelled as medics, nurses, and security guards shot past him helter-skelter in all directions, wide-eyed with panic. Someone shouted back, but Nik wasn't able to make out what they said. The rain was falling harder now, and Nik stood rooted to his spot, not certain what to do, when he was knocked from behind and spun around.

A tight knot of men and woman, all athletic-looking and identically dressed in thick boots, cargo pants, berets, and matching dark-blue windbreakers, were on a dead run in the opposite direction, back into the heart of the office park. Nik didn't hesitate. He broke into a sprint and fell in behind the small squadron.

The escaping crowd Nik had encountered when he arrived at the office park had apparently abandoned its supplies in a rush to flee, and the ground was littered with blankets, medical supplies, and rain gear. He stopped and scooped up a poncho and slipped it over his head. A patch on the breast read "Trident Security."

Nik looked up just in time to see the crew he was trailing disappear around a building. He raced to rejoin them, and when he turned the corner, he came to a dead stop. He stared out at an area the size of a ball field that had been leveled.

The blast had pancaked a four-story building, and its husk sat smoldering, cloaked in an eerie orange halo, while the acrid smells of melted electronics and burnt rubber made Nik's eyes water and nose run. Upended cars and trucks were scattered about, doors and trunks ripped from hinges. Out on the perimeter, away from the center of the explosion, damaged buildings displayed gaping windows filled with glass shards like rows of busted-out teeth.

"Who are you?" a sharp voice snapped from behind Nik. He wheeled around to face a man with yellowed eyes and a blond mustache the size of a large, woolly caterpillar nestled on his upper lip. He wore a black ball cap tightly pulled down over his head, tactical vest, and black battle dress trousers tucked inside combat boots. Strapped on his left wrist was an oversized military watch and on his right thigh, a sidearm. A name tag on his vest simply read "Colonel," no last name. Nik was about to identify himself when the man spied the patch on Nik's poncho.

"Trident Security. Good. Follow me. We need to see if we can recover any bodies. A cadaver dog is on the way," the man said and dashed off with Nik in tow.

The group Nik had been trailing made its way to the wreckage. The colonel took charge and instructed them to form a bucket brigade. "We need to make a hole," he ordered and started funneling out rubble hand over hand.

Nik took a place in the back of the line and stacked blocks of concrete around his feet and worried how he might react if they actually pulled a body from the building. Nik had an aversion to blood and got light-headed when he saw it, and, on a couple occasions, had even fainted at the sight of his own blood.

After about ten minutes, the colonel called out, "I think I hear someone." The conga line doubled its pace and quickly carved out a small cavity wide enough for one of the women to wedge into. "Throw some light in this hole," she said, and almost instantaneously, a powerful handheld spotlight bathed the area in a yellow glow, illuminating not only the opening but everyone in the rescue line as well.

That's when the woman directly in front of Nik turned and surveyed his matted-down hair, fogged wire-rimmed glasses, and soggy loafers.

"You ain't security," she said.

"Never claimed to be," Nik said.

"Who are you?" she interrogated.

"Nik Byron," he said.

"I mean, who are you with, Byron?" she said.

Nik knew better than to lie. "I'm a reporter with *Newshound*."

The woman took a half step back, swiveled her head, and, while keeping one eye fixed on Nik, shouted over her shoulder, "For fuck's sake, someone let a fucking reporter in here."

CHAPTER 4

December 15, Washington, DC

Patrick Morgan and Mia Landry reluctantly abandoned their cozy booth at the back of the Third Edition and headed for the door. Mia tucked her unruly hair under a purple-and-white beanie, slipped on a silver puffy jacket, and made her way to Georgetown University Hospital. Mo tugged on a beaten-up Red Sox baseball cap and shambled down the street to his apartment. He went to work trying to track down Homeland Security sources and, at Nik's urging, called veteran news editor Frank Rath and dispatched him to *Newshound*'s offices to monitor media reports and be prepared to edit any stories the reporters might file.

Nik's three colleagues had followed him to Washington from the Midwest when it appeared he was going to be chief editor and had stood by Nik despite his demotion. They were aware Nik had remained loyal to them as well, and that he would have resigned from *Newshound* had they not uprooted their lives and careers to make the cross-country journey to the nation's capital with him.

Ironically, all three had adapted to their new surroundings much better than Nik had.

Frank, at sixty-eight, a seasoned journalist who had covered government coups, Wall Street scandals, and presidential campaigns, had settled in as the dean of the newsroom, happy to tutor and share war stories with eager young reporters. Nik had coaxed Frank out of semiretirement back in the Midwest, and they had been together ever since.

Shortly after arriving in DC, Mia, a former intern whose superior reporting skills had turbocharged her career, had launched *Dateline Washington*, a podcast that covered the singles scene in the nation's capital. The program became an instant hit with young professionals in their early twenties, like Mia, and gained her widespread notoriety, and, in no time at all, the concept had spread to the rest of *Newshound*'s markets nationwide.

Mo had won the admiration of the staff with his unrivaled professional and personal work ethic. Not only did he spend countless hours meticulously crafting his stories, he was also a devoted bodybuilder and encouraged everyone to join him at the local Y for noontime workouts. With biceps as thick as railroad ties, fingers round and stout like shotgun shells, and a chest the size of an anvil, the thirty-six-year-old Mo cut an impressive figure in a newsroom filled with otherwise out-of-shape and flabby reporters.

Nik, on the other hand, remained unsettled and was amazed at how quickly his colleagues had acclimated to the unfamiliar terrain.

"Brah," Mo had slurred one boozy evening at the Third Edition, laying a tree trunk of an arm across Nik's stooped shoulders, "*Newshound* moved us across the country on their dime, doubled our salaries, and put us up in corporate apartments while we searched for places to live. What's to bitch about?"

It was Nik's experience that reporters could always find something to bitch about, and bitch Mo and Mia did when Nik called and told them about the Trident story.

"We ain't fuckin' ambulance chasers," Mo protested.

"No, and you aren't desk jockeys, either," Nik said, having fully anticipated the blowback. "Companies inside Trident handle a lot of highly classified work for the government, and they're trying to make this out as a ruptured gas line when it's doubtful that's what happened. Something's not right."

"What's Whetstone think?" Mo asked, knowing the question was certain to irk Nik.

"He's out of town," Nik said curtly. "It's my call."

"Remind me never to invite you to a boozehounder again," Mo grumbled.

Mia was the first to come across the trail of the bloody explosion. She spotted an ambulance driver exiting Georgetown Hospital's emergency room drop-off and approached him. "Are the Trident victims here?" she asked in a distressed voice.

"Most have been admitted to ICU," the driver said.

"How bad?" Mia said, feigning anguish and only mildly uncomfortable with the subterfuge.

"I've seen worse," the driver said, "but bad."

"I've been trying to find out what happened but can't get a straight answer. Do you know?" Mia pressed.

The driver looked around before answering, unsure of how much to divulge. "Well," he began, when his partner blew through the emergency room doors. "We got to go, Doug," she said as she sprinted toward the ambulance. "Now!"

The driver broke away from Mia and headed to the vehicle, but after he opened the door, he turned back to her and silently mouthed a word that she thought was "bomb."

"Wait," Mia said, but the driver climbed into the ambulance and was gone.

Mia dashed into the hospital and was making her way toward the intensive care unit when she was stopped by a security guard with a face full of peach fuzz and festering pimples. He looked to be about seventeen.

His name tag read "Officer Stevie P." He had a badge on his lapel, and on his hip belt, a canister of mace, handcuffs, and a nightstick.

"Can I help you?" he asked.

"I hope so. I'm trying to find the explosion victims," Mia said.

"Which one?" Officer Stevie asked.

"From Trident Park," Mia said, attempting to bluff her way past the guard.

"You family?" he asked suspiciously.

A heavyset nurse with readers perched on the tip of her nose overheard the exchange and stepped out of an office into the corridor.

She peered over her glasses and then barked, "Stevie, how many times I got to tell you you're not to bother the visitors. Now get back to the tollbooth before people leave without paying for parking."

"I just came in to use the facilities and warm up a bit, is all, Nurse Louise," Stevie said before trotting to the exit.

"Sorry about that, miss," the nurse said to Mia. "He can be a little creepy. What can I do for you?"

Mia gave the nurse a sad smile, hoping to earn some sympathy before answering. Nurse Louise was unmoved and stood motionless, arms crossed, head cocked to one side, a pensive look on her face as she appraised Mia with what the reporter considered penetrating vision.

Mia thought, *It's as if she can see right into me—my racing heart, scar tissue, chipped teeth from my field hockey days. No chance of bullshitting her.*

"I'm a reporter with *Newshound*," Mia confessed, "and I'd like to talk to some of the victims from the Trident Park explosion."

The nurse remained rigid, sighed deeply, and then said, "You better come with me," and turned on her heel and headed toward a set of double doors that read "ICU," her shoes squeaking loudly on the polished floors.

On the other side of town, Mo was striking out with Homeland Security officials. They either didn't know anything or they were being evasive.

"It's Sunday, Mo," one source told him when reached at home. "Why don't you give it a rest?"

Mo was inclined to agree. He called Frank Rath at *Newshound*'s offices to check in and see if he had heard from either Mia or Nik.

"Not a word." Frank yawned. "And as far as other media goes, they're saying it was an accident."

"Feels like a wild-goose chase," Mo said. "You think Nik's overreacting because he's itching to get his career back on track?"

"Maybe," Frank said. "Dunno. Hang on. There's Nik now on the other line."

Frank came back a couple minutes later. "Mo, you still there?"

"Yeah."

"Nik spoke with Mia. They're both headed to the office. Should arrive in about thirty minutes. He wants you in here, too," Frank said.

"Really? Is that necessary?" Mo pleaded.

"'Fraid so. Looks like we might have a mad bomber on our hands," Frank said.

CHAPTER 5

December 15/16, Washington, DC

The small team worked late into the night, carefully piecing together a story that attempted to strike the right balance between fact and informed speculation. It was Frank's job to make sure the story straddled that fine line without toppling over it. He knew firsthand that if you crossed that line one too many times, it eventually vanished.

Nik told his colleagues about the panicked stampede, the cratered building, the work to dig through the rubble, and the special ops team led by a colonel with an old-school, bushy mustache he had encountered at Trident. Everything came to a brief standstill, Nik said, when they discovered he was a reporter working for *Newshound*.

"They debated what to do with me, but, in the end, the guy running the show, with the yellow mustache, told them to escort me from the premises and make sure I left. They refused to identify themselves, the government agency they worked for, or, for that matter, if they were with the government at all. By the way they operated, it was pretty clear they were experienced and had performed rescue missions in the past," Nik said.

"So, you didn't get the colonel's name?" Mo asked.

"No, in my notes, I refer to him as Colonel Mustard. But now that I think about it, when they were rushing me off the site, I did hear a name. It sounded like Calkins, but I couldn't swear to it. It was noisy and chaotic."

"Colonel Mustard, like the character in Clue," Mo said. "Not a lot to go on. We'll see if we can track down a Colonel Calkins. At least it's a start."

Before he was evicted from the office park, Nik had taken several photos of the devastation on his cell phone, and they planned to publish those with the story. The pictures showed the flattened building and the overturned vehicles, but, unfortunately, he wasn't able to get any pictures of the rescue workers.

Mia related the story about the ambulance driver and his silently mouthed "bomb" warning and said a nurse admitted her to the intensive care unit, where she interviewed several injured office workers. They told her they didn't know what had caused the explosion, but they were surprised to hear it was being blamed on a gas-line rupture since the office park relied mainly on alternative energy sources for most of its power.

They decided not to mention the ambulance driver's "bomb" quote since Mia might have misinterpreted what he actually said, and, moreover, she didn't know his name. Mia pledged to track down the driver when she returned to work later that day.

At 2:55 a.m. early Monday morning, *Newshound* published its story under a triple byline. The headline read:

**Massive Explosion Rocks Office Park
Home to High-Tech Spy Firms
Dozens Injured**

Gas Leak or Foul Play?
"Felt like a bomb"

By Nik Byron, Mia Landry,
and Patrick Morgan
Newshound *staff reporters*

A huge fireball ripped through the controversial Trident Office Park in southeast Washington Sunday evening, sending a towering pillar of fire and smoke into the nighttime sky and injuring at least a dozen individuals and damaging scores of buildings. No fatalities were immediately reported, but property damage could exceed $25 million, according to real estate estimates.

Authorities said a ruptured gas line was the likely cause of the explosion, but that explanation was immediately questioned by witnesses, who said there was no noticeable gas odor before the blast, and office workers were quick to point out that Trident generates most of its power from hydropower and alternative energy sources and not natural gas.

"The only gas line in Trident runs to the backup generator, and it's state of the art. It's equipped with sensors that detect, self-report, and shut down instantaneously if there are leaks,"

said George Malone, an engineer who
helped design the power system for the
office complex.

Trident is home to dozens of software start-ups and technology firms,
many of which conduct highly classified and secretive work for the nation's
top intelligence operations, including
the CIA, FBI, and National Security
Agency.

The complex has been the target
of anonymous threats by anti-
government groups in the past as
well as protests by privacy advocates.

One of the office park's more
colorful and high-profile tenants is
OmniSoft Corporation, whose founder,
Cal Walker, is in a long-running legal
battle with the federal government
over intellectual property theft. The
company alleges the government
stole its proprietary monitoring software—named POOF—and forced it into
bankruptcy.

Witnesses reported a chaotic scene
at the office park shortly after the
explosion. Frantic first responders
were seen fleeing the site, fearing a
second explosion was imminent, while,
at the same moment, a small, highly
trained squad entered Trident to begin
a search-and-rescue mission for survi-
vors in the rubble.

When approached, members of

the rescue team refused to identify themselves and barred a *Newshound* reporter from the property "on the grounds of national security."

A Homeland Security spokeswoman said the department was aware of the situation at Trident but was treating it as an industrial accident. She down-played the notion of the involvement of a special forces unit.

"Sounds like someone's letting their imagination get the best of them," she said.

More than one dozen victims were admitted to Georgetown University Hospital with injuries ranging from broken bones to third-degree burns. At least four patients were listed in criti-cal condition.

Emily Hightower, a software engi-neer, said she was exiting her office building when the explosion occurred. Although her building is located more than 100 yards away from the blast site, the shock wave from the blast knocked her off her feet and left her temporarily unconscious. She said she came to in the back of an ambulance headed to the hospital.

"Honestly, it felt like a bomb went off," Hightower said, echoing the impression of several other victims who spoke to *Newshound*. Hightower said she did not recall smelling any

rotten-egg odor associated with a
natural gas leak before the explosion,
a refrain also repeated by other office
workers *Newshound* interviewed.

As of early this morning, crews
were still at the site sifting through
evidence and investigating the source
of the explosion. They said it may be
several days before the actual cause is
known.

CHAPTER 6

December 16, Washington, DC

Nik staggered into his Georgetown apartment a little before four a.m. and collapsed into an overstuffed chair. He fell asleep fully clothed with a bottle of Budweiser in one hand, his cell phone in the other, and Mose Allison on the Sonos.

He stirred awake three hours later when the phone burred and vibrated in his hand. It was Dick Whetstone, *Newshound*'s chief editor and Nik's nominal boss. Nik could hear Allison's song, "Your Mind Is on Vacation" and the refrain, "your mouth is working overtime" playing in the background.

"Yeah, Dick," Nik said, jabbing the speaker icon on the phone screen, shaking his head, and sitting up straighter in an effort to kick-start his brain.

"It's Richard. How many fucking times do I have to remind you, Byron, my name is Richard," Whetstone said peevishly.

Whetstone was barely five foot seven, gaunt, verging on malnourished, with a sallow complexion, limp hair, and a pinched mouth filled with gray teeth, and behind his back, reporters called him Li'l Dick.

"Right, sorry. Next time," Nik said groggily.

"Might not be a fucking next time for you, Byron, you publish another bullshit story like the Trident explosion," Whetstone threatened.

"How's the media conference? Your speech a big hit?" Nik asked. "Nice weather in San Diego?"

"I'm gone less than forty-eight hours, and we print a sensational story about a bomb going off at an office park. We look like fucking stooges," Whetstone sputtered. *"Home to high-tech spy firms.* What the fuck were you thinking, Byron?"

Nik made his way into the galley kitchen, dropped a coffee pod into the machine, selected Americano, and pressed Brew. His stomach rumbled. He wondered if he had any bagels left in the freezer. He opened the door and peered in. Nothing. Maybe he'd go to Au Pied du Cochon for breakfast and get an order of runny eggs Benedict and pommes frites, those little slivers of potato heaven deep-fat fried to golden perfection in lard.

"Well?" Whetstone demanded.

"Well, what?" Nik said.

"About the bomb," the chief editor said.

"Sorry, thought it was a rhetorical question," Nik said, retrieving the *Washington Post* from the vestibule outside his apartment door and scanning the newspaper for a story on the explosion.

"Don't fuck with me, Byron. You're on very thin ice here, and it's about to come crashing down on your head."

"I believe the saying is 'crash through the ice.' The 'roof is going to come crashing down on my head,'" Nik corrected.

"You're a real smart-ass, aren't you, Byron? Little wonder you didn't get the chief editor's job," Whetstone goaded.

The *Post* buried a six-inch story on page B12 with the headline "Office park blast blamed on gas leak." The last sentence in the story referred readers to its website for updates.

"Never said it was a bomb," Nik finally replied. "We said witnesses said it *felt like* a bomb. Don't you think it's odd that no one reported smelling any gas odor?"

"Just tell me that nutjob Walker didn't put you up to this," Whetstone said, referring to the OmniSoft CEO.

"Cal Walker? Haven't heard from him," Nik said. "The building where he had his office was destroyed, and it's not known if he was inside."

"You ask me, fucking blessing in disguise if he was," Whetstone said.

"Correct me if I'm wrong, but I believe you're the one who assigned me the OmniSoft story, Chief," Nik said.

"Yeah, but I didn't think you were foolish enough to take it seriously. No one else in Washington did, or does," Whetstone said.

"We done here?" Nik asked.

"Just about. I'm taking some much-deserved R&R after the conference and don't plan on returning to the office for another couple weeks. You need to put your 'Galloping Gourmet' hat back on and cover the King Kobe story, Nik," Whetstone belittled, "and leave Trident the fuck alone."

"Un-huh," Nik replied.

"You know, Byron, your career's probably unsalvageable, but that's hardly a good reason to drag Mia, Mo, and Frank down with you. You might want to think about that."

"I'll keep it in mind, Dick."

"It's Rich—" Whetstone started to say when Nik hung up.

———

Nik immediately texted Sheriff Korum and asked him to call when he got to the office. He tried Cal Walker's cell phone again but got a message saying his voice mail was full.

Nik hopped into the shower and started to plot his day, but he couldn't shake Whetstone's admonition.

As much as he hated to admit it, there was some truth to what Whetstone had said about Nik's career and the negative impact it might have on his friends. Nik couldn't help but think that none of them would be in this predicament if Rusty Mitchell, *Newshound*'s founder and benefactor, had not been jolted awake one night nine months earlier with a vision about *Newshound*'s future.

Mitchell had amassed a net worth approaching $500 million after successfully bootstrapping and selling two technology start-ups. He had launched *Newshound* on a whim to spur local media competition, especially in the business news arena, in his hometown of Kansas City.

To everyone's shock, *Newshound* was an immediate hit and was financially successful in year two, a virtually unheard-of feat for a media start-up. Mitchell didn't know anything about the media business, and that, along with an obsessive customer-centric focus he had honed in the technology industry, benefited *Newshound* enormously.

Mitchell pushed traditional boundaries and wasn't afraid to fail, which made him a rarity in publishing circles. He made rapid-fire decisions, and if something didn't work out, he abandoned it quickly and moved on to the next endeavor.

He relentlessly pursued technology solutions to give *Newshound* a competitive advantage. Mitchell issued the newsroom camera-mounted drones to cover breaking news events, incorporated natural-language technologies into the publishing system to transform data into computer-generated stories, and wrote software to help reporters sift through mounds of information to pinpoint important investigative stories and trends.

Mitchell was shrewd, data-driven, and tightfisted, but, at times, he would throw all of that to the wind and rely on gut instincts, and on that fateful night nine months earlier, his gut had told him the country was ready for *Newshound*.

The next morning, Mitchell announced he was committing tens of millions of dollars to expand *Newshound*'s operations nationwide. Virtually overnight, *Newshound* went from a single stand-alone news site to a media juggernaut.

The company opened offices at a blistering pace, and within six months had operations in San Francisco, Seattle, Atlanta, Boston, Los Angeles, Portland, Denver, Chicago, New York, and Dallas. The goal was to be in the majority of the top-twenty markets by the new year.

Mitchell's strategy was simple and direct—build, buy, or bury. Where possible, build a site from scratch; if there was competition, buy it; and if they refused to sell, bury it.

In the case of Washington, DC, Mitchell bought out the competition, but in order to close the deal, he was forced to agree to keep the existing management in place, including Nik's nemesis, Richard Whetstone, for eighteen months and granted them the authority to hire and fire personnel as they saw fit.

The agreement had effectively torpedoed Nik's promotion and sidetracked his career. Nik had pleaded with his old boss, Bo Cooper, to intercede. Cooper had been put in charge of *Newshound*'s West Coast operations and, while sympathetic to Nik's plight, was powerless to change the outcome.

"Sorry, sport," Cooper told him, "not my circus, not my clowns. You and Mitchell need to work this out between yourselves."

Mitchell admired Nik and felt bad about reneging on his promise to promote him to chief editor in DC after the banking scandal story. Mitchell explained he was bound by the contract and told Nik that his hands were tied for the next year and a half. He had tried to soften the blow by granting Nik a generous stock option package in *Newshound* that he predicted one day could be worth a small fortune if the company went public.

Yeah, Nik thought to himself bitterly, *when pigs fly,* and shoved the paperwork in the back of a drawer and forgot about it.

CHAPTER 7

December 16, Truck Stop in Indiana

Indiana State Highway Patrolman Clint Ward was just about to clock off duty when he saw the faded lime-green Dodge van limp off Interstate 70 and glide toward the Fuel King of America truck stop and convenience store.

There wasn't anything particularly suspicious about the vehicle, but he took note of it because he couldn't recall the last time he had seen a relic 1979 Dodge B100 SWB Street Van. He'd had one just like it when he was a teenager, and he had spent nearly every free minute working on it in his parents' garage in Columbus, Indiana, where he grew up. He equipped the van with a stereo system, mini-fridge, futon, and even bolted benches along the inside panels. Despite all the time he spent on it, he could never figure out how to stop the damn thing from burning oil by the case and, in the end, resorted to collecting waste oil from local gas stations to dump into the engine. He smiled, thinking of the good times he and his girl-friend, Shirley Mintz, had in the van. They used to lie in the back naked, smoking weed, sipping Rolling Rock, and fucking like minks for hours. He smiled again and wondered whatever had happened to Shirley. He just might look her up, he thought to himself, the next time he visited his folks back in Columbus.

The officer's patrol car was tucked away in a small lane between the off-ramp and the frontage road that the highway department had carved out to stow equipment when they were doing repair work on the interstate. He usually sat there at the end of his shift to write up his reports and keep an eye on vehicles entering and exiting the highway.

As the van rolled past the trooper and under a streetlight, Ward glimpsed two male occupants in an animated discussion, but mostly what he noticed was the rust along the vehicle's rocker panel and thought, *Once rust sets in, you're screwed.* He shook his head knowingly and went back to writing his reports. With his head down in his paperwork, Officer Ward didn't notice the passenger door fly open.

———

Nukowski jumped out of the van as it sputtered and stalled about fifty feet from the truck stop. Nukowski had told Cooley to pull off the interstate and get gas about thirty miles back, but Cooley had insisted he could make it to Fuel King, which he claimed had the cheapest gas along the highway.

Nukowski leaned his shoulder into the passenger doorjamb and, with a loud groan, got the van's front wheels over a little rise that provided just enough momentum to allow the vehicle to coast downhill toward the fuel island and a spot alongside the pumps. The van was the only vehicle on the premises as far as Nukowski could tell.

Cooley tumbled out of the driver's side door and started shivering. It was a little after four a.m., the air was damp and cold, and the heater in the van barely worked. He was coming down from his meth high, and that only added to his shakes. He needed both hands to steady the gas nozzle and guide it into the fuel tank.

Nukowski was halfway to the store when Cooley called out to him. "Hey, Nuky, get me a Mountain Dew and a pack of Kools. I'll pay you back."

Nukowski gave a backward wave of his hand to acknowledge the order, but muttered, "Get your own shit, fuckstick. I ain't your errand boy," and disappeared into the store.

Nukowski stocked up on Slim Jims, sunflower seeds, Red Bull, and a large hazelnut coffee that burned his tongue and the roof of his mouth when he took a drink. "Fuck," he said and spit out the boiling liquid on the floor.

"Shoulda warned you, that machine runs a little hot," the clerk said.

"No shit," Nukowski said and handed the clerk four twenties for the gas, told her to add a bag of chicken tenders and a bottle of blackberry e-juice for his vape, and asked for the key to the men's room.

When he came out of the restroom, the clerk had switched on a small television set that was sitting on the counter and was listening to a news report about a gas-line explosion in Washington, DC. The TV reporter said at least a dozen people were hospitalized, and two people, a maintenance man and an office worker, had died overnight from their injuries.

"Shit happens," the clerk said, handing Nukowski his bagged-up groceries and change.

"It does to me," Nukowski said and, with arms loaded, pushed his rump against the door and hurried back out of the store. He wanted to tell Cooley what he had just heard on the news, but when he turned around, he went stock-still. There was Cooley jawing with a state cop.

"Hey, Nuky," Cooley belted out when he saw his companion

drawing near. "Officer Ward here had a '79 Dodge Street Van just like this one. Ain't that sum'in'?"

Nukowski dropped his head and quick-stepped back to the van. There was nothing he wanted to say to no cop.

"You get my smokes?" Cooley asked, raking his mangled neck again with chewed-on fingernails. The skin was inflamed from the constant mauling, and his neck looked like a stalk of withered rhubarb, a classic tell of a meth head that Nukowski hoped the cop hadn't noticed.

"They were out," Nukowski lied.

The cop was too busy studying the van to pay attention to the pair. He circled the vehicle, all the while making little asides about its condition. He was saying something about burning oil when he stopped at the back. "Hey"—he raised his voice—"you know these tags expired six days ago?"

"Yeah, yeah, yeah," Cooley replied. "I got the new ones in the mail just before we left, and I forgot to put them on, is all, Officer. Promise I'll do it first thing when we get back."

What the fuck, Nukowski thought, *we've been driving across the country on expired plates? Shithead.*

"Okay," the cop said hesitantly. "Make sure you do. Lucky for you, I'm officially off duty or I'd write you up."

Officer Ward continued his inspection of the van and rounded the side of the vehicle just as Nukowski struggled to open the passenger's door, a steaming cup of coffee balanced in one hand, the sack of groceries in the other.

"Here, let me get that for you," the officer volunteered, and reached in front of Nukowski, grabbed the handle, and popped open the door.

Under the glare of the truck stop's bright lights, Nukowski's store of weapons was clearly visible, and when he turned his head to eye the cop, he saw a look of panic on the man's face.

CHAPTER 8

December 16, Truck Stop in Indiana

Indiana State Trooper Clint Ward rocked back on his heels, and his right hand instinctively went to his holstered side-arm. But before he could unsnap the leather strap and draw his service revolver, Nukowski doused him in the face with the scalding coffee. The cop screamed in pain and threw his arms up reflexively, like a boxer trying to shield himself from more blows.

Nukowski dropped the bag of groceries on the ground, stepped around the open door, reached in the cabin, withdrew the Smith and Wesson .500 Magnum, and shot the cop once under his upraised arms through the heart.

It happened so fast that Cooley was still carrying on his end of the conversation about the van with the officer when the violent concussion from the world's most powerful pro-duction revolver jellied his knees. Cooley looked up to see Nukowski long-striding back toward the convenience store. Nukowski was halfway there, the silver-plated handgun with the eight-inch barrel dangling at his side like an executioner's sword, when he spun around and yelled at Cooley to put the cop's body in his cruiser.

Cooley slowly crab-crawled around to the front of the van. The dead cop was lying on the ground, hands thrown behind his head like he was leaning back in a chair, walleyes staring off into the distance, a fist-size hole in his chest, crimson fingers spreading across his shirt and under his badge. Cooley gagged, and bile flooded his mouth. He rolled halfway under the van and vomited. He was still lying there in his own puke when the second gunshot shook the windows inside the store.

———

After he killed the cop, Nukowski entered the convenience store and shot the clerk in the back of the head as she desperately tried to unlock the door to a little office next to the cleaning supply closet in the rear of the building. Nukowski stepped over her body and pushed open the office door and put two rounds into a Dell tower server tucked under a metal desk, guessing that's where video from the security system was stored. He fired his last shot into the security camera mounted over the store's double doors for good measure as he exited.

Cooley was staggering to his feet when Nukowski appeared at his side.

"You're as useless as teats on a boar, Cooley," Nukowski said and pushed past him.

Nukowski grabbed Officer Ward by the coat collar and dragged his body to the police cruiser and stuffed it into the back seat. Before closing the door, he unsnapped the two-way radio from the cop's belt and tucked it into his waistband.

Cooley had climbed back into the van and was sitting in the driver's seat when Nukowski opened the passenger door and tossed the gun and handheld radio inside.

"Drive," Nukowski ordered.

"Nuky," Cooley began to say.

"Shut your face, Cooley, and drive, or I'll shut it permanently. And don't stop until we hit Michigan," Nukowski said in a low, menacing growl.

An hour after the pair fled the truck stop, the first report came over the radio that a trooper and a civilian had been found shot to death. Nukowski ordered Cooley to avoid the interstate and cling to blue highways as they steered a course for the far western regions of Michigan.

Rain fell nonstop, and the farther north they drove, the colder it got. The rain eventually turned to sleety snow, and the roadway was blanketed with an icy sheen. Even the slightest bend in the road sent the van's worn tires into a fishtail, and Cooley fought to keep the vehicle centered in his lane. The van's heater had stopped working altogether, and Cooley was forced to use a credit card to scrape frost off the inside of the windshield.

Cooley's attempts to strike up a conversation with his accomplice went nowhere. "Please, Nuky, I gotta stop and get something to drink," he pleaded. "My throat is parched."

"Swallow your spit," Nukowski said.

"I don't have enough spit to lick a stamp," Cooley whined.

Alerts about the killings continued to spill from the radio, and three hours after the shooting, a bulletin was broadcast for law enforcement to be on the lookout for an older-model, light-green van that a passing motorist had seen exiting the highway at the Fuel King truck stop around the time of the shootings.

"Fuck," Nukowski croaked.

"Jesus, Nuky, you think they made us?" Cooley asked.

"Shut up and let me think," Nukowski said.

When they were fifty miles inside the Michigan state line, Nukowski bolted upright and instructed Cooley to take the Three Rivers exit.

"We need to lay low for a few days, Cooley, ditch this van and get us a new set of wheels," he said. "And I know just the person to help us."

CHAPTER 9

December 16, Washington, DC

Nik was headed across town on Wisconsin Avenue to *Newshound*'s offices when his phone's screen lit up with an incoming call from the Northern Virginia County Sheriff's Department.

"Sheriff Korum," Nik started right in when he answered his phone. "I owe you big-time. Your instincts about Trident were spot-on. It looked like a fricking military exercise when I got over there last night."

"How interesting," a young, raspy female voice said. "Do tell."

It was Samantha Whyte, Korum's investigator.

"Sam, is that you?" Nik said. "I thought you were the sheriff."

"Disappointed?" Sam asked.

"No, I just . . . well, never mind," Nik said, caught off guard, fumbling for a clever riposte and regretting that he might have already revealed too much to the former *Washington Post* reporter. He wanted to cut this conversation short. "I have another call coming in," he fibbed. "Can you ask the sheriff to contact me when he's available?"

"Let it go to voice mail," Sam said. "Sheriff Korum's in budget meetings all day and asked me to return your message. You were a busy boy last night, Nik. I hear your story lit a fire under the ass of the reporters at the *Post*, so to speak," she said.

"It's probably nothing," Nik said, trying to downplay the story. "At least, that's what my editor told me when he chewed me out this morning."

"'Li'l Dick' Whetstone?" Sam said. "What the hell does he know about news?"

"You know him?"

"Yeah, I know of him," Sam said. "Thinks he's God's gift to journalism."

"Yup, that's him," Nik said.

"What a douchebag," Sam said.

Nik chuckled. "Pretty much."

"Listen, Nik," Sam said, her voice turning more steely as she steered the conversation toward a touchy subject between the two of them, "we need to clear the air. I get the sense you still don't fully trust me and blame me for leaking your investigation into county bid-rigging to the *Post*."

"I'm shocked you would feel that way," Nik said sarcastically. "It only took me months of filing Freedom of Information requests and threats from our lawyers to pry those documents out of the county, but somehow they miraculously fell into the *Post*'s lap the day after I let it slip in the sheriff's office what I was working on."

"I swear to God it wasn't me," Sam said defensively.

Nik and Sam had already gone several rounds about the leak to the *Post* in the past, and he didn't want to slug it out again.

"Okay," he said, "I believe you. Feel better?"

"No, you don't."

"You're right, I don't, but we're not going to get anywhere arguing about it for the umpteenth time. Let's just agree to disagree," Nik said.

"You know I'd be well within my rights to tell you to go fuck yourself, Byron," Sam said testily.

Nik laughed out loud.

"What's so goddamned funny?" Sam demanded.

"Oh, nothing," Nik said. "Just the last person to tell me that was my ex-wife, and, truly, she was well within her rights."

"Hmm, sounds like domestic bliss," Sam said mockingly.

"Not even close. For the most part, it was a rock fight. You know how it is," Nik said.

"I'm sure I don't," Sam said. "My sympathies to the lady."

"Easy for you to say, you didn't have to live with her," Nik said.

"Nik, there's not enough time in the day for us to relitigate old battles."

"Agreed, and it's been my experience that those discussions are much more productive over a drink anyhow," Nik said, more in the way of a suggestion than a passing comment.

Sam ignored the overture and said, "The reason the sheriff asked me to call is to pass along some information about the explosion. Our department has been asked to supply support to the investigation."

"Hold on," Nik said. "I need to pull over." He wheeled into a parking lot of the Giant grocery store chain and parked. He retrieved a notebook and pen from his shoulder bag and twisted the top off his coffee mug to let the liquid cool while he took notes. "Okay, go ahead," he said.

"Investigators have pulled video from a security camera mounted across the street from Trident. It's low-res, grainy, and shot from a long distance. There's one straight-on view and one side shot. Not ideal," Sam told Nik.

"Why from across the office park? Doesn't Trident have its own security cameras?" Nik asked.

"They do, but all the feeds went to servers sitting in the building that was destroyed in the explosion, and there's no backup to the cloud," Sam said.

"So what's this crappy video show?" Nik asked.

Sam said, "An old, beat-up, faded-green van, like a repairman would drive, exiting the office park late Sunday afternoon before the explosion. The van's got a couple signs on the doors, and you can definitely see two figures inside."

"When did the van enter Trident?"

"Unknown. It's not a fixed-position camera; it rotates, and it's not always trained on Trident's entrance. It was just by luck that it was aimed in that direction when the van exited. Investigators checked with tenants and maintenance crew, and no one claims to have had a repair scheduled for Sunday."

"Is there a clear view of the passengers?" Nik said.

"Not really. Outlines mostly. Appears to be two men. Technicians are working to enhance the video. And, who knows, it might be just what it appears to be, a repairman's van."

"Understood."

"A couple other things," Sam said.

"I'm listening."

"The video also shows Cal Walker's car entering Trident and driving into the parking garage at the same time the van exited. There's no video of him leaving. I thought you'd want to know, given the stories you've written about his fight with the government."

"Thanks," Nik said.

"Okay, here's the other thing," Sam said. "Investigators think someone may have tampered with the gas line that runs to the office park's backup generator that it relies on in case there's a power failure."

"So, not an industrial accident, then?" Nik said.

"Maybe not. Too soon to say. I should know more later today," Sam said.

Nik was scribbling hurriedly in his notes. "If that turns out to be the case, those people who died were murdered," Nik said.

"That's correct," Sam said.

"Besides the guys in the van, are they looking at any other possible suspects?" Nik asked.

"Feds are focusing on radical privacy groups, antifa, and a handful of lower-level militia outfits. They've assembled a terrorist task force."

"Any foreign terrorist connections?" Nik inquired.

"None that I'm aware of so far, but the feds aren't sharing everything with local law enforcement. I wouldn't be surprised if federal agents aren't kicking doors down and busting heads as we speak," Sam said.

"Really?" Nik said.

"No, of course not. I just said that to see if you were paying attention."

"So, how much of this useable?" Nik asked.

"It's all useable," Sam answered, "but none of it attributable. Proceed with caution, Nik. Things are fluid and could change in one helluva hurry."

"I need to hop on this story before they do," Nik said.

"Any more questions before you go?" Sam asked.

"Just two."

"Shoot."

"You talking to any other reporters?"

"Nope. The sheriff was clear. You have an exclusive. Next question?"

Nik hesitated. "What about that drink?"

"Don't push your luck."

"That's my job," Nik reminded her.

Sam laughed. "Tell you what, call me next week. We'll talk about it then," she said and ended the conversation.

CHAPTER 10

December 16/17, Washington, DC

Nik sped back to *Newshound*'s offices and put in a couple quick calls to the FBI, Homeland Security, and the District of Columbia's Special Investigative Unit. He asked spokespeople at the separate agencies the same basic four questions: *Was the gas line tampered with? Were they able to pull any useable information from the video? Were the men in the van suspects? Did they have any other leads?*

The FBI and Homeland Security issued blanket "no comment"s. The DC spokesperson referred Nik to Corletta Ramsey, a lieutenant detective who was heading up the District's investigation.

"I hate the press," Ramsey proclaimed even before Nik could say hello. "Furthermore, I don't trust you people. You don't get shit right."

"Mornin', Detective," Nik countered. "I was hoping to take just a minute of your time."

"But as much as I despise the media, I hate those government spooks runnin' around all over the place out at Trident even more. The first word out of their mouths when they were babies was a lie, and they only got better at lyin' over time," the detective said.

"Un-huh," Nik uttered. He thought about asking a question but decided to keep quiet and see where this conversation was headed.

"The only reason I took your call is 'cause I know Mo," Ramsey said. "We lift together over at the Y, and he's mentioned your name a time or two."

Of course, Nik thought, *Mo. That figures.*

"I'll give you what I can about the explosion," Ramsey continued, "but it's not for attribution, and you need to get another source to confirm it before you publish. It can't be traced back to me, understood?"

"Understood," Nik said.

"And Lord help you if you burn me."

"You have my word," he said and started composing a rough outline of the list of sources he would need to contact.

Nik worked the phones around the clock and, thirty-six hours later, published his second Trident story.

Investigators Open Two-Pronged Probe into Trident Blast
Evidence of Tampering
Hunt Underway for Older-Model Van
Blast Claims Four Lives

By Nik Byron
Newshound *Deputy Editor*

Authorities combing through the Trident Office Park blast site have

uncovered evidence that a gas pipeline at the complex was tampered with
prior to the explosion, *Newshound* has
learned.

Meanwhile, four blast victims
have now died as a result of their
injuries, and a half dozen others
still remain hospitalized, according
to a Georgetown University Hospital
spokeswoman.

Sources tell *Newshound* that
search crews recovered a large section
of a metal coupling that once joined
the gas pipeline to an industrial generator the office park used as a backup
power source in the event of an elec-
trical failure. Trident relies mostly on
alternative energy for its operations.

The section of coupling that investigators retrieved appears to have been
scored with a series of small drill taps,
possibly suggesting another device was
attached to the pipeline, sources said.

Authorities have sent the metal
fragment to a lab in Maryland for
analysis, but one law enforcement individual close to the investigation who
requested anonymity said, "It's pretty
clear a foreign object was affixed to
that pipeline, and that foreign object
was likely an incendiary device."

A joint task force consisting of
the FBI, Homeland Security, and
the District of Columbia's Special

Investigative Unit has been placed in charge of the Trident investigation. A task force spokesperson refused to comment on the probe.

While field investigators continue to hunt for clues in the wreckage, authorities have also launched a search for an older-model light-green van seen exiting the office park shortly before the blast occurred. A video from a surveillance camera across the street from the office park shows what appear to be two men inside the van, which was described as a "typical repairman's vehicle."

The video footage is low resolution and grainy, but investigators are working to enhance the quality.

The video also reportedly shows OmniSoft Corporation CEO Cal Walker driving his car into the parking garage of Building 8 just prior to the blast. OmniSoft's office building was destroyed by the explosion, and Walker, who has accused the federal government of intellectual property theft, has not been heard from since Sunday night.

In addition to OmniSoft, Trident is home to a number of technology companies that conduct highly sensitive work for some of the nation's top spy and counterintelligence agencies.

The southeast Washington office

park has been the target of protests by
privacy and anti-government groups
in the past, and those groups, along
with some militia-style organizations,
are currently drawing the attention of
authorities, sources said.

No one has yet claimed responsibil-
ity for the blast, and investigators have
all but ruled out foreign involvement,
sources said.

The four victims who died as a
result of injuries they sustained in the
explosion were described as a 42-year-
old software developer, a 33-year-old
office manager, a 62-year-old security
guard, and a 44-year-old landscaper.
Their identities were being withheld
pending notification of next of kin, a
hospital spokeswoman said.

CHAPTER 11

Two Days Earlier, Trident Office Park

On the afternoon of the explosion, Cal Walker pulled into Trident's driveway and noticed the rickety van with the lopsided business signs exiting the office park and turning south toward the interstate. It had been years since Walker had worked for the National Security Agency and CIA as an analyst, but his spy training had never completely abandoned him, and, out of old habits, he would unconsciously make mental notes of seemingly small inconsistencies in his surroundings.

Take the van, for instance. It looked ordinary enough, the type of vehicle any repairman might drive, but Walker wondered why the van's signs didn't have any contact information. There wasn't a phone number, email, or website address. Just the name: "Washington Service & Repair." That was odd. And what was it doing in the office park on a Sunday, when most businesses were closed and the place nearly deserted?

Indeed, Walker himself would not have been there had he not received a message from an unidentified caller promising to provide him with damaging evidence against the federal government to use in his upcoming trial.

The readout on his answering machine had shown the call was coming from a blocked number, but he had hacked the phone company and was able to retrieve the caller's number. It was from a cell phone. He scribbled down the number and stuck it in his wallet. He'd try to track down the phone's owner later when he had time but suspected it was probably a burner phone.

Walker had become used to these anonymous promises over the years, and, ninety-nine times out of a hundred they turned out to be dead ends, more likely than not ploys by someone trying to enlist Walker in their own fight against the government, or an around-the-bend conspiracy nut who wanted to bounce their ideas off Walker. And, ninety-nine times out of a hundred the tipsters were men, but this time, it was a woman who had left a message on his answering machine, and for that reason, he was more hopeful the caller might actually possess some useful information.

The unidentified caller said she'd meet Walker at his Trident office at six p.m. Walker had some work he needed to catch up on, so he arrived early on Sunday, at four thirty, and that's when he spotted the two men in the van leaving the office park.

Walker wrapped up his work by five thirty, closed down his laptop, and made a few handwritten notes in preparation for the meeting. He decided to brew a pot of coffee and ice some drinks in the hope the discussion turned productive. He didn't have any snacks in the office to offer the visitor since he'd been trying to lose weight. His battle with the government had taken its toll and had drained Walker financially, emotionally, and physically. He had easily packed on an extra twenty pounds, and it showed noticeably on his five-foot-nine frame.

He fished two dusty bottles of sparkling water out from under the sink in the break room and filled the coffee machine reservoir with tap water. He opened the cupboard above the refrigerator to retrieve the coffee, but the shelf was empty. Damn. He could offer his guest tea, but he only had a couple stale Earl Grey pouches in a drawer, and he really could use the caffeine himself.

He glanced at the clock: 5:40. If he hustled, he could make it to the small country store down the road and back again in time. He scribbled a quick note and tacked it to the door. "Went out for coffee. Will be back 6-ish" and signed it "Cal." He cursed when he got stuck behind a church bus on his way to the store and realized he'd be late for his appointment.

Walker hurried out of the store and into the wintertime darkness and a light drizzle with a can of Folgers Coffee, a pint of half-and-half, a six-pack of diet soda, and some low-fat snacks.

He was backing out of his parking spot when he heard the explosion and saw the flash over the office park. Walker wheeled his Prius around and spun out of the store's lot, heading away from Trident as fast as his little hybrid car would take him.

———

Walker exited Maryland State Route 5 at Trinity Church Road and pulled into the gravel parking lot of a little boatyard where he moored his Catalina 375 sailboat. He had made the drive from DC in just under three hours, a trip that normally took two hours and change even in heavy traffic, but he drove well under the speed limit for most of the journey to avoid attracting attention and to milk every drop of power possible from his rapidly dwindling Prius battery. Walker had planned to plug the car in Sunday night, as was his habit, and have it fully charged for the workweek Monday morning. Now he was praying he could make it to a recharging station before the battery pack went completely dead and left him hoping the fumes in the reserve gas tank were enough to keep him from getting stranded.

On the drive down, Walker had anxiously flipped back and forth between radio stations, hoping to catch reports about the explosion. So far, details were skimpy—a dozen or so victims transported and admitted to Georgetown University Hospital for treatment and at least one office building—Building 8— totally destroyed by the blast, the building that had housed OmniSoft Corporation.

Initial reports claimed the blast was the result of a gas pipeline leak, but Walker wasn't buying it. He was convinced he had been intentionally lured to his office and that the explosion was meant for him. It was only by sheer luck that he had avoided being at his desk when the building came down.

He saw reporter Nik Byron's calls come in while he drove south out of the nation's capital but let them go to voice mail. He debated whether he should pick up, but decided it would be safer, in the near term, if people didn't know his whereabouts, let alone if he were dead or alive. It would take days, if not weeks, to clear the rubble and discover that Walker was not in the building, nor his car in the underground parking garage. Walker eschewed traditional cell phones and exclusively used burner phones so he couldn't be tracked, another holdover from his NSA days. He had hacked his home and office phones to forward his calls to the endless supply of burner phones he used.

He avoided going back to his Dupont Circle condominium to pack belongings for the trip and instead drove straight to St. Mary's on Maryland's southernmost tip on the western banks of the Chesapeake Bay. Walker had once dated a coed who attended Saint Mary's College, and he was familiar with the area.

The first thing Walker did after unlocking the boat's cabin was to shave the grizzly hipster beard that had taken him six months to grow. Walker was anything but hip, but he was a geek, and inevitably, nearly every story written about him and OmniSoft's skirmish with the government either had a picture with him and the full beard or mentioned it in passing. It had become his trademark.

Shorn of the chestnut facial hair, Walker applied several coats of bronzer to his milky skin to give him a weathered appearance. Next, he cut and dyed his brown hair a distinguished silver and strung a pair of reading glasses around his neck. He now looked more like a bookish live-aboard sailor and less like Ulysses S. Grant. He vowed to drop fifteen pounds as soon as possible to complete the makeover.

It was only a few years earlier that Walker had bought the secondhand sloop and stashed it in the St. Mary's boatyard for just such an occasion. He had stocked the boat with a month's provisions, clothing, a few disguises, $10,000 in cash, passports, and outfitted it with top-of-the-line navigation gear, Wi-Fi, dozens of burner phones, calling cards, backup computer equipment, and files.

The location offered him a number of escape routes—he could lie low in St. Mary's, sail up and down the Chesapeake Bay, or head east to open water and the Atlantic Ocean and then north to Canada or south to the Florida Keys.

For the time being, Walker would remain in St. Mary's, working on the boat, waiting, watching, and listening. And when he felt the time was right, he'd resurface.

CHAPTER 12

December 21, Georgetown

Samantha Whyte met Nik for drinks at Nora's, a charming café tucked away on a side street off Wisconsin Avenue in Georgetown. Sam had picked the location after rejecting Nik's first two suggestions—the Stagecoach Inn in Arlington and Fifteen Minutes in Adams Morgan.

"Loved those places," she told Nik when he called the following week as promised, "when I was in college."

The bar at Nora's was intimate, elegant, quiet, and tastefully adorned with garlands for the holidays. A restored tin ceiling hung overhead, and the floor was covered in a honeycomb-patterned tile. The plastered walls were covered with dozens of black-and-white photos of Scottish terriers in all shapes and sizes staring down at the patrons. The bartender—his name tag read "Charles"—gave Nik a stiff-necked sideways glance when he called him Charlie and asked for a longneck Budweiser. After debating several drink options, Sam ordered a vodka martini. When the drinks arrived, Charles started to pour Nik's beer into a fluted glass when Nik stopped him with a wave of his hand, pushed the glass aside, and picked up the bottle and took a long pull.

"Thanks, Charles," Sam said and gave Nik a smirk and a shake of the head.

"Cheers," she said, and she and Nik clinked glasses.

"Cheers," Nik said, "to burying the hatchet."

"To burying the hatchet," Sam agreed, and they clinked glasses again.

When Nik had called Sam and suggested they get together for a drink, he informed her that he had discovered how the *Post* had gotten wind of *Newshound*'s county bid-rigging story. Turns out, the clerk in the county commissioner's office who had handled Nik's documents request had leaked it to a *Post* reporter.

"Place is a sieve, and I owe you an apology," Nik had told her during the call.

"Well, whaddya know, it wasn't me after all," Sam had chided. "Apology accepted."

No sooner had she forgiven him than Nik had asked her out for a drink. Sam had halfway anticipated the invitation when she saw Nik's number pop up on her caller ID. She had already decided she'd accept if he asked. It was late in the year, and it wasn't as if her calendar was overflowing with invitations.

"But it's not a date," she had insisted.

"Fine. Call it whatever you like," Nik said.

"Besides," Sam had added, "I've been meaning to call you. There's some new information Sheriff Korum received that he asked me to pass along to you." Sam wouldn't say what the information was over the phone but promised to share it with Nik when they met.

"So, do you have big plans for the holidays?" Nik asked after the toasts, resisting the impulse to talk shop right away.

Sam appreciated his stab at chitchat and gave him a quick smile as she pushed a pair of red Tom Fords to the top of her head. Nik had not seen her wearing glasses before. They had the dual effect of making her look smart and sexy at the same time.

"I'll see some friends, visit family, catch up on some rest, read the new John Grisham novel. Guy's a machine," she said. "You?"

"A quick trip to see the family, drink eggnog, eat too much turkey. Looking forward to seeing the sibs."

"Brothers and sisters?"

"Yeah, one each. I'm the oldest of three. You?"

"Just my older sister and me. What about Mrs. Byron?"

"My mother?"

"Your wife."

"My *ex*-wife, Maggie?"

"Right. You guys get together over the holidays?"

"If that's your way of asking if we have kids, the answer is no, we do not. No little Byrons running around, at least not that I'm aware of."

"So does she still live in the Midwest?"

"No. She's here."

"In Nora's?" Sam asked, looking around.

"No, DC. By sheer coincidence, she got transferred to Washington around the same time I moved out here. She works for the US Attorney's office."

"How . . ." Several thoughts crossed Sam's mind—*convenient, manipulative, unfortunate.* She settled on "interesting."

"Believe me, I know. So far, we've avoided any head-on collisions, though I did see her the other day in Adams Morgan walking arm in arm with this block of granite who looked like he could play middle linebacker for the Chicago Bears. She was dwarfed by him, and I wouldn't even have recognized her had I not heard her voice. That you don't forget," Nik said without any trace of malice.

"Some women like men with a little more meat on their bones," Sam said.

"Apparently, and my New Year's resolution is to hit the gym more often," Nik said, flexing his biceps.

"You might want to consider a lifetime membership," Sam teased.

It was chilly in the bar when they first arrived, as customers and staff shuttled in and out a side entrance to smoke and vape, letting in microbursts of frigid air each time the door swung open. Sam's cheeks and the tip of her nose were raspberry red from her walk to the restaurant, and she had remained bundled up in her coat.

Charles lit a fire in the fireplace, and the bar's small interior quickly turned toasty. Sam peeled off her coat and draped it over a barstool, revealing a black cashmere crewneck sweater, caramel-colored slacks, a jewel-encrusted belt cinched tightly around her waist, with black knee-high boots. Sam had a light sandy-colored complexion with a band of freckles running across the bridge of her nose and under her eyes. Her shoulder-length strawberry-blonde hair was tucked behind her ears, and the glow from the fireplace lit up her pale-blue eyes.

"What are you doing for New Year's Eve?" Nik asked casually.

Sam was ready for that question, too, but she wanted to be careful how she answered. She didn't want to give Nik the impression she was either desperate or too available, but she also didn't want to be rude. She was mulling over her response when Nik volunteered, "Can't stand it, personally. It's for amateurs. I agreed to work."

"Oh," Sam said, equally relieved and miffed by his response. She didn't have any plans, but told Nik, "I'm still trying to decide. I've got a couple options." If she had been totally honest, she would have told Nik she'd probably order Chinese, watch *When Harry Met Sally* or *Sleepless in Seattle*, and be in bed before midnight.

"Good," he said, sounding genuinely pleased for her. "Hey, Charlie," Nik shouted to the barkeep, "how about another round of drinks, and no need to pour my beer this time."

The bartender had his back to the couple, but Sam could see his shoulders tense when Nik called him Charlie again. Sam wondered if Nik was intentionally provoking their server or if he was truly so—*what was the word she was searching for*—Midwestern? If he was being genuine, it was charming in an unadorned sort of way. If it was a shtick, it would wear thin pretty quickly. For the time being, she'd give him the benefit of the doubt.

"So," Nik asked, propping an elbow on the bar and resting his chin in his palm, "what's your story?"

"Whatever do you mean?" Sam asked.

"Well, I'd hardly call you a typical civil servant. Not often you come across a reporter who's jumped ship to work in law enforcement."

This was true. Sam had started her reporting career at a small daily newspaper on Maryland's Eastern Shore after graduating from Georgetown. After a year, she took a job in Annapolis covering state politics, and three years later, the *Washington Post* came calling with an offer to cover the Hill.

She had earned a reputation as a tough but fair reporter from both sides of the aisle, and it wasn't long before she was appearing on cable news outlets for her numerous scoops. She loved politics and had chosen Georgetown specifically to pursue a career in public affairs or in the foreign services, but she had gotten bit by the journalism bug when she was a sophomore and spent the next three years practically living at the campus newspaper offices.

After two years of covering the Hill, Sam was offered the White House beat, a plum job, but before she could start, she and fellow reporter Gregg Robbins needed to wrap up an investigation they were conducting into foreign campaign contributions to Lisa Cunningham, the second-ranking member of the House and chair of the House Ways and Means Committee.

Robbins and Sam had been digging into the story on and off for eight months, and on one particularly long evening near the conclusion of their investigation, they had wound up in bed together. It might have been inevitable, but it was nonetheless complicated.

Sam was single, but Robbins was married to another *Post* reporter, although recently separated. Their secret affair was about two months old when they chartered a turboprop plane to Cunningham's vacation home off the coast of Georgia to confront her with their findings.

They had light cocktails on the plane and arrived at the small airport that served Sea Island a little after four p.m. on a Friday afternoon. The plan was to meet a source, grab an early dinner, and prep for their nine a.m. interview the next morning with Congresswoman Cunningham.

Sam had exited the plane with her carry-on luggage ahead of her colleague and turned right at the bottom of the stairway toward the terminal. What transpired next was still a mystery. Robbins had an overnight bag and small briefcase in one hand and his cell phone cradled between his shoulder and ear when he, inexplicably, turned left at the bottom of the gangway and walked straight into the churning propeller and was decapitated.

There were plenty of theories as to what happened— Robbins's head was down and he was distracted by the call; he was light-headed from too many drinks on the plane; the antianxiety medication he had been prescribed after he and his wife separated had clouded his judgment.

Sam remained on Sea Island for two days while the accident was under investigation. Blood tests revealed trace amounts of alcohol and medication in Robbins's system, but hardly enough to impair his judgment. Sam never interviewed the congresswoman, and she never told anyone that she and Robbins were having an affair. There was nothing to gain by causing more grief for his widow, and she kept the secret even now.

Two days after Robbins's funeral, she had resigned from the *Post* and dropped out of sight for the next twelve months, eventually resurfacing as a spokesperson and investigator for Sheriff Korum's department. Sam seldom dated and had not been romantically involved with anyone since.

Of course, it had been a couple years since the tragedy, and Nik, new to town, wouldn't have been aware of her history.

"Wanted a change of scenery, I guess," Sam said, issuing her standard reply. "And I like Korum. He's a good soul. Why'd you decide to move to DC?"

"For the climate," Nik said. "Who doesn't like walking around in a steam bath for half the year and over the carcasses of thousands of dying cicadas? Only place I've ever lived where they sweep the bugs off the sidewalks in the morning. Then there's the Duke University graduates. They're thicker than the cicadas but infinitely more annoying."

"Dook, as we Hoyas call it, sucks," Sam said.

They clinked glasses and cheers-ed to that, too.

"Go ahead and ask," Sam said eventually. "I know you've been dying to."

"Is it that obvious?" Nik said.

"Only since the moment you arrived, but you put up a good front."

"Okay," Nik said, "what is it that Sheriff Korum wanted you to tell me?"

"It's about Cal Walker, OmniSoft's CEO."

Nik sat straighter in his chair. "Yeah, what about him? They identify his body?" Nik asked.

Rescue workers had pulled three mangled corpses from what was left of Walker's building in the office park and were awaiting DNA results, bringing the total casualties from the explosion to seven.

"He's not dead, or, at least, he wasn't in that building when it collapsed," Sam said.

"You sure about that?"

"Positive. The guy who owns the little country grocery store 'bout a mile down the road from Trident said Walker was in his parking lot when the gas line blew. He said Walker bought coffee, soft drinks, and some snacks and said he was in a hurry to get back to his office for a meeting. Store owner said Walker's been going there for years and they were on a first-name basis."

"I'll be damned," Nik said.

"There's something else," Sam said.

"You know where he is?" Nik asked.

"No. It has to do with the guys in the van."

"Oh?"

"Investigators think they may have stumbled across them," Sam said.

"Really, where?"

"Indiana, a truck stop."

"What the hell they doing in Indiana?" Nik asked.

"Apparently killing a cop and a store clerk," Sam said.

———

After Nik pumped Sam for all the information she had on Walker and the guys in the van, they spent the rest of the evening at Nora's sipping drinks, nibbling on crab cakes, and slurping raw oysters while swapping stories about their favorite pastimes—Sam was an avid downhill skier, mountain biker, and backcountry camper. Nik loved fly-fishing and bridge and was struggling with Chinese. They compared notes on restaurants, books, and Netflix series they binge-watched. When Nora's emptied and Charles wiped down the bar in front of them for the fifth time, they decided it was time to call it a night. Nik left Charles a 25 percent tip, and that seemed to soothe the barkeep's ruffled feathers. Nik helped Sam on with her coat and offered to give her a ride home. She resisted at first, planning to summon an Uber, but when she stepped outside and saw how deserted the streets were and how cold it was, she reconsidered.

Maybe it was the alcohol, the holiday spirit, or Nik's easy manner, but Sam found herself warming to Nik as the night drifted pleasantly along. He reminded her of a goofy, if somewhat misguided, boy next door with a good heart. Sam's weakness had always been what she called a guy's S&S—smile and shoulders. She insisted both be broad, and Nik's features fit the bill.

"Nice place," Nik said when he nudged his vehicle to the curb in front of her house, a restored Craftsman just off Foxhall Road.

"It was my aunt Sally's. She left it to me. I've done quite a bit of cosmetic work on it. New roof, windows, steps, paint, but the bones are good."

Nik sighed.

"Everything okay?" Sam said.

He nodded. "Reminds me of a place I once had."

"What happened to it?" Sam asked.

"Life happened," Nik said, and leaned across the seat to give Sam a good-night peck on the cheek. He was surprised when Sam didn't turn away and instead met him full on the lips, but perhaps no more surprised than Sam was herself as she lingered in the moment.

"That was . . ." she began to say when she pulled back.

"Unexpected," Nik chimed in.

"No. Well, yes, but what I was going to say was 'nice.'"

Sam reached for the handle, pushed on the passenger door, and slipped out of the seat, sensing she just might wind up in Nik's lap if they were to continue kissing.

She dropped down and popped her head back inside and said, "I have a confession to make, Nik."

"Oh," he responded. "Is this the point in the evening when you tell me you have a boyfriend?"

"No." She laughed. "Nothing like that. But I told you a white lie. I don't have any New Year's Eve plans."

"Fantastic," Nik said, "because I'm not really working. I know a great little jazz club that's hosting a party. Whaddya say?"

"It's a date," Sam said and bent in and gave Nik another kiss, putting a little extra charge in it this time.

She withdrew her head but, after a moment, bent down again and said, "Nik, do you know the inside of your vehicle smells like dog?"

"Is that a problem?" Nik said.

"Only if you don't have a dog," Sam said and turned and walked to her front door.

CHAPTER 13

December 22, Washington, DC

Other than the brief encounter in Adams Morgan, Nik had not seen or spoken to his ex-wife in months. After a rocky marriage and at times contentious separation, the couple eventually had an amicable divorce and remained, if not friends, friendly. But neither went out of their way to stay in close contact, and while they shared memories—some great, others painful—and a few close friends, they didn't have children to keep them bound together. At times, Nik regretted not staying in touch, if only because he had a sense that he was losing a part of his past. After the divorce was finalized, he had to fight the impulse to reach out to Maggie just to check in, but eventually those urges subsided. He often wondered if she felt the same way, though somehow he rather doubted it. Maggie's unvarnished advice to Nik—"It was real, but it's really over"—stayed with him long after the divorce and propelled him to move forward.

He had not given a lot of thought to Maggie until now, but when Sam asked about a wife, it sparked an idea.

Nik and Maggie's professional relationship was nearly as

fraught as their personal one. As an assistant US attorney, Maggie was often in a position to have firsthand knowledge about government information Nik was pursuing as a reporter. The opposite was also true. Nik's sources would reveal secrets to him the government was trying to discover. He and Maggie had always been guarded about what information they shared with one another and were careful not to leave sensitive documents or notes lying around the house where the other person could find them, even if unwittingly.

Their efforts to conceal information led to a strange Kabuki dance, which was the cause of endless frustration and friction between the couple when they were married and living in the Midwest. Both were pleasantly surprised to discover how much their separation had dialed down the tension. The only issue that remained between them was Gyp, a copper-colored vizsla Nik got when it was an eight-week-old puppy. Maggie didn't want a dog but was stuck raising it when Nik moved out of their house to a small apartment during their separation.

Maggie saw in the dog the same undisciplined and at times ill-mannered attitude that she found so maddening in Nik and was thrilled when he announced he would be taking Gyp to DC with him once he was settled.

Nik was uncertain what work Maggie had been assigned in the US Attorney's office in DC, but he knew she was a rising star and had been actively recruited to the nation's capital to get her more exposure to the top brass at the Justice Department.

Nik figured if she didn't have direct information about the Trident explosion, she'd at least know someone who did. The question was, would she share it with him? And there was only one way to find out.

———

Maggie had just stepped into a meeting with her assistant about a money-laundering case she was prosecuting when her cell phone buzzed and Nik's name popped up on the screen. Her first thought was *What's he want?* And she debated whether to answer.

"Go ahead and start the meeting without me, Louis," she said to her colleague. "I need to take this call. It shouldn't be long." Maggie stepped back out in the hallway and answered the phone.

"Is everything all right?" she asked worriedly. She and Nik had agreed to keep each other informed in the event something happened to someone in their immediate families.

"Everything's fine, Maggs," Nik said. "No deaths, serious illness, missing persons."

"So, why are you calling?" Maggie said, a sharper note in her voice now.

"I'll get to that in a second," Nik said, "but before I located your new cell number, I called the AG's switchboard and they said they didn't have a Maggie Byron working there."

"That's right, Nik. I went back to using my maiden name, Stone, Margaret Stone. Now, what is this about? I'm very busy."

The news wasn't totally unexpected, but it still caused Nik's voice to catch in his throat, even if just a little. "I'm calling about the Trident Park explosion. I need some help with information."

Maggie wasn't involved with the case, but she knew about it. Her colleague Gaylord Spence—an ex-college jock and one-time semiprofessional weight lifter—had told her the Justice Department had quietly launched an investigation into the explosion, and she had been following the events ever since.

Spence was a political appointee with a degree from a third-rate law school whose father, an ethanol fuel titan, had raised millions of dollars for the president's campaign, and when his man won, old man Spence's reward was a patronage job for his slow-witted son with the Justice Department. Spence Junior's title was special assistant to the attorney general, which meant he created PowerPoint presentations and ran the audiovisual equipment for his boss.

It was a meaningless job, but it gave Spence access to sensitive information, and in his desire to impress Maggie and get into her pants, he blabbed to her about the Trident investigation.

"The AG doesn't believe a fucking word those cocksuckers at the CIA or the NSA say," Spence had confided one evening to Maggie when she suspected he was particularly horny and desperate for something more satisfying than a hand job. "One lies and the other swears to it. If this Trident thing's dirty, you can bet they'll try to pin it on the FBI, which means the Justice Department. The AG has assigned a dozen agents, and that's just for starters."

Maggie found Spence to be a useful diversion, though she still hadn't slept with him and wasn't sure she would. He was good-looking enough and as randy as a bachelor at an all-girls boarding school, but he was also divorced with two kids, alimony payments, a mortgage, and a law degree from some college she'd never heard of until she met him.

"What sort of information you looking for?" Maggie asked Nik suspiciously.

"Don't worry. I won't ask you to violate your oath or any laws," Nik said. "I just need to know if I'm on the right track or if I'm headed off a cliff."

Nik told Maggie what he knew and what he suspected: that two men driving an older-model van might be linked to the explosion at Trident and possibly the deaths of a cop and a store clerk in Indiana; that Cal Walker, the CEO of OmniSoft, might have been targeted in the blast and apparently was on the lam; that a highly trained military unit had appeared on-site almost immediately after the explosion, as if they had been anticipating it, and that the guy in charge of the unit was a colonel.

"We call him Colonel Mustard because of his yellow mustache. We don't have a last name, though it could be Calkins, but we haven't had any luck verifying that so far. I don't have any idea how any of it fits together," Nik said, "and on top of that, my editor has threatened to fire me if I keep pursuing the story."

Maggie entered a vacant office in the Robert F. Kennedy Department of Justice Building. She could see the top half of the Washington Monument down Connecticut Avenue from a small window in the office. She closed the door and propped herself on the edge of a desk and weighed what to divulge to Nik, if anything.

"All the old ground rules still apply?" she said.

"Yes," Nik said. "I won't use your name or identify you in any way."

"And if you get anything significant, you'll give me fair warning before it's printed?"

This was the one part of the agreement Nik wished she'd forgotten. It made him cringe to release information before it was published, but he rationalized it by telling himself that East Coast news broadcasts were often delayed for viewers in West Coast markets.

"Deal," he reluctantly conceded.

"You're headed in the right direction. After the cop and store clerk were killed, the criminals shot up the computer server where the security video was stored," Maggie said, "but our techs were able to retrieve the damaged files and are now working on restoring the images."

"How's that possible?" Nik asked.

"It's called digital harmonics," Maggie said, "and it applies technology that allows users to experience images that are otherwise too degraded or obscure for the human eye alone.

The software tools analyze embedded data in waveforms to render the images decipherable."

"That's surreal," Nik said. "You think I might—"

"Get a look at the files?" Maggie cut in. "Dunno. My understanding is the best we can hope for is that the images will confirm that the van is the same make and model as the one observed at Trident and that the two guys share similar structural, facial, and hair characteristics. It's not like we'll have actual mug shots. I might be able to supply you with an image, but no guarantees. I'll know more in twenty-four hours. I gotta go now, Nik."

"Thanks, Maggs, I owe you."

"Listen, you took that damn dog off my hands, so I figure we're even. By the way, how's Gyp doing anyhow?"

"He's had a little setback," Nik admitted. "I left Gyp in my vehicle a couple weeks ago when I ran into the dry cleaners for about five minutes, and I think he may have had a panic attack. He chewed through all the seat belts. I had to send him to finishing school."

"What's he finishing, his brain? I don't get your attachment to that dog," Maggie said.

"Well, it's like this, Maggs," Nik said, "unlike women and cats, the later I come home, the happier Gyp is to see me."

"Maybe next time get yourself a fish, Nik," Maggie said, and then hung up.

CHAPTER 14

December 22, Three Rivers, Michigan

Nukowski.

That was Grant Dilworth's first thought, lying in bed at night, when he heard the engine whine and saw headlights dance over the treetops as a vehicle bounced down the rutted lane that led to his secluded cabin in the pines. His second thought was *Run.*

And he would have, too, but his wife and newborn were asleep across the hallway and it wasn't an option.

Dilworth scrambled from his bed and to the window just in time to see a dull-green van with the windows down pass under a sodium vapor yard light and roll to a stop in front of his machine shop. The light snow that had begun falling when he turned in for bed had intensified overnight, and the ground, trees, and the sculptures he forged for a living were covered in a blanket of powdered sugar. He glanced at the clock: three fifteen a.m.

His dog, Pontiac, an eighty-five-pound black-and-tan sway-back German shepherd, thankfully, was at the vet's recuperating from an injury he had received after getting ensnared in a coyote leg trap, or he would have been bringing down the house with his barking and howling.

Dilworth darted across the hallway and looked in on his wife and daughter. Still asleep. He gently closed their door and went back to the window. He could see two figures inside the van, but so far, neither one had made a move to get out of the vehicle.

Maybe it isn't Nukowski after all, but just someone who's lost, he thought hopefully, but knew better.

More likely, Nukowski was getting his bearings. It had been, what, at least five years since he was there last, and a lot had changed. Then, the only structure was a piss-yellow double-wide trailer with a bowed axle mounted on cinder blocks, no outbuildings, and an overgrown pasture full of rusted-out farming equipment. The trailer was gone now, and in its place stood a two-story log cabin with a shiny metal roof and wraparound porch and attached garage. The pasture was mowed and dotted with various stainless-steel sculptures of grizzlies, bison, and wolves that Dilworth created in his machine shop and sold online around the world.

Any doubt Dilworth had about who was in the vehicle vanished when the passenger door sprang open and out stepped a wiry bantamweight with a limp mullet whose hips and rounded shoulders rolled like waves when he walked. It was Nukowski all right.

Dilworth grabbed a pair of jeans from a bedside chair, pulled a ragg-wool sweater over his head, stepped into a pair of ropers, and tucked a .32 revolver into the small of his back. He opened the front door just as Nukowski set his foot on the bottom porch step.

"Long time no see, Grant," Nukowski said, bounding up the stairs and thrusting out a powerful hand.

Dilworth ignored the gesture and said, "When'd you lose the ankle monitor, Nuky?"

"Ha-ha," Nukowski said.

"What are you doing here?" Dilworth demanded. "At this time of night. Can't be anything good."

"Is that any way to greet your former partner?" Nukowski said and leaned back against the porch railing and looked around. "I swear, you're prosperous, Grant. I hardly recognized the property at first, but when I saw those sculptures, I know'd it was your place. You always talked about metalworking if you ever got ahead. You should at least give me a little credit for getting you back on your feet."

"Only to nearly get me killed."

"You survived, didn't you?"

As much as he tried to put it out of his memory, Dilworth knew if not for Nukowski, he likely would have died well before his time. Nukowski had found him living on the streets of Detroit when he was young, alone, and scared. For food, Dilworth waylaid KFC customers carrying buckets of chicken as they exited the restaurants or wrestled bags of groceries from old ladies as they made their way to their cars. He was always careful not to injure his victims if he could help it.

A photo Dilworth had saved from that time in his life showed him emaciated; his ribs poking through a ratty T-shirt; his eyes lifeless, sunken, and dark as the bottom of a well. Nukowski had given him a place to live, fed him, and taught him how to chop cars, cook meth, run guns, and steal credit card numbers online. They were small-time hoods who flew under law enforcement's radar for the most part, but two scores at the end of their crime spree changed that.

Nukowski had been tipped off that a Mexican mule was in Detroit with a cache of cocaine for distribution in the Midwest, and he, Dilworth, and another accomplice, a woman, staged a car accident with the mule's vehicle as it turned onto a ramp for Interstate 94. Nukowski pistol-whipped the mule, and they made off with ten kilos of pure cocaine. After they cut and resold the coke on the street, the take was split three ways, with each pocketing nearly $75,000. Dilworth used his proceeds to buy the farm where he now lived with his wife and daughter.

That would have been the end of Dilworth's criminal career had not Nukowski strong-armed him into making one last run to St. Louis to deliver stolen guns to a motorcycle gang, the Rivertown Rebels. Unbeknownst to them, they walked into a sting by the Missouri Compliance and Investigation Bureau and had to shoot their way out. Two undercover officers, one a thirty-one-year-old woman with a husband and twin toddlers at home, were killed in the firefight along with three members of the motorcycle club.

Dilworth and Nukowski escaped and were never identified, but the case remained active, and the killings hung over the pair and knitted them together forever. Dilworth blamed Nukowski for the botched operation, and their parting was acrimonious.

"Who's your friend?" Dilworth asked, chinning toward Cooley.

"Don't worry about him. He doesn't know anything."

"He knows where I live."

"Couldn't be helped."

"I'll ask again, what do you want?" Dilworth said and let go of the door handle with his right hand and slid two steps to the left of Nukowski to create space in case he needed to draw the gun.

"We need a vehicle."

"What's wrong with the one you're driving?"

"It's a little too popular for my taste."

"There's a used-car lot in town. O'Neil's. You probably passed by it. They can fix you up. They open at nine."

"No paperwork."

"What'd you do?"

"Believe me, the less you know, the better," Nukowski said. "You do this favor for me, Grant, and we're done. You got my word on that."

Dilworth heard a disturbance from inside the house and flinched, and Nukowski pushed off the railing and cocked his head toward the front door.

"Who's inside?" Nukowski asked.

"It's Pontiac, my German shepherd."

"How come he didn't bark when we pulled in?"

"He's old. Deaf, half blind, and stove up. It's all he can do to scoot his ass across the floor."

Nukowski threw Dilworth a *you better not be fucking with me* look.

To distract him, Dilworth said, "I'll make a call. There's an old, abandoned homestead about four miles back on the east side of the road. Your new vehicle will be behind the barn this time six days from now, fueled. Leave the van with the keys in it. It'll be chopped before daylight."

"That's my ol' pard," Nukowski said and edged slowly backward off the porch. When he reached the bottom of the stairs, he looked up at Dilworth. "You ever see Sara again after the coke heist?"

"Sara? No, never did," Dilworth said. "Why?"

"Oh, no reason," he said with a soft chuckle. "Just wondered, is all." Nukowski climbed into the idling van, and Cooley nosed it back down the rutted lane. The van braked and Nukowski cranked down the window. "Don't make me come back here a second time, Grant, if you know what's good for you," he called out before the van rolled on. Threat delivered.

The front door cracked open. "That Nukowski?"

"Yeah," Dilworth said.

"Jesus."

"Yeah."

A gust of wind caught the hem of Sara's patchwork-quilt robe and parted the front, revealing a pair of long, silky legs, black bikini panties, and a 12-gauge Winchester pump shotgun pressed up against her right thigh.

CHAPTER 15

December 24, Washington, DC

Nik glanced down at his trilling phone as he stepped inside the elevator in *Newshound*'s parking garage. It was Dick Whetstone. Nik hit the End Call button and patiently waited for the alert informing him that he had a voice mail. It was the eighth call in the last few days from his editor, and each time, Whetstone left Nik a lengthy message, which he summarily deleted without opening. Nik reasoned if he avoided the calls and messages, then Whetstone couldn't actually fire him, at least not until he returned from his West Coast media junket. And as appealing as the prospect of firing Nik might be, Nik knew Whetstone well enough to know he was not about to cut his all-expenses-paid travels and vacation short to accomplish it.

Nik had already blocked all incoming text messages from Whetstone's mobile number and had his emails automatically routed to a junk mail folder, which was emptied routinely. Nik knew his actions were grounds for dismissal and that

Whetstone would likely sack him the moment he set foot back in the office. By then, Nik hoped the Trident story would have taken on a life of its own.

But, with Whetstone's looming return and DC grinding to a halt during the holidays, it was a race against time, and Nik needed help. Which was why he summoned Mo, Mia, and Frank Rath for an early-morning meeting at *Newshound*'s offices on Christmas Eve.

It was officially an office holiday, but Nik needed to bring the trio up to speed on his reporting and make it clear to them that they could be jeopardizing their jobs by remaining on the Trident story.

Nik made a pit stop at Sugar Shack Donuts & Coffee before heading to the office, and the sweet smell of freshly baked pastries and the earthy aroma of just-brewed coffee reached the conference room thirty seconds before Nik. Mo's head snapped up from its resting position on the conference room table when he scented the coffee.

"Bless you, son," he said groggily, eyes bleary. Despite the temperature being barely above freezing, Mo was dressed in cutoff jeans, a ripped Gold's Gym T-shirt, and flip-flops.

"Late night?" Nik asked.

"Stayed too long at the Third Edition," Mo croaked.

"You know what they say," Frank said, helping himself to a cup of coffee.

"No," Mo managed to answer. "Tell me?"

"Dogs that chase cars and men who close down bars don't live long lives," Frank said philosophically and stabbed a couple of donuts.

"That's rich, coming from you," Mo said.

Notwithstanding years of heavy drinking, smoking, and an unhealthy diet, Frank Rath looked remarkably fit for someone pushing seventy. There wasn't a trace of gray in his tar-black hair, and he was as lean as a whippet. That was on the outside. On the inside, it was an entirely different story. Frank's kidneys were failing.

Mo had inadvertently learned of Frank's condition one day when he overheard a phone call Frank was having with his insurance provider. Frank had sworn Mo to secrecy about it, but one night, when he had too much to drink, Mo had let it slip to Mia. Frank had not shared his illness with Nik, nor had Mo or Mia breathed a word to their colleague.

A voice sang out, "Did I miss anything?" It was Mia. She was as cheery as Mo was hungover.

Dressed in green cargo pants, hiking boots, and a long-sleeved plaid shirt with a red kerchief knotted around her neck, her dark hair braided in the back, Mia looked like a park ranger, which was fitting since she apparently planned to lead a hike up Maryland's Catoctin Mountain with two dozen young, single professionals who subscribed to her podcast— *Dateline Washington*.

"Grab a cup of coffee and snag a donut before Mo eats them all," Nik said. "We're just getting started."

After Mia took a seat, Nik began: "Before I share with you where the Trident story stands, you need to know that there's a very good chance I'll be fired for pursuing the story when Whetstone returns. He has explicitly ordered me to, quote, 'leave it the fuck alone,' unquote, or words to that effect. I've chosen to ignore his wishes. I have every reason to believe he's serious and will carry out his threat. Each of you needs to understand you could be risking your careers if you decide to work with me."

It wasn't much of a speech, as speeches go, but Nik had rehearsed it on his drive over to the office that morning. He didn't know how'd they react, and as he looked around the table, he was a little unnerved by the silence. The only sound was Mia tapping out a group text message to her fellow hikers that she would be running a few minutes late. Frank stared out the window and scratched his chin, and Mo's head remained planted on the table.

The stillness was shattered by a thunderous, window-rattling burp from Mo, followed by: "Fuck it, I'm in."

"That was impressive," Mia said, fanning her nose and face with her hand. "I can't belch like that, but, yeah, sign me up, too."

Nik turned to face Frank. "One way or the other, this is probably my last rodeo, so, sure, why not," Frank said.

Nik wasn't certain what to make of Frank's comment. He made a mental note of it and would follow up with him later.

"Good," Nik said and proceeded to tell the three about what he had learned from Maggie and Sam, without revealing his sources. When he was finished, he said, "I'm going to write a quick story on the new information, and after that, I'll hand out assignments. I realize it's your day off, so I'll text them to you. We should avoid using company emails to discuss the story in case Whetstone has access to our accounts. I've secured all the necessary permissions for platforms and systems, so there's nothing he can do to stop us from publishing the story, and he can't kill it after it's on the site or social media."

After the meeting, Nik hurried back to his desk and began composing a story. He had promised his parents he'd be home for Christmas and had a flight booked for later that afternoon. Never a particularly fast writer, Nik worked diligently and sent the finished story over to Frank in record time, along with images of the van lifted from the video that Maggie had supplied. Less than forty-five minutes later, the article and pictures were live on *Newshound*'s site.

Manhunt Underway for Suspects in Trident Office Park Explosion
Pair Linked to Killings in Indiana?

By Nik Byron
Newshound *Deputy Editor*

Authorities have identified an older-
model van seen at an Indiana truck
stop where two people were killed as
one similar to, if not the same as, a
vehicle that was spotted exiting Trident
Office Park shortly before a devastating explosion leveled buildings and left
several people dead earlier this month.

The truck-stop victims—a seven-
year veteran of the Indiana State
Police's highway patrol and a 29-year-
old female store clerk—were each shot
once with a high-powered handgun.

It is not clear what provoked the
shootings.

According to sources, investigators used sophisticated software to
compare video from both the Trident
and truck-stop crime scenes and have
determined the men seen in the van
share "similar structural and facial
characteristics."

The driver of the van was described
as having an elongated neck with a
wedge-shaped head. The passenger's
head was characterized as square, and
he wore his hair in what is considered
a mullet style—short in the front and
sides and long in the back.

The van is described as a

late-1970s Dodge Street Van, either
white or a faded green.

In a related development, sources
tell *Newshound* that investigators are
now confident that Cal Walker, the
CEO of OmniSoft Corporation, was
not killed in the explosion, as initially
feared.

Walker was seen on video entering
his Trident Park Office building just
prior to the blast, and it was believed
he was buried in the rubble when the
building collapsed. However, the owner
of a country store near the office park
said Walker was sitting in his car in
the store's parking lot when the explosion occurred.

Walker and OmniSoft are in a
long-running legal battle with the federal government, alleging government
employees stole the company's proprietary monitoring software and forced
it into bankruptcy. There has been
unconfirmed speculation on a number
of internet sites that OmniSoft and
Walker were targeted in the Trident explosion, but with the unrelated killings
in Indiana, authorities have pushed
back hard against those rumors.

While investigators now believe
Walker is alive, they do not know his
whereabouts.

Authorities have concluded that
a gas pipeline in the office park was

tampered with prior to the explosion, and they have questioned a number of potential suspects, but no arrests have been made.

The blast is now responsible for the deaths of seven people, four of whom died while being treated for injuries at Georgetown Hospital, and three still unidentified bodies recovered by rescue workers. Several other victims remain hospitalized.

CHAPTER 16

December 24

Hawk hated loose ends. They could get you killed if you weren't careful, but loose ends were what he had a fistful of.

By all rights, Cooley and Nukowski should have been killed in that Trident Park explosion along with Cal Walker. Instead, all three were alive and on the run.

No use beating himself up about it. He'd have to improvise, but that's what he was trained to do, from the deserts of Iraq to the craggy outcroppings of Afghanistan and dozens of black sites in between. He had no idea where Walker was. He'd gone to ground after the explosion, but that was okay. Hawk would eventually find him and deal with him later.

The more pressing problem was Cooley and Nukowski. There was a manhunt underway, and given the bloody trail those two fools were leaving in their wake, even the Blind Boys of Alabama could cut their track eventually.

He figured the pair was holed up somewhere, probably with one of their militia buddies. It didn't matter, though, because, as a precaution, they had agreed to meet at a prearranged location after the bombing, and Hawk knew exactly where they were headed. He planned to be there when they arrived. He'd personally see to it that those loose ends were tied up permanently this time.

CHAPTER 17

December 28, Northern Virginia

Three days after Christmas and feeling more than a little roly-poly from all the cookies and heavy meals he had consumed at his parents' house, Nik spilled out of his Land Cruiser before it came to a complete stop and lurched across Courthouse Road, nearly falling as he bounced up a set of icy steps to the Circuit Court of Arlington, Virginia.

A pretrial hearing was scheduled that morning in a lawsuit filed against King Kobe, the packaged food and Wagyu beef mogul who was accused of mixing horseflesh in with the high-end delicacy before selling it to local restaurants. As much as Nik wished he'd never heard of the guy, he felt an obligation to continue reporting on the story.

Nik slid into a pew near the back of the courtroom just as the judge exited his chambers and took the bench. The owner of the Bluebird Restaurant, a Northern Virginia landmark, was suing King Kobe—whose real name was Curtis Spinks—for fraud for selling him beef that had been tainted with horseflesh. Lawsuits were also starting to pile up in the District of

Columbia, but this was the first one to receive a hearing, and Nik wanted to be on hand to hear how the judge ruled on the defense's motion for a directed verdict to dismiss the case.

Spinks claimed that he had no knowledge the meat had been adulterated and that a disgruntled ex-trainer at the dressage-riding academy he operated had spiked the beef with horseflesh to get back at Spinks over a labor dispute. Spinks's lawyer told Nik they had a videotape of the former employee caught red-handed in the act of tainting the meat and planned to submit it to the court. Nik wanted to get a copy of the video to post on *Newshound*'s site once it was in the public record.

At the front of the courtroom, lawyers for both sides exchanged documents and consulted with their clients as the judge reviewed the case file. Spinks, a squat man with a florid face, shaved head, and multiple chins, looked like he was dressed for a rodeo. He wore a fringed buckskin jacket, bolo tie, snap-button shirt, and dark-brown dressage riding boots, an interesting wardrobe choice at any time of the year but a particularly odd selection on a cold, sleety December morning for a courtroom appearance.

It was becoming clear to Nik the proceedings were not going to start on time, and he regretted racing across town to the courthouse, skidding around corners, and running at least one traffic light in order not to be late.

To kill time, he opened his laptop and scanned the headlines on *Newshound*'s site before switching over to the *Washington Post* and other media outlets. It didn't take him long to scroll through the stories. Generally, the weeks around the holidays were a slow time of the year, news-wise.

Nik clicked on his email folder and was delighted to see a note from Sam. It had been a week since they had spent an evening together at Nora's, and he was beginning to wonder if she was getting cold feet about their New Year's Eve plans. He was relieved to learn she was not.

Nik—thanks for a wonderful evening, and I'm looking
forward to our first official date and spending New
Year's Eve with you—Samantha.

Nik immediately zeroed in on the phrase "spending New
Year's Eve with you." Was she suggesting they were going to
spend the night together? He hoped so. Or was she just dangling a romantic possibility in front of him? If he weren't careful, he knew he was capable of spending the next seventy-two
hours tying himself in emotional and mental knots parsing
the meaning behind what likely was nothing more than an innocent, quickly dashed-off line.

"Is it the court's understanding that your client possesses
a video recording that purportedly shows a former employee
of King Kobe blending horsemeat with the beef?" The hearing
was officially underway.

"Not exactly, Your Honor," Spinks's lawyer replied. "What
we have is a video that shows the ex-trainer entering the food-
processing area with a bucket from the stables and then, thirty
minutes later, exiting the same area empty-handed."

"That's it?" the judge asked incredulously. "That's the reason you petitioned for this hearing?"

"Yes, Your Honor."

"Motion denied. Any other matters?"

Nik sagged in his seat. He had squandered his morning
when he could ill afford to take any time away from the Trident
story. He cursed, shook his head, closed his laptop, and started
to rise when he was tapped on the shoulder from behind.

Nik twisted in his seat. Sitting directly behind him was
a man wearing a pair of yellow-tinted shooting glasses, an
old maroon-and-yellow Washington Redskins beanie tugged
snugly over his ears, with a matching scarf coiled around his
neck. His nose and mouth were the only exposed features.

"You need to drive more carefully, Nik. You almost lost me

back there when you blew through that stoplight at the foot of the Key Bridge," Cal Walker said as he got up from his seat and headed out of the courtroom with the reporter nipping at his heels.

"I didn't recognize you in the mummy getup, Cal," Nik was saying as he tried to keep pace with Walker as they steamed out of the courthouse and across the street.

"Wasn't my intention to surface so soon," Walker said, "but after your big scoop that I was still alive, it changed the calculus."

"Hey, thanks," Nik said.

"It wasn't a compliment," Walker said.

Walker paused alongside his car and swept his eyes over the parking lot for any signs of trouble. "Follow me," he said, "and try not to get lost."

"Where we headed?" Nik asked.

"You'll see," Walker said and climbed into his car and sped away.

CHAPTER 18

December 28, Three Rivers, Michigan

Grant Dilworth was squatting just inside an old tumble-down chicken coop when he heard the van turn into the farm lane shortly before two a.m. on a cloudless night. It had snowed most of the day, and light from a waning moon sparkled off the snow and cast a glow as shiny as a new quarter over the ground and his surroundings.

The van coughed and spewed as it crept down the narrow strip, lights off, toward the barn at the back of the property where Grant had stashed the getaway vehicle, a nondescript fawn-colored Toyota Camry with 79,256 miles on the odometer. The car had been stolen from outside a Chicago shopping mall ten days earlier and wiped clean of nearly all identification and was virtually untraceable.

Sara and Grant had fought almost nonstop ever since Nukowski had shown up unannounced at their home. She was adamant that she did not want her husband to get any more entangled with Nukowski, and she certainly did not want him staking out the barnyard when Nukowski showed up to claim the stolen car.

"He's a psychopath, Grant, can't you get that through your head?" she had pleaded. Sara had relented reluctantly when Grant showed her the story from the Washington, DC, news site about authorities searching for two men driving a late-1970s Dodge van wanted in connection with the deaths of several people in a multistate area. Sara read the story carefully and noticed the reporter had included his contact information at the bottom of the piece.

Dilworth hadn't gotten a good look at the van's driver the night Nukowski had appeared on his porch, but the description of the vehicle and the passenger matched. While he felt certain the driver would resemble the news-story description, he needed to confirm it for himself.

As the van approached, Dilworth could easily make out Nukowski sitting in the passenger seat, but just as the vehicle drew alongside the chicken coop, the driver turned to look at Nukowski, and all Grant could see was the back of his head.

The van rolled past and pulled off into a small clearing. The driver parked the van at an angle, obstructing Dilworth's view even further. He heard doors open and slam shut, and he saw Nukowski round the back of the van toting a bulging canvas gym bag, which he suspected was full of weapons.

"Why do we need to wipe it down if he's going to chop it?" Dilworth could hear the driver ask Nukowski.

"Just do as I fuckin' say and make it quick," Nukowski replied.

Nukowski pried the license plate off the back of the vehicle and stashed it in the bag. "Let's go," he commanded and climbed into the Camry. Dilworth still had not gotten a good look at the driver, and now, when the car exited the property, he would be on the opposite side of the chicken coop where Dilworth was stationed.

He heard the car start and saw its headlights sweep across a stubble field as it made its way back toward the road. Dilworth had all but given up hope he would see the driver's face when the car came to an abrupt stop and the driver leapt out and slip-slided on the snowpack back toward the van.

Nukowski rolled down his window and called out, "What now?"

The driver opened the van's door and tossed something inside. "I almost forgot to leave the keys."

"Get the lead out of your ass, Cooley. We need to get on the road," Nukowski said. Cooley slammed the van door shut and ran-shambled back to the Camry, providing Dilworth with a full-on view of his face, cartoonishly long neck, and bullet-shaped head.

Cooley, Dilworth thought. *Good, now I have a name to go with the face.*

Dilworth could hear the low-riding Toyota drag bottom as it made its way slowly down the weed-choked lane toward the road and past the chicken coop. The car dipped down into a little hollow in the lane and momentarily disappeared from his view.

He drew a deep breath, exhaled, and started to relax. His next breath got caught in the back of his throat when he saw the brake lights flash and heard a car door open. The next thing he knew, Nukowski was standing in the lane holding a weapon the size of a bazooka in his right hand.

Nukowski stood still as a post, panning the ground all around him with his eyes. He slowly lifted his head and stopped when his gaze came even with the chicken coop.

Cooley cracked his window. "What is it, Nuky? You see something?"

Nukowski didn't answer, just kept staring straight ahead. Dilworth was certain he had covered all traces of his footsteps in the snow, but he knew Nukowski to be an expert tracker who would stalk prey for days when hunting, to say nothing of his marksmanship skills.

"You're starting to make me nervous, Nuky," Cooley persisted.

"Shut the fuck up, Cooley," Nukowski barked.

Dilworth crouched into a shooting position and squirmed backward in the coop as far as he could scoot. He was a lousy pistol shot and would almost certainly miss Nukowski at this range with the .32 he clutched in his hand. Give him one of his custom-made hunting bows with its modified scope, and he could thread a needle at a hundred yards, but he bordered on incompetent with an open-sight handgun at any distance. He had considered bringing the bow but knew he'd be too constricted by the dilapidated outbuilding to get a full extension on the pull, and, besides, a gun gave him multiple chances to hit his target.

"Grant," Nukowski shouted. "You there?"

If Dilworth fired first and missed, which he surely would, Nukowski would return fire and knock over the falling-down chicken coop with that rocket launcher he was holding and then finish him off with the next round. Better to sit tight and see what played out, he reasoned.

The wind whipped the car's exhaust, and it encircled Nukowski's legs. One minute he was standing there, the next he disappeared into a bank of vapor. Dilworth's heart pounded against his chest, and he cursed himself for not listening to Sara's pleadings to stay home.

In the next moment, he heard a door shut and saw the taillights flash again as the car continued its slow crawl toward the road.

Dilworth crumpled on the coop's floor and reached into his coat pocket and withdrew a black fob the size of a garage door opener with a small screen and thumbed it on. A green light blinked, indicating the GPS unit attached to the Camry was activated and tracking the car as it headed north.

CHAPTER 19

December 28, Northern Virginia

Nik followed Cal Walker's car as it snaked through the back streets of Arlington, down George Washington Parkway, back across the Key Bridge, into Georgetown, and then across the Maryland state line, where it finally pulled into a dilapidated industrial park clogged with decommissioned tractor trailers, aging heavy earth-moving equipment, and lifeless railcars sitting on an abandoned spur. Walker hustled out of his car and into a side door of a warehouse and motioned Nik inside.

"What is this place?" Nik asked as he stepped through the door.

"It's a redundancy site," Walker said, switching on overhead lights that flooded the cavernous interior, revealing stacks of servers sitting behind locked cages.

"I thought you'd have everything in the cloud," Nik observed.

"Not a chance. That's what they expect you to do," Walker said.

"Is this where you've been hiding out?" Nik asked.

"No, and hold off on the questions for just a moment."

"Okay, but you're going to need to tell me what this is all about," Nik said as he trailed Walker down a narrow corridor.

Walker stopped at a large metal-plated door and punched a code into a keypad. "In here," he said and closed the door after Nik entered.

It was a small tomb-like space, maybe eight by eight, with dull gray walls, a fluorescent light in the ceiling, and a folding card table and chairs in the middle of the room.

"Hardened against electronic surveillance," Walker informed Nik when he saw the quizzical look on his face.

"Ahhh, I see," Nik said, pulling out one of the chairs. "Little paranoid, aren't we?"

"Maybe, but they didn't try to blow *you* up, did they?" Walker said and grabbed the other chair.

Walker removed the shooting glasses, Washington Redskins beanie, scarf, and the peacoat he was wearing. His brown hair was now a steel gray, cut short, and his signature giant pinecone-shaped beard was gone. It also looked to Nik like Walker had lost weight.

Nik pulled a notebook and pen out of his satchel. "Who exactly is the 'they' you refer to?"

"For starters, the two guys in the van," Walker said and rubbed his bloodshot eyes. "Beyond that, I don't know for certain."

"But you're convinced that bomb was intended for you and wasn't an anarchist or some domestic terrorist trying to send a message to the government by striking a soft target?"

"Absolutely."

"And why's that?"

"Because I was intentionally lured to my office for a meeting at six p.m., exactly the same time the explosion occurred. It was just sheer dumb luck that I ran out of coffee and decided, at the last moment, to dash down to that little country grocery to resupply. Had I not, I would have been sitting at my desk when the building came down."

Nik was racing to keep up with his note-taking. "Who was the meeting with?"

"I don't know. It was an anonymous caller promising me dirt on the government that would help my lawsuit. I've gotten plenty of similar calls in the past," Walker said. He pulled a cell phone out of his pocket and played the voice mail for Nik.

"Can I get a copy of that?"

"Sure."

"You recognize the voice?"

"Nope, but that was the first time the tipster was a woman."

"Any thoughts on who the guys in the van are?" Nik asked.

"No idea. Button man, or men, I'm guessing, recruited to carry out a hit on me."

"Assuming that's the case and that bomb was meant for you, who would want to kill you and why?"

"I think the why is obvious. They want to take control of POOF, and I'm standing in the way."

"Cal, the federal government doesn't go around hiring hit men."

"Don't be so sure about that. I worked in the intelligence community, and I can tell you our government does a lot of shit it's not supposed to do."

"Come on. It's one thing to accuse the feds of trying to steal your software, it's a whole other matter to accuse them of attempted murder. I report something like that, I might just as well draw up my resignation papers now."

"Don't worry. I don't think the feds tried to bump me off— at least, I don't any longer," Walker said and pushed back from the table, stood, and started pacing around the claustrophobic room. "Fact is, I don't know who's trying to kill me, but I'm developing a new theory."

"Oh, and what might that be?" Nik asked suspiciously and

jotted down "conspiracy" in front of "theory" in his notebook. Nik was feeling panicked that Walker might launch into yet another tangled tale of intrigue that would be impossible to prove or, even more maddening, disprove. A dull, throbbing pain started forming just above his eyes, and he pinched the bridge of his nose to ease the tension.

"That it's much bigger than the US government. That it's an international plot."

The dull throb Nik felt inside his head turned into a pulsating tremble, and he thought, *The skeptics are right. Walker's delusional. Why didn't I listen? I should have steered clear of him and OmniSoft. Countless hours spent on the story wasted, my career in tatters.* He thought he might start weeping.

Before Nik could respond, Walker said, "I know what you're thinking, but stay right where you are. There's someone I want to introduce you to."

He stepped out of the room. Moments later, he reappeared with a stout Asian man wearing a three-piece suit and Nike running shoes.

"Nik, I'd like you to meet Mr. Liu Li, the former deputy chief of intelligence for China's Ministry of State Security, the country's premier espionage agency."

Mr. Liu looked at Nik seated at the table, blinked, and bowed slightly.

What the fuck, Nik thought and slumped deeper into his chair, where he remained for the better part of an hour trying, but failing, to pry any meaningful information out of Mr. Liu.

CHAPTER 20

December 31, Washington, DC

It was nearly seven p.m. on New Year's Eve, and Mia and Mo were at their cubicles in *Newshound*'s office, having spent another fruitless and lonely day trying to track down the mysterious colonel Nik had encountered at Trident Office Park the night of the explosion.

Mia had combed through scores of military databases looking for the elusive Colonel Calkins while Mo had worked his human sources in Homeland Security, the Department of Defense, and the FBI. Mia came across a handful of Calkinses, but, compared with Nik's description, they were either too young, too old, or deceased. Mo's sources had never heard of or knew a Colonel Calkins, and Nik, while he said he was sure he would recognize the man if he saw him again, wasn't able to provide much of a physical description beyond the yellowish mustache and eyes.

Mia was anxious to wrap up her work, such as it was, and head home to get ready for a night out on the town. Her New Year's Eve plans included dinner, drinks, and dancing with her growing *Dateline Washington* fan base. *Newshound* had rented out a DC nightclub for the festivities and sold five hundred tickets to the event at $150 apiece. Mia's podcast was not only making her a minor celebrity, but it was a profit center for the media company, as well.

Mo's plans were much more low-key. He had a dinner date with Corletta Ramsey, the Washington, DC, lieutenant detective he worked out with at the local Y, and afterward he was headed back to his apartment alone to stream *Pumping Iron*, the bodybuilding docudrama that featured a young Arnold Schwarzenegger.

As Mo and Mia sat at their desks staring at their empty notebooks, they were both in a silent funk. When they had signed on with Nik to pursue the Trident story, they assumed it would be a fairly easy task to locate Colonel Calkins and piece together a story on his background and his role in the rescue operations the night of the bombing. Now, they weren't so sure, and, furthermore, they were having second thoughts about their snap decision to join Nik's crusade.

Mia broke the silence. "I've exhausted every possible lead, Mo, and I'm at a dead end. I'm not even sure this guy exists."

"My last call was to a night janitor at the Pentagon, that's how desperate I am," Mo countered. "I've run down every LinkedIn and Twitter connection I can think of and have reached out to dozens of military Facebook groups. I've got nothing to show for it."

This was the unglamorous part of reporting: unproductive endless hours pursuing shreds of information from reluctant, if not downright hostile, sources. It could be a soul-crushing experience and was not a line of work recommended for anyone who had a hard time handling rejection.

Mia rolled her chair away from her desk, stretched out her legs, and pressed the palms of her hands to her eyelids.

Mo crossed his massive forearms on his desk and dropped his head in the space between and stared down at the floor.

They were sitting like this when Frank Rath strolled into the newsroom. He was wearing a University of Kansas baseball cap, camel-hair overcoat, scarf, and rubber boots. The bill of his cap was covered in a wintery stew of snow, sleet, and ice. Frank, having given up driving years ago, lived near *Newshound*'s office and walked to work.

"What's wrong with you two? Someone die?" he asked.

"Not yet, but I fear our careers are on life support," Mia said and explained their dilemma.

"Maybe you're looking in the wrong places," Frank said, pulling off his overcoat and scarf. "It's getting real nasty out there, and unless the two of you want to spend New Year's Eve stuck in this office, I'd advise you to get moving before the roads become impassable."

"Where do you suggest we look?" Mo asked.

"What?" Frank said. "Oh, I don't know, but maybe the guy's not military. Maybe he's with one of those private security firms the government contracts with to do their dirty work."

"I hadn't thought of that," Mo said and snatched his cell phone off his desk and started scrolling through the contact list. When he found the name he was searching for, he punched the Call button. It rang four times before a male voice answered. "Yeah?"

"Lance, this is Patrick Morgan with *Newshound*. I don't know if you remember me."

"I remember you, Mo. Those ex-Navy SEALs are still pissed at you for showing them up on our little training exercise, but why are you calling me on New Year's Eve? You need to get a life."

Months earlier, Mo had participated in a public recruiting event sponsored by Lance's company, Yellow Jacket Defense, for a story he was writing on private military contractors. Mo finished in first place in the strength endurance exercise, to the chagrin of many of the military veterans.

Mo quickly explained the reason for the call and described Colonel Calkins. After a long pause, Mo asked, "Lance, did you hear me okay?"

"Yeah, I heard you," Lance answered flatly.

"Well?"

"Don't know any Calkins."

"Aw, it was a long shot," Mo said. "Sorry for bothering you, and happy New Year's."

"I don't know him," Lance continued, "at least, not by that name, but I just might know the guy you're looking for."

CHAPTER 21

December 31, Washington, DC

Nik knocked on Samantha Whyte's front door at ten p.m., exactly two hours late for their New Year's Eve date. Normally the drive along Canal Road from his Georgetown apartment to the Foxhall section of Washington, DC, would take twenty minutes, but the wintry mix that had been spitting off and on all day had started to freeze and turned the roads into a treacherous ice rink. DC street crews, not known for their quick response times to weather events during normal working hours, didn't even bother to send out the salt trucks to combat the storm. To make matters worse, the power failed around nine o'clock in pockets around DC and had not been restored by the time Nik arrived at Sam's place.

When Sam answered the door, Nik was greeted by fingers of orange and yellow flames from dozens of votive candles scattered about the house, and in the hearth, a fire cast long, dancing shadows on the walls. The backlighting made it appear as if Sam were literally shimmering as she stood in the doorway in her sequined top, bangle earrings, and turquoise-and-silver rope necklace.

"My intrepid date," she said and grabbed Nik's free hand, pulling him across the threshold before giving him a peck on the cheek.

"Not fit for man, nor beast," Nik said, "but I came fortified." He held up a bag brimming with provisions from his favorite Georgetown delicatessen. Sam relieved Nik of his belongings and walked to the kitchen, where she spilled the contents onto a countertop. French bread, olives, charcuterie, goat cheese, crudités, dark chocolate, wine, and champagne tumbled out of the bottomless bag.

"This looks amazing," Sam said. "You plan on spending the week?"

"Is that an invitation?" he said, and Sam turned, blushing slightly, and winked at him.

"I'm starving," she said. "How about you?"

"It was all I could do not to tear into that bag of groceries on the way over here," Nik said.

"You open the wine," Sam instructed, "and I'll set out some appetizers."

The two had exchanged text messages earlier in the day when the weather had started to turn questionable. They had arrived at a backup plan to have dinner at her house in case of a power failure, not an uncommon occurrence in DC in the wintertime, since many of Sam's kitchen appliances ran off natural gas.

Nik removed his overcoat and scarf, and Sam was impressed to see he was wearing a tuxedo with an emerald-green waistcoat and matching hand-knotted bow tie.

"Very debonair," she said approvingly.

"Mind if I put on some music?" Nik asked, withdrawing a Bluetooth speaker from his overcoat pocket.

Sam said, "Your playlist or mine?"

"Mine, I think, at least to start," Nik said, and up came the distinctive xylophone notes of the Modern Jazz Quartet performing live at Monterey.

Sam called out from the kitchen, "I hope you like beef bourguignon. I've never made it before, but my butcher assured me it would be fine if I followed his recipe and didn't overcook the meat. He said the secret was in the sauce."

"Ah, the magical secret sauce we've all heard so much about," Nik said. "Hope he's right."

As it turned out, it was exquisite. After a leisurely dinner where they swapped stories about their favorite childhood adventures—Nik's were summers in northern Michigan with his family, Sam's taking long car trips to see distant relatives in Mississippi and Louisiana—Nik opened the champagne, and Sam served ice cream for dessert, vanilla with sea salt, hazelnuts, and a caramel swirl.

Sam revealed that she had been taking hot yoga classes three days a week before work for the past six months and that one major benefit, besides being incredibly limber, was that she could eat what she wanted without gaining an ounce of weight, and, with that, she served herself a second helping of ice cream. Nik declined an offer for more, patting his stomach and explaining, "I haven't worked out since the Trident story broke."

Without going into great detail, Nik quickly updated Sam on the investigation. He wanted to avoid talking shop on New Year's Eve, and wrapped up his thoughts by saying, "I'm still trying to sort everything out. Maybe I can bounce some ideas off you after I get a better grip on all the moving parts."

Sam hesitated, recalling the memories of the last story she had a hand in before she abandoned reporting, but said, "Sure. I'd love to help, if I can."

At midnight, they toasted the new year, and Sam spread a white down comforter and fleece blanket on the floor in front of the fireplace. The power still had not come back on, and lying in front of the fire, Sam rolled atop Nik as quick as a cat, pinning his arms back. With her strawberry-blonde hair dangling in his face, she leaned forward and kissed him and then stretched and elongated her limbs, melding her body to his, and within minutes, they were naked. They made love twice before falling asleep entwined in each other's arms and legs. They awoke and made love again. Sam dozed off, breathing peacefully, but Nik, preoccupied with the Trident story and the strange meeting with Walker, couldn't quiet his restless mind and lay awake staring into the dying fire.

At two forty-five, Nik's cell phone trilled. Without hesitating, he snatched it up and answered. It was a woman's voice, but she was slurring so heavily, he had a difficult time understanding what she was saying.

Sam stirred awake. "Is it your ex?" she mouthed silently, clutching the blanket to her bare chest.

Nik shook his head no, thumbed the Record button on the phone, pressed his ear to the speaker, and, with his free hand, covered his other ear. "I'm sorry, could you repeat that? I couldn't hear you clearly."

The woman spoke more deliberately this time but still sounded like she was talking with a mouthful of ash. "'Those two guyz inna van who blup the building, killed a cop and store clerk, I know who they are."

Just then, Nik heard a man's groggy voice in the background. "Sara, who are you talking to?"

The line went dead. Nik looked down at his phone. He had recorded the call and captured the incoming number successfully.

———

After the late-night call from the mysterious woman, Sam and Nik scooped up their belongings from in front of the fireplace and straggled back to Sam's bedroom, where they were startled awake by the blare of the television, radio, and glare of house lights when the power was restored at precisely 6:24 a.m.

Sam felt fuzzy-headed from the champagne and a bit self-conscious about the prior night's sexual escapades and the fact that a naked man was lying next to her. It's not that she hadn't enjoyed the evening, she had, but it was the first time she had gone to bed with a man since Gregg Robbins, and that was more than two years ago.

As she lay there, Sam struggled with what to say. With each passing moment, she felt more and more anxious and started to regret her impulsiveness. She was on the verge of blurting out, *This whole thing was a mistake,* when Nik rolled over and kissed her gently on the lips and told her she looked beautiful.

He bounded out of bed and pulled on his boxers. "How 'bout I make us some coffee?"

"Great idea," Sam said, relieved. "Coffee's in the pantry on the top shelf in a tin. Make sure you don't grab the decaf by mistake."

"Please, give me a little credit," Nik said and danced out of the bedroom, humming.

Sam sank back into the bed and thought about Gregg, her last lover, and wondered if he and Nik would have gotten along. Both were reporters, but that didn't necessarily mean much, since reporters were fiercely competitive and independent. Sam often thought she and Robbins would have stayed together for a long time had he not died, perhaps even married, though it would have been complicated. It was too early to form any expectations about Nik, but one thing was clear: he'd test her patience if he were an incurably cheery morning person who liked to hum.

As if Nik could read her thoughts, he called out from the kitchen, "You know, I can't get over the fact that you're single. How'd I get so lucky?"

"I was seeing someone," Sam said sadly, "a reporter. At the *Post*, but he passed away."

"Oh," Nik said. "I didn't know. I'm so sorry."

"It's okay. I'm going to jump in the shower," Sam said, thinking it would be a good place to have a quiet moment to compose herself.

"Breakfast, such as it is, will be ready when you get out."

Over coffee and bagels, they quickly read a slender *Washington Post* and discussed the upcoming college football games. Nik's Michigan Wolverines were playing in a bowl game, and he was looking forward to watching it, though he was certain they would disappoint him once again.

Sam didn't have any rooting interests and checked movie schedules and showtimes on her iPad. There were several Academy Award contenders she wanted to see before the Oscars ceremony. She bought a ticket for a three-thirty movie and then flipped over to an astrology site and read aloud a synopsis of their respective horoscopes for the year ahead.

Sam, a Gemini, had a four-and-a-half-star year out of five. She was going to travel abroad ("My sister and I are talking about a trip to Ireland"); come into money ("I'm expecting a nice tax refund"); find love ("Huh, no clue what that could be"); and rekindle friendships ("My college class reunion is this year").

Nik was an Aquarius and he had three stars ("Figures"). Don't expect much rest during the first half of the year ("Great"); career pitfalls on the horizon ("Can't wait"); things are not what they first appear to be ("Never are"); you will get help from an unexpected ally ("Finally").

CHAPTER 22

January 1, Northern Virginia

Mo and Mia huddled in a crammed, airless, frigid office on the site of a former girls' summer camp in Loudoun County, Virginia. It was January 1, New Year's Day, and Mia was still wearing the strapless, above-the-knee black satin dress with the yellow sash from the night before. Mo was dressed in gray sweatpants, a dark-red hoodie, and an old pair of high-top Converse basketball shoes. They had arrived at the office a little after sunup, Mia thick-headed from too much partying and too little sleep, Mo alert as a rooster at dawn, having fallen asleep on his couch before ten thirty. They were there to interview Lance Duvall, the commander of a private military contractor, Yellow Jacket Defense, who was shipping out later that day for an overseas assignment that he'd "rather not talk about," he had told Mo the day before when they had arranged the early-morning rendezvous.

Duvall refused to discuss any details about the enigmatic Colonel Calkins over the phone and insisted on a face-to-face meeting. Lacking any leverage, Mo agreed.

Duvall was perched on the corner of a metal desk, dressed head to toe in desert fatigues, trouser legs tucked neatly inside a pair of sand-colored combat boots. He slid off the desk and walked over to a four-drawer olive-green filing cabinet stationed against the wall.

"I remember him, if he's the guy I'm thinking of. He caught our eye because of his combination of technology chops and combat exposure. That's a rare skill set, and we're always on the lookout for folks who match the profile."

"But you didn't hire him?" Mo said.

"Nope. Too many red flags." Duvall unlocked the cabinet and riffled through a column of folders. "To be honest, our records are a little disorganized. Hope I can find the file," he said.

"Great." Mia moaned loudly, tipped her neck and head over the back of the plastic chair she was occupying, and emitted a soft belch. "Couldn't you have told us that over the phone and saved us the trouble of driving all the way out here on New Year's Day in a sleet storm?"

"Hey," Duvall snapped, turning back toward the pair with a thin folder in his hands, "I don't have to give you jack shit. That'd be fine with me."

"No, no, no. We appreciate the help," Mo jumped in. "Don't mind her. She had a long night, s'all."

Mo prodded Mia with the toe of his shoe and hissed at her to sit up straight. She shimmied forward in the chair, satin crinkling like cellophane, and struggled to focus her mind. Duvall threw her a hard, unsympathetic look, but Mia totally missed it. Her eyes were shuttered.

"As I told you yesterday, I'm not a hundred percent certain it's the same guy, but it sure sounds like him from what you described," Duvall said and withdrew several sheets of paper from the folder and fanned them out in front of him on the desktop.

"We didn't know him as Colonel Calkins. He registered his

last name as Brick, but I doubt that was his real name. Guys around here called him Custer, because of his yellow hair," he said. Anticipating the reporters' question, he quickly added, throwing up a hand, "It's not unusual for new recruits to conceal their true identities in the initial phase of the onboarding process. Lot of these guys have records, some criminal, others military related, that they don't want to unnecessarily reveal. If they make it through the first round of vetting, then they're required to provide full disclosure."

Duvall continued to sift through the pages. "Here it is," he said, and slid a document across the desk. Mo and Mia scraped their chairs closer. When Mia leaned in to read the material, Mo got a strong whiff of perfume and stale whiskey.

The document was titled "Reasons for Disqualification" and read in part:

> Recruit displayed an impressive knowledge of software operating systems, networking capabilities, and information technologies. He possessed a working understanding of military tactics and strategy. He was competent in marksmanship, orienteering, hand-to-hand combat, and detonation techniques. He was keenly aware of geopolitical issues in a number of international hot spots where Yellow Jacket operates. Despite these attributes, however, we cannot recommend offering the recruit a field position or a follow-up session at this time.
>
> In his 1:1 interviews and written psychological profile, the candidate exhibited a strong anti-authority, anti-government disposition. When pressed to clarify certain statements, he was evasive, dissembling, and combative. We also found the recruit given to exaggeration

and self-aggrandizement. Furthermore, several of his verbal and written responses to questions suggest an individual prone to confrontation and unprovoked violence that could quickly escalate to gunplay. As it is Yellow Jacket's stated goal to defuse tensions in the field, we do not believe the candidate, for all his qualities, would further the organization's mission. APPLICATION DENIED.

Mo clucked his tongue a couple times and nodded to himself as Mia scribbled in a small notebook that she pulled from the clutch she was carrying. "Know what became of him?" Mo asked.

"No idea, but my guess is he signed on with some other outfit. As you can see, that application is dated," Duvall said, and eyed Mia suspiciously as she rapidly copied passages from the document. "Remember our agreement, you can't identify Yellow Jacket as the source of the material."

"We won't," Mo assured him.

"I've got to push off," Duvall said and started gathering up the documents and shoving them back into the folder. "Mind telling me what he's done, or don't I want to know?"

Mo looked at Mia. He had not been able to get in touch with Nik to tell him about the interview with Duvall and was uncertain what to reveal.

"We don't know that he's done anything," Mo said, "but we believe he was at the Trident Office Park the night of the explosion with a military-style team on a search-and-rescue mission. We're trying to find out who sent him and how it was that he was able to get to the site so quickly after the blast. It was almost like he had planned to be there."

Duvall rocked back in his chair, dropped his chin to his chest, and rubbed the fingers of his outstretched left hand together contemplatively. "Trident is where all those high-tech companies are located, right?"

"Yeah," Mo said. "They conduct a lot of top-secret work for the government."

"Maybe he did."

"Maybe he did what?" Mo said.

"Plan it," Duvall said.

CHAPTER 23

Several Years Earlier, Washington, DC

Joint Base Anacostia-Bolling sits on a 905-acre campus in southwest Washington, DC, and is home to the Defense Intelligence Agency.

The DIA, as it is known, is the military's top spy organization and operates out of a modern six-story office building and employs more than 16,500 workers worldwide in 104 countries, about 30 percent of whom work at the Anacostia headquarters. Nearly three-quarters of the workforce are civilians, and they have expertise in a wide range of skills, including cyber warfare, biosciences, economics, intelligence gathering, terrorism, and computer science.

The DIA is one of three branches of the US intelligence community—the CIA and the State Department's Bureau of Intelligence and Research are the other two. All three are unique in that they are considered "all-source agencies," meaning they use all manner of intelligence, regardless if it's collected by human sources in the field, satellite transmissions, or cyber, in conducting their analysis. It is at the forefront of evaluating the potential of quantum computing, encryption, sensing, and communications, considered to be the battlefield of the twenty-first century.

Its stated mission is to provide "military intelligence to war fighters, defense policymakers, and force planners in the Department of Defense and Intelligence Community."

Ever since it was established in 1961 by then President John F. Kennedy, the organization has been outwardly focused, concentrating its manpower and assets on overseas military threats and conflicts, both real and perceived.

Post 9/11, the DIA took a more active, if somewhat nuanced, role in assessing potential threats on US soil, a move that was and remains a controversial decision both inside and outside the agency to this day. At the same time, the agency stepped up its efforts to identify and evaluate leading-edge technologies to help in its campaign to counter threats by terrorist organizations and military foes in warfare.

To that end, it created a secretive internal unit modeled on the CIA's In-Q-Tel venture capital arm and charged it with investing in promising technologies and companies. Over the years, the DIA quietly scoured universities, Silicon Valley, think tanks, hackathons, and incubators for software tools and talent.

It was during one of these routine evaluations that a counterterrorism analyst stumbled upon a small DC technology company with a potentially interesting surveillance software program, with the impossible, tongue-twisting name of Phantom Omniscient Ocular Functionality, or POOF for short.

Since the company was only a few miles from DIA's headquarters, the analyst—who held the government's highest security clearance available, top secret/sensitive compartmentalized information—decided to drop in and pay its owner a visit.

What the DIA employee found on that hot, sticky Washington afternoon was an underfunded, overworked, harried but brilliant company founder with a buggy, half-baked software program that was incapable of successfully repeating simple tasks without hopelessly crashing.

The analyst also saw something else that muggy day.

She saw the future. Not only POOF's but hers as well, if she could only somehow manage to get her hands on the software. It was a gold mine just waiting to be tapped.

CHAPTER 24

January 1, Northern Michigan

Lucky Stars Gentlemen's Club is housed in a squat, one-story cinder-block building situated halfway between Interstate 75 and Bliss, Michigan, ten miles south of the Mackinac Bridge and the gateway to the Upper Peninsula, as the crow flies. Its gravel parking lot is generally full of rusted-out pickup trucks, aging SUVs, and, depending on the season, either snowmobiles or Harley-Davidson motorcycles. The clientele is mainly local and steady. There's parking around back, and that's where a beige Toyota Camry with Wisconsin license plates was tucked, shielded from the road.

Regular customers didn't recognize the car, nor the two men it belonged to, who were now sitting in a back booth with a couple of the newer dancers, a flaming redhead who went by the stage name Rosie Bush and a dishwater blonde that everyone called Myrtle the Turtle, a name she had acquired because her signature dance move was to flop on her back, arms and legs outstretched, and squirm across the stage like an upside-down turtle.

Lucky Stars' interior was pretty much like every other back-water strip joint—a bar to one side; chairs crammed around the stage; high-top tables and stools a little farther back; and booths, on risers, lining the walls. Since it was the holiday season, the dancers had strung twinkling white Christmas lights above the stage, and someone had hung a poster over the bar that showed Santa in a hot tub with a bare-chested young woman surrounded by elves in various forms of copulation.

The air in the strip club smelled of sweet perfume, flat beer, and pine-scented air freshener. Away from the stage, the lighting was low and dim, and when customers entered the business, it took a moment for their eyes and noses to adjust to the dank atmosphere and heavily perfumed air.

Rosie sat in the booth next to Nukowski and across from Cooley. Myrtle was practically in Cooley's lap, whispering something to him, the tip of her tongue flicking in and out of his ear.

Nukowski and Cooley had been there nearly an hour when the two girls joined them for a drink, Jack Daniel's for Nukowski, a Seven and Seven for Cooley, and wine spritzers for the women. The dancers had just finished their performance and were swaddled in crocheted wraps that partially covered their pasties and G-strings.

"I've never been so cold in my life," Rosie complained. "Look at these goose bumps. They're the size of cherry pits," she said and stuck out an arm for Nukowski to inspect. When he didn't respond, she flopped a leg on the table. "My legs are like icebergs."

Nukowski, spying the red thatch between Rosie's legs, grunted and ran his hand up the inside of her thigh. "Feels pretty warm to me." Rosie frowned, folded her leg back under the table, and took a drink of wine.

"Global warming can't get here fast enough for me," Myrtle said. "Me and Rosie never expected we'd still be here come winter, but we're stuck now because her car broke down and we can't afford to get it fixed."

"Why, where you goin'?" Cooley asked.

"Florida, or maybe Arizona. Somewheres warm," Myrtle said with a pout.

"I'd like to go to Florida," Cooley said. "Nuky, wouldn't you like to go to Florida and get out of this fuckin' frozen tundra?"

Nukowski gave Cooley a puzzled look. "We got to meet a man."

"I know that, but after. Maybe we can go to Florida after we meet Hawk."

Nukowski stared coldly at his companion and wanted to reach across the table and wring his skinny neck for mentioning Hawk's name.

"Oooh, take me and Rosie with you," Myrtle said and slid her hand under the table and cupped Cooley's sack.

Two new dancers took the stage, and the patrons started rhythmically banging wooden lollipops on tabletops to get the girls to disrobe faster.

"Those girls are good," Rosie said as one shinnied up a pole in the middle of the stage while the other high-kicked around its edges.

"Nowhere as good as you, Rosie," Myrtle said.

"Aren't you sweet," Rosie said and stood. "I need to use the little girls' room."

"Yeah, I need to hit the head, too," Nukowski said and slipped out of the booth behind Rosie. He tossed a twenty on the table and told Cooley to order another round of drinks.

Cooley waved a waitress over and gave her the drink order. When she disappeared, he said to Myrtle, "Me and Nuky, we're famous."

"How's that?" Myrtle said.

"You've probably heard about us but just don't know it. We've been on the news."

"I don't believe you."

"God's honest truth. You might say we made a real bang, but I can't talk about that just now. If we go to Florida, I'll tell you then."

Rosie and Nukowski reappeared at the booth and had just reclaimed their seats when Myrtle blurted out, "They's famous. They've been on TV."

"I didn't say on TV," Cooley protested and gave Nukowski a nervous look.

"You need to keep your fuckin' trap shut, Cooley," Nukowski said and slowly stirred his drink. "I've warned you about that."

"I was just making conversation, s'all, Nuky," Cooley defended himself.

Nukowski hammered back his drink and slammed the empty glass down on the table when it was finished. "Let's get the fuck out of here before Cooley starts telling you his boring life story," he said.

"Where we gonna go?" Myrtle whined. "There's nothin' to do around here."

"We can go to our motel," Nukowski said with a dark grin, "and I guaran-fuckin'-tee you we'll find something to do."

A husband and wife from Kalamazoo, foraging for mushrooms in the springtime, found the two dancers' bodies partially buried under the roots of an old tree. It was apparent to law enforcement that wild animals had been feeding on their remains.

No one at Lucky Stars had thought to report the two girls missing because dancers came and went, especially in the winter when the weather turned cold. Happened all the time.

Rosie Bush's real name was Margie Anne Cox, 26, from

Lima, Ohio. The last time her family had seen her was two years before when she had checked herself out of a methadone clinic. Myrtle was really Sue Ellen Cooke, 24, from Erie, Pennsylvania. No known relatives.

Rosie's body was transported back to Ohio for burial, while some of the Lucky Stars' dancers and patrons passed the hat and held a small memorial service at the club for Myrtle, followed by cremation.

The bodies were too decomposed to determine if the women had been sexually assaulted, but the cause of death was conclusive: both had been shot once each, point blank, in the back of the head with a high-power handgun, the autopsy revealed.

"Those two girls may have worked at Lucky Stars," the coroner told the investigating officer, "but they sure as hell weren't born under one."

CHAPTER 25

January 1, Washington, DC

Hawk had a couple days to kill before his prearranged rendezvous with Nukowski and Cooley, and as he sat in his car on a quiet residential street, motor running, radio playing softly, he puzzled over how best to eliminate the pair.

An ambush was out of the question. Not that it wouldn't succeed, but then he'd never know what they knew or how they had avoided getting killed in the Trident explosion. He also wanted to find out why they had shot that cop and store clerk in Indiana and if there were any other unaccounted-for dead bodies lying around. He had a lot of questions, and he needed the pair alive if he was going to get any answers.

The upcoming reunion could go several ways, but he was determined to put them at ease, make them relax. That might take some work, especially if they blamed him for the malfunctioning bomb. He needed to keep a close eye on Nukowski, that was for certain. He was the dangerous one. Cooley, he could handle.

When he had first met Cooley in Afghanistan, the kid—
he wasn't much older than twenty-one then—was one hell of
an explosives expert. Not only could he build and detonate all
manner of military ordnance, Cooley was fearless and would
walk through a Taliban minefield methodically defusing
crude, but nonetheless lethal, explosives.

Hawk knew Nukowski didn't hold Cooley in high re-
gard and belittled him, but he hadn't known the kid before
he got addicted to drugs. First, it was Afghani heroin. Hawk
suspected Cooley had gotten hooked from a combination of
boredom and the pressure of his bomb-handling occupation.
Cooley turned to meth after he returned to the States when he
couldn't score heroin.

If Hawk had to guess, it was Nukowski who had killed that
cop and store clerk, not Cooley, no matter how high he might
have been. Nukowski loathed cops, despised all law enforcement figures, for that matter, a trait they shared.

"I'd lay down my life for a brother-in-arms, but I wouldn't
spit on a cop if he was burning to death," Nukowski had
told him.

They had their separate reasons for their common an-
imosity toward government officials—Nukowski blamed
banks, government programs, and the sheriff's department for
foreclosing on his family farm and driving his father to suicide
and his mother into poverty; Hawk held a grudge for getting
drummed out of West Point for hacking into the academy's
computer system to change his test scores. Cooley harbored
a dull memory of resenting the government, but he couldn't
remember exactly what for or why. Mostly he liked to blow shit
up and was just along for the ride.

Hawk had stayed in contact with Cooley after Afghanistan
out of a sense that the kid's skills could prove useful down
the road. He visited Cooley in Michigan a couple times, and

on one trip, he met Nukowski and some of Nukowski's Three Percenter buddies—the far-right, anti-government militia group. They bonded over their love of guns and hatred of government.

Together, the three of them would talk late into the night about how to inflict damage on the government. Hawk introduced them to *The Turner Diaries* and other anti-government literature, and slowly, over time, he seeded the idea to blow up a government facility outside of Washington, DC.

He promised it would just be the first in a long string of government targets that they would go after, each one bigger and bolder than the one before.

Of course, there weren't going to be any other attacks after Trident. If all had gone according to plan, Nukowski and Cooley would have been killed in the explosion along with Walker. Investigators would have discovered their bodies in the rubble and traced them back to their Michigan base camp, where they would find anti-government manifestos, a weapons cache, and plans to attack other installations and conclude the pair were a couple of white nationalist dirtbags who were out to destabilize the US government.

That plan went sideways, for reasons still unknown to Hawk. Nonetheless, he believed he could piece it back together. *But it will require that the* Newshound *reporter lead me to Walker,* Hawk thought to himself as he watched Nik emerge from Samantha Whyte's house on New Year's Day and skid down the ice-covered sidewalk toward his vehicle.

CHAPTER 26

January 1, Washington, DC

Nik briefly considered swinging by *Newshound*'s offices after leaving Sam's house, to take care of some paperwork, but decided against it because he wanted to be sure to catch the opening kickoff of the college bowl game. He headed back to his Georgetown apartment instead.

Nik's place was situated on the corner of Thirty-First and N Streets, just a block off Wisconsin Avenue. He lived on the first floor of a four-story historic redbrick Georgetown Federalist-style home. It had white plastered walls and bay windows with built-in seating that looked out onto a small courtyard encircled by a black wrought-iron fence.

While Nik's apartment was charming, it also was quirky. His bedroom was wedged into an area that was once the landing for a massive staircase that descended from the upper floors. The owners had removed the lower portion of the staircase when they converted the bottom floor into an apartment, but they failed to completely wall off the space, so, at one end, it had a door that led to the apartment's entryway and, at the other, an arched opening that poured out onto a breakfast nook, galley kitchen, and claustrophobic bathroom, which had at one time served as a butler's pantry. The bathroom contained the skinniest shower Nik had ever encountered, and he barely could turn around in it, forget about ever sharing an intimate scrubbing with another person.

His favorite spot in the apartment was the sun-filled front room, with its leaded-glass windows, wide pinewood plank floors, high ceilings, and fireplace. On Sundays, he'd sit there working at his desk, Gyp at his feet, after they returned from a run in Rock Creek Park.

He missed Gyp's company, and he made a mental note to call his trainer to find out when he could reclaim the dog. When Nik had dropped Gyp off at the Charlottesville kennel for obedience training after he had chewed through his vehicle's seat belts, the handler told him that Gyp would need to be there from two to six weeks. The boarding and training weren't cheap, but Nik knew he didn't have either the time or the patience to instill discipline in the rambunctious hound.

Nik's landlord, his wife, and their children occupied the three floors above him in the house, but they were away for the holidays, which reminded Nik he had promised to feed their fish. The house was unusually quiet, and that was a blessing for several reasons. Nik could play his music as loud as he wanted, he could scream profanities at the TV during cable news programs or Michigan football games, and he could catch up on work without any distractions.

Nik arrived back at his apartment from Sam's fifteen minutes before kickoff, enough time for a quick shower. He stepped out of the shower, toweled off, and heated a pot of chili on the stove that he had prepared a few days before in anticipation of the game. Nik prided himself on his chili, made with expensive cuts of sirloin, spices from a Mexican bodega, beer, onions, peppers, and black beans, served on a bed of rice. He covered the chili with shredded cheese, opened a Budweiser, and plopped down in his favorite leather chair in front of the television to watch the game.

He had invited Mo, Mia, and Frank over earlier in the week to watch the game and had stocked up on enough beer and snacks to feed a small army. But with the weather turning bad, he wasn't certain they'd show, and he had neglected to check his recent messages.

In typical Michigan football fashion, the game was a grind-it-out-on-the-ground, low-scoring affair, and at halftime, it was Michigan 10, USC 7. Nik hoisted himself out of his chair and padded to the kitchen, where he got another beer and put his dishes in the sink to soak. He grabbed his laptop from his desk and returned to his chair and started checking emails. It didn't take long. Most people were out for the holidays, and he didn't have many emails, none that were urgent. That wasn't true for his voice mails. His mailbox was full.

About a third of the calls were from Dick Whetstone, who, Nik was certain, would soon be his ex-boss if he continued to ignore Whetstone's increasingly frantic calls. He'd listen to those last, if at all, though he could pretty much guess what they said.

The first message he played was from Maggie, his ex-wife, who had called to wish him a happy new year and tell him she had some more information on the Trident Park explosion that he might be interested in hearing. She'd be back in the office January 2, and he should call her then.

His parents and his sister, Hanna, also called to wish him a happy new year.

There was a message from Mo telling him that he might have a lead on Colonel Calkins and that he and Mia were going to meet with a source on New Year's Day to follow up.

The attorney for King Kobe called to inform Nik that his client was in settlement discussions with several restaurant owners, and he predicted a favorable outcome after the first of the year. "It's all been a huge misunderstanding," the lawyer said and promised to give Nik an exclusive story when the settlement was reached.

There were several calls from public relations flacks pitching story ideas for their clients. Nik deleted those messages.

A second message from Mo said he and Mia had a productive meeting with their source and that they were driving back to DC, but road conditions made the going slow and he was pretty certain they would not be back in time for the football game. Either way, Mia had no interest in the game, and she was going home to sleep. Mo suggested they all meet the next day. Frank left a message to say he was under the weather and planned to stay in bed all day. His call ended with the cheer "Go Blue."

The last message was from Cal Walker. He told Nik they needed to talk and that Nik should call him on the burner phone he had given the reporter the last time they met. Nik deleted the message after listening to the call, walked over to the desk to retrieve the phone from his shoulder bag, and called Walker. He answered on the first ring.

"Mr. Liu wants to meet," Walker announced when he picked up the phone.

"Hope it's more productive than the last time. I wasn't even certain he could understand me. He barely uttered two words."

"That was my fault," Walker said. "I pushed him to meet with you when he wasn't ready. He needs to feel he can trust you."

"Yeah, but can I trust him?" Nik said.

"That's up to you. Listen to what he has to say and make up your own mind," Walker said. "He needs to be cautious. There are a lot of people connected to his government that want to silence him."

"Okay, when's he want to meet?" Nik asked, mildly annoyed

that he was talking on the phone as the second-half kickoff was about to take place.

"Now," Walker said.

"No way. Michigan's playing in the Rose Bowl, and the second half is just about to start," Nik complained.

"Suit yourself. He's leaving town tonight. So it's now or never."

Nik stewed. "I'm having a hard time verifying he is who he claims to be," he said, "and I'll need to confirm everything he tells me, which means I'm going to need to be able to reach him after he leaves."

"Understood," Walker said, "and I have some information that might help you with that as well."

"Hmmmm," Nik replied, his mind half on the game and half on the mound of documents Walker had already buried him under in the past six months.

"Hey, you can take it or leave it. I'm just trying to make your life a little easier," Walker said.

"Any easier and I'll be catatonic. Where do you want to meet? The warehouse?" Nik asked.

"No. I'll text you an address as soon as we hang up. It'll take you about an hour to get here in this weather."

"All right," Nik said and exited the call.

He was buttoning up his coat when he heard the football announcer exclaim, "Michigan recovers the kickoff on USC's six-yard line. What a break for the Wolverines to start the second half."

CHAPTER 27

January 1, St. Mary's, Maryland

A gust of raw, sleety wind slapped Nik in the face and snapped his head around when he stepped out of his apartment and into the street. His eyes watered, and he double-timed it to his Land Cruiser, chin tucked tightly to his chest, and regretted, not for the first time, his decision to save a few bucks and forgo having the SUV's heater rebuilt. He was preoccupied with trying to find a radio station that carried the Rose Bowl game and didn't see the dark-blue sedan slip in behind him when he turned onto Wisconsin Avenue.

Nik had never been to Maryland's Eastern Shore or St. Mary's before, and he was surprised at how desolate and un-inhabited the village felt when he crossed the city limits. He knew St. Mary's was the state's first colonial settlement, once its capital, and also home to Saint Mary's College, but that was the extent of his knowledge.

Walker texted him directions to the Sand Bar, a roadside tavern, and told Nik to find a spot and park out front, which wasn't difficult since there were only a couple other vehicles in the lot. When he entered the bar, Nik was thrilled to see they had the Rose Bowl game playing on the bar's 1980s-era, washing-machine-size television suspended in an upper corner of the room. The bar had a low-slung timber-planked ceiling and uneven flooring and smelled briny and damp, like an outgoing tide. Walker was in the rear of the place, sitting in a booth with his back to the wall, same old Washington Redskins stocking hat stretched over his head, scarf knotted around his neck, and blue peacoat opened in front. Nik took a stool at the bar near the TV, ordered a Budweiser, and turned his attention to the game. Walker pushed out of the booth and slouched toward him. Nik was concentrating on the game and didn't notice when Walker occupied the stool next to him and sat down.

The score was Michigan 18, USC 20, with less than a minute to go in the fourth quarter. Michigan had the ball at USC's forty-five-yard line and was marching down the field when a USC linebacker intercepted a tipped pass to seal what appeared to be a victory, but an interference penalty against USC nullified the interception, and Michigan found itself inside the thirty with time running out. Michigan's coach sent in the team's field-goal kicker to win the game, exactly how they drew it up. Unfortunately, the kick sailed left, hit the upright, and bounced back into the field of play as time expired.

"We're cursed," Nik cried and dropped his head on the bar. After several moments, he looked up and, for the first time, realized Walker was sitting next to him, alone. "Where's Mr. Liu?" he asked, perplexed. "Don't tell me I drove all the way out here for nothing."

"Keep your shirt on," Walker said gruffly, and looked over his shoulder to make sure no one was listening, a futile gesture since the place was nearly deserted except for some old-timers talking among themselves at the end of the bar. "He hasn't left yet. He needs to limit his exposure. He's risking his life just meeting with us. You park out front?"

"I did."

"Okay, follow me," Walker said and headed to a back exit and an alley where his Prius was parked. Nik, tired of the cat-and-mouse game and feeling used, swiveled in his stool toward the fleeing Walker and snapped, "Cal, I'm not leaving here until you tell me where we're going, where Liu is, and what the fuck this is all about."

Walker spun back around to face Nik. "Lower your voice," he pleaded, hands outstretched in front of him, pushing downward like he was trying to dampen the air. "I promise, Nik, just fifteen more minutes, and all your questions will be answered."

Nik doubted that, but he drained his beer, boosted himself off the stool, and reluctantly followed Walker out of the bar.

"Do me a favor," Walker said when they reached the car, "duck down in the seat so no one can see you."

"Christ, why didn't you just have me crawl into the trunk?" Nik protested.

"I would," Walker said, "but these cars don't have trunks."

Hawk had stationed himself so he could keep an eye on the reporter's car and the front door of the bar. As far as a stakeout went, it was fairly routine. There was virtually no traffic on the road, and the Sand Bar wasn't a very popular spot. He didn't know why the reporter had left his warm apartment on a winter's late afternoon to drive across the state line in shitty weather to this tidewater outpost, but his hunch was that it had something to do with Walker.

Hawk saw the compact car swing out of a side street that paralleled the bar's parking lot and turn his way. As the car approached, he averted his eyes to avoid being blinded by the headlights and only returned his gaze momentarily when the vehicle pulled alongside. He caught a brief glimpse of the car, a Prius, and the driver's profile, or what he could see of it. The driver continued to look straight forward and had a knit cap pulled snugly over his head and a scarf wrapped around his neck, obscuring most of his features.

After about thirty more minutes of sitting in his car, Hawk decided to enter the bar and have a look around. He also needed to relieve himself. There were only three people in the place, not counting the bartender, and the reporter wasn't one of them.

"Whaddya drinking?" the bartender asked when Hawk returned from the men's room and approached the bar.

He scanned the back wall of the bar where all the liquor bottles were stationed. "Dewar's, straight up," he said and took a stool. The bartender poured three fingers in a highball glass. "That'll be four bucks."

"That all? I need to drink here more often," Hawk said and peeled a twenty from a bankroll he pulled from his pocket.

"Why, where you from?" the bartender asked, wiping down the bar in front of Hawk. The other customers turned toward the stranger, waiting for his reply.

"Oh, here, there, everywhere. You know." Their curiosity unrewarded, the other customers went back to talking among themselves.

"I was supposed to meet a guy here," Hawk said, peering around, "but I was out in my car on a call and I'm a little late. Youngish-looking fellow, light hair, glasses. You seen him, by any chance?"

"Yeah, he was in here. Watched the end of the football game and then left about a half hour ago. Seemed upset his team lost."

"Musta just missed him, then, but I didn't see him come out the front door, though."

"That's 'cause he didn't. He went out back," the bartender said and motioned to the rear of the bar, "with an older guy."

"The older guy, what did he look like?" Hawk asked casually, finishing his whiskey.

"Like a hundred other live-aboard sailors that blow through here every year. You want another drink?"

Hawk took his time answering as if he was giving the question serious weight, when what he was really thinking was: *St. Mary's ain't that big of a place. If Walker's hiding out, how hard could it be to find him?*

"Sure. Why not. I'll have one more. Tell me, where can a man rent a quiet, out-of-the-way boat slip around here?" Hawk asked.

CHAPTER 28

January 1, Maryland's Eastern Shore

An alarm tripped inside Cal Walker's head as he rolled slowly past the dark-blue sedan parked out front of the Sand Bar with the lone, mustached man sitting rigidly inside. It could mean only one thing: his enemies were a helluva lot closer than he feared.

Walker's eyes flashed to the rearview mirror, and he exhaled deeply when the sedan remained stationary and didn't pull out to follow him. Only then did it occur to him, *It's not me they're tailing, it's Nik.* But they—whoever they were—would quickly discover Nik was no longer in the bar and that he had left with another customer out the back way and was likely in the car that had exited from the back parking lot. St. Mary's was small, and there weren't a lot of locals driving Priuses, and he mentally kicked himself for not ditching the Prius sooner. It would only be a matter of time before they tracked him down.

"Can I get up now?" Nik, still curled up on the floorboard, called out.

"What? Oh, sure. You can sit up."

"How much farther?" Nik said after he unfurled his body and craned his neck to get the kinks out.

"Not far now," Walker replied. "Tell me, Nik, did you notice anyone following you on your drive over?"

"Not particularly, but I remember thinking there was only one other car on the road besides me. Then again, it is New Year's Day."

"This car, was it behind you the whole way?"

"Yeah, pretty much."

Walker then told Nik about the dark-colored sedan parked out front of the Sand Bar with the single male occupant and his suspicion that Nik had been followed from DC.

Nik generally dismissed Walker's paranoia. Cal tended to see spies lurking in every doorway, Nik believed, but having once nearly been run over by a couple of thugs who didn't like him nosing around in their business back in Kansas City, he was inclined to give Walker the benefit of the doubt this time. "You see what the guy looked like?"

"I got a quick look, but I didn't want to stare and be obvious," Walker said. "He had a prominent light-colored mustache and, if I had to guess, I'd say he was mid- to late forties."

"Colonel Mustard," Nik said offhandedly.

"What the hell's that supposed to mean?" Walker said.

"That's the nickname we've given the guy who I saw the night of the Trident explosion. He had this giant yellow mustache. You know, a push-broom mustache, so we named him after the character in Clue," Nik said.

"Whatever," Walker said.

"You see the color of his mustache?"

"Too dark. Here we are," Walker said and pulled into a parking lot, killing the car's engine.

Nik hopped out the door and heard gravel crunch underfoot when he stood. In the near distance, he could make out sailboats bobbing in the bay. "So this is your hideaway. Which one of these junks belongs to you?"

"The one at the far end," Walker said, motioning to the tall-masted sloop. Walker unlocked a gate that led out onto a dock where the boats were moored. It was quiet, and there didn't appear to be anyone else living aboard the vessels.

As they made their way down the dock, Nik could see a faint light coming from Walker's craft, and when they reached the boat, a man emerged from the cabin. It was Mr. Liu. He was dressed similar to Walker: peacoat, watch cap, jeans. He held a cigarette in his right hand, which he flicked into the air, and it made a soft hissing sound when it landed in a puddle of water on the dock. In his left, he palmed a small revolver, which he slipped into the pocket of his jacket.

"Good to see you again, Nik," Liu said in a reedy voice and extended a hand. "Come aboard and let's talk."

There was a heavy chop to the waves, and Nik had to steady himself as he stepped from the dock onto the undulating boat, thinking the whole time, *His English is flawless.*

———

For the next seventy-five minutes, Liu related his story to Nik while Walker busied himself brewing tea for Liu, setting out plates of cheese and sweets, tidying up the small galley kitchen, and playing classical music to drown out their voices. Liu sat on a padded bench, arms resting on a small tabletop, a glowing cigarette clamped between his fingers, gray smoke encircling his head. Nik sat opposite Liu, the bobbing boat unsettling his stomach, a closed porthole above his head like a halo that he wished were open to let the fresh air in and the smoke out, but it was wintertime and the cabin was already chilly.

While Liu's English was perfect, he spoke quickly, and his sentences tumbled out of him in daisy-chain fashion and rear-ended one another. Nik unsuccessfully raced to keep up with the narrative and asked to tape-record the conversation, but Liu refused "out of an abundance of caution." He offered to slow down but would soon forget his pledge and start talking in rapid sentences again after only a few minutes. Nik reverted to a chicken-scratch shorthand and hoped he'd be able to read his notes when the interview concluded.

As Walker bustled about, it was clear Liu and Walker were comfortable in each other's company, and occasionally fin-ished one another's sentences like a married couple might. At first, Nik was suspicious and wondered if Liu and Walker had rehearsed their answers for his benefit, but then realized the men, both ex-spies, shared a common background, and maybe he shouldn't be surprised that they thought and acted alike.

Liu's story began a few years earlier when he was assigned to China's United Nations delegation in New York as an in-terpreter. In addition to English, Liu said he spoke Japanese, French, and Russian.

Liu said he had been tapped for the undercover post be-cause his bosses in the Ministry of State Security wanted to expose him to the United States. A UN posting was quite normal for rising Chinese spies, according to Liu, and he esti-mated that at least 40 percent of his country's diplomatic corps were intelligence agents working for the government, and that didn't even include the students and businesswomen and -men working under nonofficial cover.

Liu told Nik that he had been posted to the UN for about a year when, on a Saturday morning in late autumn, a stylish, dark-haired woman had approached him as he ate breakfast at the small Midtown diner he frequented on the weekends. The woman said she was visiting from out of town and had asked for directions to the Boathouse in Central Park, where she was supposed to meet a friend at eleven that morning and worried she would be late.

Liu said he tried to steer the woman in the right direction, but couldn't help but think it was odd that, of all the people in the busy café, she had chosen him, a middle-aged Asian man, to ask for directions. But still, it was New York, and customers around him were carrying on conversations in several different languages.

Liu said he finished his breakfast, paid his bill, left, and was enjoying the cool weather and stroll back to his apartment when he turned a corner and ran headlong into the woman. She was walking in the opposite direction of the park, and Liu immediately knew their meeting wasn't a coincidence.

His suspicions were confirmed a second later when she leaned in and whispered, "My friend at the Boathouse told me to tell Mr. Liu that we can provide him a product one thousand times better than Dragon Eyes. It's the crown jewels of US intelligence." Then she was gone.

Liu explained to Nik that Dragon Eyes was a camera with a resolution five times more detailed than the human eye, capable of monitoring thousands of people in real time and identifying individual faces. The People's Liberation Army was working to marry Dragon Eyes with tracking and encryption-penetrating spyware, but, to date, the efforts had been a complete failure. The PLA and State Ministry, Liu said, were now working together to steal US military technology in an effort to catch up.

The Chinese were behind other nations in developing advanced spy software and discreetly put the word out that they were willing to acquire the technology by any means necessary.

"All of this started after Edward Snowden leaked the CIA cables revealing how extensively the US was spying on its allies by breaking encrypted intercepts and diplomatic communications. It was obvious that the United States possessed superior electronic monitoring technologies, and China couldn't afford to fall any further behind in the arms race. Snowden's actions set off a panic in Beijing, and we've been playing defense ever since," Liu said. He paused to take a sip of tea and let Nik catch up with his scribbling.

"So, did you go to the Central Park meeting?" Nik asked.

"No. Of course not. That's not how tradecraft works, and I'm pretty certain they didn't expect me to," Liu said dismissively. Walker nodded his head in agreement. "I reported the approach to my superiors, and we were confident that there would be another attempt."

"And was there?" Nik said.

"Yes, this time by a man as I was hailing a cab on Lexington Avenue. More information was quickly exchanged and a meeting arranged."

"Okay," Nik said without looking up from his notes, "so I assume you met and ended up acquiring the spyware. Who was the seller?"

"Actually, Nik, we met several times, but we did not carry out the transaction, even though the technology was exactly what we were looking for," Liu said. "As for the sellers, they were either a couple of rogue ex-military or intelligence community operatives. Code names only, but former or active US agents for certain, and perhaps Mossad is mixed up in this, too, somehow. Hard to know."

"Why didn't you acquire the technology. Too expensive?"

"No. Because we thought it was a trap. The Americans knew we were desperate to get our hands on the technology, and we became suspicious that your government was setting us up and that we would receive compromised software that would allow the US to spy on us while we were spying on our enemies," Liu said.

"It's a wonder your head doesn't explode with all this spy-versus-spy stuff," Nik said.

Liu only shrugged in response.

"So, if you didn't acquire the spyware, what's the purpose in telling me all this? I'm not following," Nik said.

"I said we didn't acquire it then, but we did get our hands on it eventually. We used the North Koreans as a cutout to obtain the technology for us. That way, we have plausible deniability, but, of course, everyone knew China was behind the multimillion-dollar transaction because the North Koreans don't have a pot to piss in," Liu said.

Nik said, "And what was this technology the North Koreans acquired for China?"

"POOF," Liu said. "It was POOF, Dr. Walker's surveillance program."

Nik shot a quick look at Walker, who was leaning against a doorjamb studying his fingernails.

"And now for the sixty-four-thousand-dollar question," Nik said, looking up from his notepad and at Liu, "why did you defect, and why are you revealing these secrets?"

Liu extracted another cigarette from a pack and used the coals from a smoldering butt to light the end. His eyes watered from the smoke, and he squinted before continuing. "I don't know what this means, sixty-four-thousand-dollar question."

"It's an expression," Walker chimed in. "Just another way of saying it's a very important question."

"That's right," Nik said.

"Oh, I see," Liu said. "Don't misunderstand me, Nik, I believe we should use every means of technology available to defend the Chinese people against our enemies, but that's not how our leaders see it. They want to apply the technology to suppress, control, and spy on our own citizenry, and then they want to export Dr. Walker's product to other regimes to do the same. Their goal is, in essence, to build a digital Great Wall that spans the globe. They were already halfway there with advances in facial-recognition technology. POOF is the last piece to the puzzle."

Nik just nodded and continued his note-taking, all the while thinking, *Liu's as bat-shit crazy as Cal.*

"International plot," Walker offered.

"Riiight," Nik answered.

"My country is more powerful now than ever, but far less free. Yet, there's still time. That's why I defected. That's why I sought out Dr. Walker. Together—" Liu began to say, but before he could finish his thought, there was a sharp crack and the porthole behind Nik's head exploded, glass shards raining down on him.

Instinctively, Nik crouched and covered. He stole a quick look in Walker's direction, but Walker had vanished. He could hear foreign voices yelling on the deck above him, pounding footsteps, a gunshot, then another, and finally the cough of an outboard motor.

Nik lifted his head to survey the cabin. Liu was facedown on the table in a dark pool of blood, the cigarette still gripped tightly in his fingers, embers searing his skin. The sight of blood made Nik light-headed, and he could feel himself slowly blacking out.

CHAPTER 29

January 1, Maryland's Eastern Shore

The Sand Bar's weathered-looking customers and bartender turned out to be quite chatty after Hawk bought several rounds of drinks for the house. The barkeep, Wink Simons, told Hawk the older guy who had left with his friend had been hanging around the tavern for several days.

"He'd nurse a drink, two at the most, for a couple hours like he was waiting on someone, and then leave. Day before yesterday, he was in here late afternoon when this Asian gentleman shows up, and they left together," Simons said, and confirmed the customer drove a Prius.

When Hawk asked about boat slips, the customers provided him with three locations and drew him a map to each. He thanked them, left Wink a twenty-dollar tip, and was reaching for the door when one of the customers asked, "Whatcha piloting?"

"How's that?" Hawk said, halfway out the door.

"Your boat. What is it?"

Hawk didn't know the first thing about boats. He had

spent the last several years in the deserts of the Middle East and the mountains of Afghanistan. He noticed a framed picture of a vintage boat hanging on the wall next to the door. "Chris-Craft," he said, reading the nameplate.

"I thought you said it was a sailboat," the old man replied.

Hawk stammered. "It will be when I'm finished converting it."

The old man gave Hawk a quizzical look. "Good luck with that," he said as everyone at the bar guffawed and turned back to their free drinks.

Hawk heard loud voices and what sounded like a gunshot when he pulled into the parking lot of the last marina the customers had directed him to. He quietly opened his car door and crept toward the boat slips, and that's when he saw the Prius parked behind a small utility shed. He heard the whine of a boat's motor and then a second pop. Definitely gunfire. He didn't know what was happening, but he didn't plan to stick around and find out, either. Gunplay tended to draw the attention of neighbors and then cops, especially in a town as small as St. Mary's.

Hawk piled back into his car, confident he had found Cal Walker's hideout, but wondering who was doing the shooting and why.

CHAPTER 30

January 2, Washington, DC

The sun was coming up as Nik exited the Beltway and crossed back over the Maryland state line into the District of Columbia. He was beyond exhausted. His stomach ached from the thick-as-molasses coffee he had purchased from a roadside store, and the inside of his mouth tasted like dirt.

He longed for sleep, but there was work to do before then, and he made a mental list of the things he needed to accomplish: reschedule a meeting with his *Newshound* colleagues; arrange a call with his ex-wife later in the day; check in with Sam to see if she was able to trace the call he received early New Year's Day from the woman claiming to know who had killed the state trooper and clerk and bombed Trident. When he had attempted to redial the caller later that morning, he had gotten a message saying the number had been disconnected.

As he drove back to Washington, Nik replayed the night's events in his mind, and even now, it seemed like a dream.

The sight of Liu's head swimming in a bloody soup made Nik woozy, and he had nearly passed out, but in an instant, there was Walker, towering over him, barking orders, sweeping the table free of plates, cups, ashtrays, and broken glass with his forearm, a pistol at his waistband.

Nik launched himself from the booth and sprinted to the head to retrieve towels, gauze, scissors, bandages, ointment, and anything else he could carry. Walker bandaged the wound and said Liu was lucky. The shooter had not taken into account the pitch of the boat on the water and had fired just as a wave rolled and crested, instead of in the trough where the water is flat and the boat steady. Had he waited another moment, the bullet likely would have caught Liu right between the eyes. As it was, the shot came in high and the bullet creased the top of Liu's skull, opening an ugly, but nonfatal, five-inch gash that gushed blood. After he tended to Liu, Walker had dug the slug out of the cabin's panel behind where Liu was seated.

Walker told Nik that after the shot was fired he had disappeared to the back of the boat and retrieved a pistol from his sleeping quarters. He said he surfaced on deck just as two men ran to the end of the dock where a Boston Whaler was idling. Walker said he got off one round as the pair hurdled over the side of the boat and a second shot as it pulled away. He heard one of the men scream in Chinese and thought he might have been hit.

"I'm embarrassed," Walker confessed, "that they were able to get close enough to get a shot off. It won't happen again, and, for sure, I won't play the music so loud next time."

After Liu was stabilized and conscious, Walker drove Nik back to his vehicle. Both Walker and Liu agreed that the people who had tried to kill him weren't likely to return that night, but just in case, Walker set a trip wire on the dock and furnished Liu with an AK-47 that he pulled from a sea trunk.

Walker ditched the Prius for an old Ford pickup truck he had stashed nearby at an all-night storage lot. The truck had an NRA decal in the rear window and a bumper sticker that read: "If you're going to ride my ass, at least pull my hair." He discarded the Washington Redskins beanie and put on a long blond wig and black thick-framed glasses. He made a quick pass by the Sand Bar to confirm the blue sedan was gone before depositing Nik back at his vehicle.

"I don't expect you'll have any problems, but just in case, you should take the back roads home. Might take a little longer, but you'll know immediately if you have a tail," Walker advised. Nik no longer thought Walker paranoid and followed his advice. He also agreed that they would use only encrypted apps for future communications.

Nik was relieved to see there was a parking space right out front of his apartment when he turned onto Thirty-First Street. That was a rarity in Georgetown, in his experience. Usually he had to circle the block countless times hunting for a spot and, as often as not, park illegally. He had a glove box full of parking tickets to show for it.

Nik quickly fired off notes to his *Newshound* colleagues; his ex-wife, Maggie; and Sam. That finished, he kicked off his shoes, tugged his shirt over his head, unbuckled his belt, and dropped his pants to the floor before falling facedown into bed. He lay there in his boxers, suspended in a semiconscious mist, and struggled to arrange all the facts in his head and make sense of what had happened the night before. It was a tangle, and as he closed his eyes, his last thought was: *What did Liu mean there was still time? Time for what?*

CHAPTER 31

January 2, Washington, DC

Nik had just stepped out of the shower when he heard his cell phone chirp with an incoming text. He wrapped a towel around his waist and gingerly stepped over to the bedside table where the phone was charging. He had twisted his ankle on the boat when he had run to retrieve bandages for Walker, and the swelling in his foot had not gone down. Standing in a small pool of dripping water, he scanned a series of messages from Maggie, Mo, and Sam.

Maggie didn't have time for a call during the day and instead proposed they meet after work, at six thirty, at the Hay-Adams hotel across the street from the White House. I have dinner plans, so it's gotta be quick, she wrote. Nik replied he'd meet her there promptly.

Sam informed him she had been able to get the information he wanted but refused to put it in an email or text and said he should call her when he had a free minute. He texted back, Thanks and will do. He then added, Miss you.

Mo said he had spoken to Frank and Mia and suggested

they all meet for lunch at Clyde's in Georgetown at noon. Nik responded, See you then. It was already eleven forty-five. He'd have to hustle.

Nik limped into Clyde's ten minutes late, his hair slicked back, still damp from the shower, eyes red-rimmed and puffy from lack of sleep, his perpetual three-day stubble unkempt and nearly a week old, dressed in black jeans, a North Face down jacket, and work boots. Clyde's atmosphere could best be described as beer hall meets French bistro, with walls covered in eclectic prints and posters, and a menu offering hearty upscale pub food. It strived for a neighborhood bar ambiance, but the stampeding tourist traffic in Georgetown made that a challenge.

"You look more like a hobbled horse than the Galloping Gourmet," Mo said.

Nik ignored the jab and asked, "Have you ordered yet?"

"Just drinks," Mia said. "We were waiting for you before we got around to lunch."

The waiter arrived with their drinks and took their lunch order. Nik asked for a double espresso, hoping it would clear out the fog that had settled in his head.

"So, what have you been up to?" Mo asked. "Besides not sleeping."

"Following OmniSoft leads, but before I tell you about my adventures, first fill me in on what you found out about Colonel Mustard," Nik said.

Mo looked at Mia and nodded, and she recapped their conversation with Lance Duvall, the private security officer. "Pretty sure Calkins is not his last name and he went by an alias when he applied to Yellow Jacket. Registered as Brick, but we're fairly confident it's the same guy you encountered at

Trident the night of the explosion. Unfortunately, they didn't have a picture of him in their files, but he fits the physical description. I got a request in to my Pentagon sources to pull recent photos of military personnel with the surname of Brick. I'll let you know when I hear back."

"Duvall have any idea what happened to this guy?" Nik asked.

"Nope. It was a while ago. Duvall thinks there's a good chance he signed on with some other outfit that wasn't as picky as Yellow Jacket. Apparently soldiers of fortune are in high demand, especially ones with some technology experience," Mia said.

"Okay, that's us. Now, what about you?" Mo said.

"Last night," Nik said, stopping briefly to inhale the espresso, "I was interviewing this guy when someone took a shot at him and nearly blew the top of his head off, and would have, too, had they fired a fraction of a second later."

"Bullshit," Mo said.

"God's honest truth. He was sitting as close to me as you are now when they opened fire on him and parted his hair with a slug. It's a miracle he's alive."

"Hold on," Mia said, concern in her voice, "and rewind. Who got shot, who was doing the shooting, where did this happen, and what's it got to do with OmniSoft?"

"I know," Nik said, tilting back in his chair and throwing up his hands to ward off the skeptical looks around the table, "it sounds crazy. It *is* crazy. I wouldn't believe it myself had I not been sitting right there when it happened."

The waiter appeared with their lunch order, and Nik paused. Mia offered to share her plate with the table.

"What is it?" Mo asked skeptically.

"Avocado toast. It's delicious. Try it."

"No, thanks," Mo said. "I don't put peanut butter on tacos, and I don't put guacamole on toast."

"Suit yourself."

When the waiter left, Nik told them about meeting Walker at the Sand Bar, the stakeout in front of the bar, going to Walker's boat, and Mr. Liu.

"We're in the cabin and Liu's telling me this fantastical story, and just when I'm thinking this guy is nuts, all hell breaks loose. The porthole shatters, Liu slams facedown into the table, Walker storms on deck and starts firing at the guys who tried to kill Liu, and I'm sitting there covered in glass and in shock. I only snap out of it when Walker starts screaming at me."

Mo said, "What the fuck."

"Yeah, WTF," Mia added.

"So, what now?" Mo asked.

"Dunno," Nik said. "I was hoping we might figure that out together. I've got a few ideas, but nothing approaching a plan."

"I have one." It was Frank. He had been silent during most of the conversation. "Want to hear it?"

"Sure," they answered in unison and turned toward him.

Frank, the wizened veteran, who always seemed to grow calmer and measured the more chaotic things became, said: "First order of business, we need to confirm Liu's identity. Even if he says who he is, we still don't know if we can believe his story. We need to establish his credibility. If he's a defector, you can bet the Chinese government will either paint him as a traitor who can't be trusted or claim he's an insignificant bureaucrat."

"We should start at the United Nations. They would have a record of his service," Nik said.

"I can take that on," Mia said. "I have a college classmate who went to work for the UN as a communications specialist. We follow each other on Twitter. I'll reach out to her."

"See if you can get your hands on a picture of him and send it to me," Nik said.

"Will do," Mia said.

"Next, we need to pin down this Calkins-slash-Brick guy and figure out his role," Frank said.

"Mo should handle that," Mia volunteered. "He's got the best military and intelligence sources."

"Agreed," Nik said. "Mo?"

"Do my best," Mo mumbled, wrestling to get his mouth around a football-size hamburger.

"That leaves the guys in the van and the federal government's involvement with OmniSoft. I'll take those," Nik said.

"Good," Frank said.

After paying the tab, Nik asked, "You sure you're up for this, Frank? You don't look so good."

"You might want to take a look in the mirror," Frank said.

Nik pulled Mo aside when they were outside. "Is everything all right with Frank?"

"No, it's not, but you need to hear it from him, not me," Mo said.

When Nik looked up, Frank was already gone.

CHAPTER 32

January 2, Washington, DC

Nik's ex-wife was sitting in a tall, red-tufted chair, sipping a champagne cocktail and talking on her cell phone when Nik limped into the bar of the Hay-Adams hotel at six thirty on the dot as they had arranged. Maggie, dressed in a light-gray blazer, matching skirt, and a sky-blue blouse, hurriedly finished her call and lifted her face to Nik when he leaned in over the table to give her a kiss, but she quickly jerked back when his stubble rasped her cheek.

"You know there are companies now that deliver razor blades directly to your doorstep. Might want to look into that," she said, rubbing a palm across her cheek and shoving a chair out with her foot. "Have a seat, Nik. Good to see you."

"Sorry. Haven't had time to shave," he said, dropping into the chair.

The Hay-Adams personified Establishment Washington, genteel, conservative, and moneyed, and Nik guessed that was why Maggie was drawn to it. Nik had been there once before to meet with a congressional staffer who was investigating the

OmniSoft complaint. He thought the place staid, pretentious, and overpriced.

He ordered a Budweiser—$16.50—and they exchanged small talk.

Maggie said she had been looking at condos to buy but couldn't decide if she wanted to live in the District or in one of the close-in suburbs. She had narrowed her choices to McLean, Virginia; Chevy Chase, Maryland; and Kalorama in the District. When she and Nik had divorced, he had agreed to a sixty-forty split of their assets, and she had invested wisely and could afford a place in an upscale neighborhood.

"Sounds like a First World problem," Nik said.

"You still like living in Georgetown?" she asked.

"I do. The place is small, but it suits me," he said.

Maggie asked Nik about his love life, and he told her about Sam. "She's an investigator for the sheriff's department in Northern Virginia," he said. "We just sorta clicked."

"That's good to hear, Nik," she said without a trace of jealousy. "Try not to screw it up this time."

Nik didn't want to open old wounds by pointing out that it was Maggie who, when their marriage was faltering, had the wandering eye. Instead, he said, "Thanks, Maggs. I'll take that under advisement."

Maggie handed Nik her phone and showed him a picture of her with a group of skiers on a snow-covered mountaintop. She told Nik she had been in Vail over the holidays on a ski trip with new friends from a book club she had joined. She also shared a picture of Gaylord Spence, an assistant to the attorney general, and told him they were officially dating. The photo was Spence in a contorted position on a mat.

"We take yoga classes together," Maggie said with a smile.

Maggie freely admitted Spence wasn't particularly bright or ambitious, but he was good-looking and, because of his position, had a direct pipeline into everything important that was happening in the attorney general's office.

Nik swiped through the pictures on Maggie's phone and longed for some time off for himself, if for no other reason than to sleep. But he didn't see a ski vacation in his future anytime soon, even if he could afford one, which he couldn't. He was envious of Maggie's lifestyle and the way she had landed on her feet after the divorce.

Her good fortune irritated him, and he snapped, "I'm happy for you, Maggie. Really, I am, but I'm not here to look at your Instagram account. Can we talk about OmniSoft? That's why we're meeting, right?"

"Don't bite my head off. I was just making conversation."

"Sorry, Maggs," Nik said again, realizing that being rude to her wasn't going to help his cause. "I haven't been sleeping much lately."

"Forget it," Maggie said, an edge creeping into her voice, becoming more businesslike. "Yes, we're here to talk about OmniSoft. I've been authorized to speak to you on background. We're offering you this information so you have a better perspective on what really transpired between the government and Cal Walker. It's not as Walker paints it, but you can't use anything I tell you in a story unless you confirm it independently, understood?"

"I know what background is, Maggie," Nik said and spun around to search for their waiter. When he caught the server's eye, he asked Maggie if she wanted another cocktail. She did.

"What you pay for alcohol in this place would keep me in beer for a month," he said when their drinks arrived. "So, what do you got for me?"

"The US government was Walker's primary client and financial supporter, pumping tens of millions of dollars into POOF. The FBI, CIA, and DIA were all excited about the technology's potential. In return for the government's invest-ment, Walker signed over certain rights to the software to the United States government, as well as issuing it stock in his company," she said.

"What's the DIA?" Nik asked.

"Defense Intelligence Agency. They were the first ones to spot POOF's potential applications, but the Justice Department and FBI took the lead role since OmniSoft was domiciled in the US," Maggie said, stopping momentarily to answer an in-coming text message on her phone.

"Sorry," she said. "It's Spence. Just confirming dinner reservations."

"How nice," Nik said.

Maggie continued: "Walker's technology, while buggy, was superior to anything we'd ever seen and, properly deployed, would give the United States an edge in identifying, surveil-ling, and neutralizing terrorists. It also had the benefit of being virtually invisible."

Nik cut in, in an exasperated tone, "So, what's new? I know most of this already, Maggie."

She nodded. "But what you don't know could fill a wing at the Smithsonian. First, Walker's not quite the innocent by-stander he likes to make himself out to be. Do you know what he did at the CIA?" she asked.

Nik shook his head.

"He was assigned to the division that carried out wet work."

"What, assassinations?"

"I'm sure as hell not talking about skinny-dipping. I'm not saying he was directly involved, but he was attached to that particular unit as an analyst. Ask him, if you don't believe me."

"I will," Nik said, "but what's that got to do with OmniSoft?"

"That's point number two. Some higher-ups in the in-telligence community became alarmed about OmniSoft's precarious financial condition and Walker's general lack of management oversight of the company and the government's investment. There was legitimate concern Walker could be compromised and that POOF would fall into the hands of our adversaries and be turned against us. There was little confidence in Walker's ability to lock it down and prohibit that from happening. For national security reasons, the decision was made to pull the plug on funding; seize the asset, which was rightfully ours; and, in essence, force OmniSoft out of business and into bankruptcy. No one felt particularly good about the decision, but Walker had already been paid millions. Some might say *squandered* millions."

"What would stop Walker from just re-creating the technology?" Nik asked.

"We own the patents, and, anyway, you're talking about very sophisticated algorithms. They would take years to replicate, even if he had the money, which he doesn't," Maggie said.

"So the government didn't grab POOF to commercialize as Cal claims but . . ."

"Quite the opposite, in fact. Quarantine it, contain it, compartmentalize it."

"But that's not what happened, is it, Maggie?" Nik said matter-of-factly.

"No, it's not," she said, an off-putting note in her voice at Nik's cocky reply. "Somebody—we believe an intelligence operative with a technology background—got their hands on it. We don't know who, but we think they're tied to the Trident bombing," she said.

"But why kill Walker if they already got POOF? That doesn't make sense," Nik said.

"We can only speculate about the motive since we don't know who's behind it," she said. "Cover their tracks, perhaps. Maybe Walker can identify the person. With Walker out of the picture, interest in the story goes away."

"Seems that would also benefit the government," Nik said.

"The United States government did not attempt to kill Cal Walker, Nik," she said icily.

Nik said, "So now your bosses are worried that their fears have been realized and that someone is trying to sell POOF on the black market. Do I have that about right?"

"There's absolutely no proof that has happened, but, yes, naturally it's a concern," she said. "You know something you're not telling me?"

Nik considered confiding in Maggie about Mr. Liu and the scene on Walker's boat but decided against it. "Maggie, you've known me long enough to know I can't reveal information before it's printed," he said and finished his beer.

She shot back, "Here's what I know, Nik Byron, and that is you manipulate situations and people and never play by the rules you expect others to follow."

Her comment stung, because it rang true. Maggie got up to leave, and Nik stood to help her on with her coat. She swatted his hand away and stormed off. Nik left a tip and trailed after her as they made their way to their vehicles. Nik was glad to see that the hotel's valet had called ahead and their cars were waiting when they arrived at the entrance to the parking garage. He didn't want to stand around and have Maggie glowering or, worse, berating him.

Nik gave Maggie a quick peck on the cheek, told her he'd be in touch, handed the attendant a couple bucks, and slid into the driver's seat. He started to pull away, stopped, and rolled down his window. "Your bosses are worried about the wrong thing, Maggie," he said.

"What are you talking about, Nik?"

"You said they're worried POOF may fall into the wrong hands."

"And they are."

"Too late," Nik said. "It already has."

As he pulled away, Nik glanced in his rearview mirror and saw Maggie standing next to her car, the parking lot attendant patiently holding the driver's door open for her while she held an animated conversation with someone on the other end of her cell phone.

CHAPTER 33

January 3, Washington, DC

Nik was headed down Pennsylvania Avenue when his phone vibrated. It was Mo. He picked up just as another call was coming in from the sheriff's department. "I need to take this other call, Mo," Nik said. "Can it wait?"

"Yeah, just wanted to give you a quick update on our progress. Nothing urgent. Call me when you can."

He switched over to the other call. "This is Nik."

"Hey, it's me," Sam said. "Sorry I've been so tough to reach. It's been a little crazy around here."

"Been a little busy myself," Nik said, "but it's good to hear your voice. Any luck tracking down that phone number?"

"That's why I'm calling. Number's registered to a Sara Conway. It's a Detroit area code, but the cell tower the call came from is located just outside of a place called Three Rivers, Michigan, and when we look at other recent calls, they all ping that same tower."

"I can find Three Rivers on a map, but trying to identify where Sara Conway is living might be a challenge," he said, a little disappointed the news wasn't better.

"I got something on that, too," Sam said. "Her cell phone bill is being sent to a Three Rivers rural route address. Owner's name is a Grant Dilworth."

"Hang on," Nik said, and pulled his car onto the shoulder of the road. "Okay, give it to me," he said and scribbled the address down in his notebook.

"You plan on going there?" Sam asked.

"That's what I'm thinking. Better to do this face-to-face. Cold calling wouldn't work and would only tip them off. Not an easy place to get to, though, if memory serves from my college days in Ann Arbor. Probably need to fly to Detroit and catch a small charter. Thank God Whetstone's out of the office. He'd never approve the expense."

Nik had not heard from his editor in several days.

"You think that's wise?" Sam asked, a note of caution in her voice.

"I figure I'm going to get demoted or fired one way or the other. Might as well run up a tab while I still can."

"I don't care about Whetstone. I mean taking one of those small planes in the middle of the winter. I hate those things."

Nik brushed off Sam's concerns and assured her he had flown plenty on puddle jumpers. "Saw half of Alaska one summer on Beavers that you'd swear couldn't get off the ground, let alone stay aloft," he said.

"I wish you wouldn't," Sam said.

"I'll be fine. Listen, I need to talk to Mo. I'll call you when I get back and we'll go out to dinner," Nik said.

"You do that," Sam said and the line went dead. Given the abruptness with which the call ended, Nik looked down at his phone to confirm he still had cell coverage before dialing Mo.

Mo picked up on the first ring and told Nik his source at the Department of Defense was emailing him mug shots of recent military officers with the last name of Brick, or whose spellings were similar. Mo said he would send them to Nik as soon as he downloaded the files.

"It's a long shot, but what the hell, it's worth a try," Mo said.

Nik told Mo he was about fifteen minutes from his apartment and would look at the mug shots after he got home. He asked about Mia, and Mo said she had exchanged messages with her former classmate at the United Nations but that they hadn't actually spoken yet.

Nik stopped at a Five Guys and purchased two burgers, fries, and a chocolate shake for dinner. He spread the food out on the coffee table in his living room, popped out his laptop, and clicked on the email from Mo.

Mo had forwarded twenty-five pictures. None matched the description of the man Nik had seen at Trident Office Park the night of the explosion.

Nik then made a reservation for a flight to Detroit Metro Airport and booked a small charter flight to an airfield near Three Rivers. Next, he reserved a car at the airport's only car rental agency.

He plugged Sara Conway's name into Google and got a smattering of search results, mostly for a teenage Sara Conway from Pine Bluff, Arkansas, who had been awarded first place in the Quarter Horse category at the State Fair. There were also three obituaries, two birth announcements, and a promotion for an upcoming concert in Texas. No mention of a Sara Conway from Michigan.

He next typed in Grant Dilworth's name, and the screen filled with images of stainless-steel sculptures Dilworth had created in his studio in Three Rivers. The pieces of work ranged from a $7,500 silver fox to a $25,000 bull elk.

Nik clicked on Dilworth's website and hit the Contact Us button. He fired off a quick email saying he was a collector and was going to be in the Three Rivers area and wanted to come by to view Dilworth's artwork. He received an automated reply with the studio's business hours that assured him someone would be in touch shortly.

Nik was about to close his laptop when he decided to check out the *Washington Post*'s website to see if it had any new stories on the Trident explosion. He had not come across any *Post* staffers in the course of his own reporting and was starting to wonder if the newspaper had lost interest in the story. He knew *Post* reporters treated anything remotely connected to Cal Walker with skepticism. He couldn't blame them.

A quick scan of the site didn't reveal any new stories, and he used the *Post*'s search feature to broaden his inquiry. Still nothing.

On a whim, he typed Samantha Whyte's name into the search box. The page momentarily froze, sputtered, and then spit out scores of headlines with Sam's byline when she had been a reporter at the *Post*.

Nik was impressed by how prolific Sam had been when she was still at the paper. He admired anyone who could write fast, clean, and concise. His writing was clean and concise—but fast it was not. He knew reporters who sneezed and produced two thousand words on deadline. He was not one of them. He labored over every word, sentence, and paragraph, and it had irritated the hell out of his editors over the years.

Nik scrolled through the headlines, clicking on stories that caught his eye. Many of the stories were about politics, politicians, and political scandal, with a mix of hard news and softer features. One of his favorites was a story on the annual softball tournament between Republicans and Democrats on the Hill.

Sam had a nice conversational writing voice, an easy style to identify but actually very hard to produce. She also had a keen eye for capturing small but telling details: like noting the black notebook one congresswoman always had on her that contained the names and histories of all the military personnel in her district who had lost their lives in the service of their country.

Nik was closing down his laptop when a headline at the bottom of the page drew his attention. It read: "Reporter killed in freak airplane mishap."

He clicked on the headline and began reading:

> Gregg Robbins, a seasoned political reporter and twelve-year veteran of the *Washington Post*, was killed earlier today when he accidentally walked into the churning propeller of a prop plane while on assignment with fellow reporter Samantha Whyte in the oceanside community of Sea Island, Georgia. Robbins leaves behind his wife, fellow *Washington Post* reporter Victoria Kostner, and two small children.

Nik stared at his screen, stunned. He read the story a second time. Then a third. Next, he searched Gregg Robbins's name and scanned the volumes of stories he had written over the years at the *Post*. Lastly, he called up Robbins's obit and read that, too. Evidently, the reporter had been something of a legend at the newspaper.

He recalled the sadness he'd heard in Sam's voice when she had mentioned the relationship just days earlier. The circumstances of Robbins's death were grim, and to think that she'd witnessed it made Nik shudder. He closed down his laptop and wandered outside. Not long after, he found himself standing on Sam's stoop, in shirtsleeves in the freezing winter air, pounding on the door.

"Sami," Nik said, stepping across the threshold and hugging her when she opened the door. "I'm so sorry. I had no idea about Gregg. I don't know what to say. I'm just terribly sorry."

Sam dropped her head into Nik's chest and quietly wept.

CHAPTER 34

January 4, Three Rivers, Michigan

Nik glided his rented SUV to a stop on the icy drive in front of Grant Dilworth's metalworking studio late in the afternoon of the next day as the sun was sliding behind what looked to be storm clouds. He and Dilworth had exchanged messages and arranged to meet to discuss several of his sculptures.

Nik's mother sculpted, and he was impressed with Dilworth's decision to use stainless steel as his medium. It had to be one of the more difficult materials to configure.

Dilworth was in his studio when Nik pulled in, and he threw open the overhead door to his shop. He was wearing a welder's helmet and leather apron and held a flaring acetylene torch in his hand. He turned the knobs on the torch to extinguish the flame. He tipped the helmet back on his forehead, revealing a thick mane of black hair, wide-set eyes, and an arrowhead-shaped nose. A powerfully built German shepherd with a bandaged hind leg sat obediently at his side. Various big game trophies—elk, grizzly bear, bighorn sheep—were mounted on the wall of his shop, and a dozen crossbows and compound bows sat behind a glassed-in cabinet in the back.

Nik had corresponded with Dilworth using a personal email account that only identified him by his given first name—Nikolas. He did not mention his last name or his occupation, and Dilworth had not inquired.

Dilworth removed his helmet, unsnapped the apron, laid the torch on a table, and walked out of the shop toward Nik. "Nikolas?" he said, extending a beefy hand.

"Call me Nik," Nik said, pumping Dilworth's hand. "Grant?"

"Yup. Good to meet you. How are the roads?"

"Not bad. What happened to your dog's leg?"

"Oh, Pontiac, he got it caught in a coyote trap. Bad bruise, mainly, the vet said. Near as I can tell, he hasn't lost a step. Let me show you around the shop," Dilworth said. "Coffee?"

"Thanks. Love some. You take all these yourself?" Nik asked, gesturing to the mounted heads.

Dilworth ladled two tablespoons of freeze-dried coffee out of a jar and dumped them into a mug of hot water. "I did. I used the mounts to model my sculptures," he said and handed the steaming cup to Nik, who couldn't remember the last time he'd had instant coffee. It smelled like singed hair.

"How close do you have to be to take a shot?" Nik asked.

"Depends," Dilworth said.

"On?" Nik followed up.

"On all sorts of things. Wind conditions, what you're hunting, if you're shooting to kill or cripple. For a competent bow hunter, the average range is about forty yards for deer. I feel comfortable sixty-five to eighty-five yards, again depending on conditions and whatnot. The shaft itself can travel well over four hundred yards, and I've made kill shots at ninety-plus yards, but that was a unique situation where I was firing downgrade."

"Had no idea," Nik said.

When Nik pulled up, Dilworth had been working on a commissioned sculpture of an Arabian horse and a yearling standing side by side for a customer in Abu Dhabi. He told Nik it was one of the most demanding pieces he'd ever worked on, and then spent the next twenty minutes giving Nik a tour of the shop and explaining the complexities and benefits of working with stainless steel.

"Archaeologists," Dilworth explained to Nik, "believe stainless steel is one of the few permanent man-made materials on Earth. It is essentially resistant to corrosion and could, theoretically, last for a million years."

"Buyers better be damn sure they really love a sculpture if it's going to last that long," Nik quipped. Dilworth ignored the comment.

"Yet, despite its strength and durability, it's relatively easy to work. Correctly joined, welds are virtually unbreakable, and I can texture the surface with a wire brush, sander, or polish it to a mirrored finish," Dilworth said.

"Absolutely incredible," Nik said. "It's truly impressive."

"Thank you, and, exactly, what sculptures are you most interested in?" Dilworth asked.

This was the jumping-off point for Nik. He could continue pretending to be an interested buyer and hope Dilworth would reveal enough information in casual conversation to help him identify the two men in the van, or he could state his real intentions. Both choices had inherent risks.

"I need to confess something first," Nik said levelly after admiring a sculpture of a hunting dog lunging at a flushing pheasant.

"What's that?" Dilworth said suspiciously and floated his hand over a pair of blacksmith tongs resting on his workbench.

"I'm here kinda under false pretenses. My name is Nik Byron, and I'm a reporter with *Newshound*. A woman called me from this location on New Year's Eve to say she knew the two men who authorities are looking for in connection with setting off a bomb in an office park in Washington, DC, and killing a police officer and store clerk in Indiana."

Dilworth closed his eyes, shook his head, and pushed out a deep breath, the name "Sara" forming on his lips.

"That's right," Nik said. "The call came from a phone belonging to a Sara Conway."

Dead air. Dilworth remained motionless, leaning against his workbench, eyes closed. Nik fought the urge to fill the void. He had learned long ago as a young reporter that silence could be more powerful than asking another question.

Dilworth eventually said, "She's my wife. She's in the house. Wait here while I go talk to her."

With the German shepherd still sitting silently at his side, Dilworth pushed off the table and stepped toward the door. Then he stopped and turned back toward the dog. "Pontiac," he commanded, "eyes on."

With that, the dog lifted from its haunches, cocked its ears forward, and fixed Nik with a stare. Even with only three good legs, the dog would be on him in an instant, Nik knew, if he attempted a sudden move. He was envious and wondered, *How come Gyp can't be more like that?*

Five hundred miles north of Three Rivers, it was high-stakes bingo night at the Thunder Bay Lodge and Casino in Escanaba, Michigan, and the place was wall-to-wall customers, despite the three feet of fresh snow on the ground outside. The crowd of mostly senior citizens dressed in bulky sweatshirts and felt-lined boots sat at long bingo tables as an announcer called out numbers, or they force-fed coins into the mouths of the blinking slot machines that clogged the floor, a yellowish thunderhead of cigarette smoke rolling beneath the ceiling. Cooley stood at a nickel slot, small towers of coins stacked like checkers in front of him. He and Nukowski had been there two days, and all he had to show for it was a voucher for a free buffet dinner that he had won playing bingo.

Cooley was morose and blamed himself for Rosie's and Myrtle's deaths. He realized he should never have mentioned Hawk, or the fact he and Nukowski were famous and on the news. His careless slip of the tongue had cost them their lives. Nukowski was growing more and more unpredictable and bloody, and Cooley was anxious for the meeting with Hawk to set things right again.

It was Nukowski who had insisted they visit the casino. Cooley wasn't much of a gambler, but his partner liked to play blackjack and Texas Hold'em. He was up a couple thousand dollars, and the winnings seemed to lift his black mood.

Before arriving at the casino, Cooley and Nukowski had made a quick stop in the small fishing village of Pellston to get a change of clothes and collect past wages owed them from a fruit farmer and bait shop owner they worked for during harvest season.

The employer, Jud Beck, was once an active member of the Three Percenters, an anti-government group, and had introduced Cooley and Nukowski to the organization. Beck publicly distanced himself from the group after he was jailed for three months for failure to pay back taxes, but privately, he still supported it by occasionally providing shelter and employment to its members.

Beck, like most of the anti-government crowd, was a keyboard warrior, content to sit at his computer and contribute venom to online forums and feed dark conspiracy theories about the government's intentions to imprison patriots and confiscate their weapons, but not given to actual violence. That was not true of Nukowski. He was different, and Beck had told associates that Nukowski terrified him, right down to the soles of his feet.

"Don't worry, we don't plan on hanging around," Nukowski told the nervous-looking Beck when the pair appeared at the door of his bait shop unannounced. "We're only passing through and will be on our way once we collect our money."

Nukowski and Cooley stayed just long enough to swap some gossip and sample a bottle of blackberry brandy Beck had put up two summers prior. When he asked the boys what they had been up to, he laughed when Nukowski said "blowing up buildings and killing cops."

"Ha, that's a good one." Beck snorted and passed around the jug.

Cooley shot Nukowski a nervous look and changed the subject by volunteering that they were headed to the casino and then on to their hunting camp for a few days.

"Pack extra provisions is my advice, boys. They're calling for one helluva snowstorm, and you might never get out," Beck warned.

Truer words were never spoken.

CHAPTER 35

January 5, Pellston, Michigan

Nik drove through the night and arrived in Pellston just as Jud Beck was unlocking the front door to Beck's Bait & Tackle shop. "Mr. Beck," Nik called out as he crossed the street in front of the shop.

Beck swiveled his shaggy head toward the sound, startled that someone would be waiting in the predawn cold to buy bait, and even more confused that someone was referring to him as Mr. Beck. The last person to address him that way was an IRS agent, and that didn't turn out so well for Beck. Most people called him Jud or, if they thought they were being clever, Judy, but never Mr. Beck. That was his first clue that the stranger approaching him wasn't bearing good news.

Before Beck could respond, Nik mounted the stairs to the building and introduced himself. "Mr. Beck, my name is Nik Byron, and I'm a reporter with *Newshound* in Washington, DC. I'm looking for a couple of men by the name of Nukowski and Cooley, and I'm told they spent a few hours here with you recently."

Beck started to respond, stopped midreply, jaw unhinged, mouth open, and shook his head like he was trying to dislodge an unpleasant thought. Finally, looking lost, he said, "What's your name again, son, and what's a newshound?"

It had taken Nik the better part of the evening to pry information out of Grant Dilworth and Sara Conway about Nukowski and Cooley. He had to swear to them that he would not reveal their names, and even then, Dilworth wasn't convinced.

"You lied about who you were," Dilworth said. "Why should we believe you?"

Nik bristled. "I'll admit I wasn't totally forthcoming, but I never lied. Look, I came all this way to meet you in person. If I were going to screw you, I could have saved myself a lot of time and aggravation and just given Sara's phone number to investigators back in DC."

Eventually, slowly, they dribbled out their story. Without going into detail, they said they had known Nukowski for the better part of a decade but hadn't seen or heard from him in years until he literally showed up on their doorstep in late December looking for a favor. Neither claimed to know Cooley.

"He needed a vehicle. The van he and his partner were driving no longer suited their needs. I asked why, but he told me I was better off not knowing. I didn't push it."

Dilworth told Nik about the GPS tracking unit he'd affixed to the car. "I didn't want Nukowski doubling back on us and showing up here again unannounced," he explained.

"But you're still tracking them and know where they are?" Nik asked.

"I know where they've been. Last I checked, they were on the move again." Dilworth said the pair had visited the Thunder Bay Lodge and Casino for two days and, before that, they stopped for a couple hours at Beck's Bait & Tackle in Pellston, and that's where Nik started his search.

Standing outside of the bait shop, Nik explained to Beck that *Newshound* was a national online news operation with locations throughout the United States and that he was attached to the Washington office. When he finished, he suggested they move inside where it was warmer.

Beck hesitated for a moment, then invited Nik in. "Now, who is it you're looking for again?" he asked, turning on the lights and removing the "Closed" sign from the front window.

"Nukowski and Cooley," Nik reminded him. "They were here a couple days ago."

"Oh, that's right. They just dropped by to collect some back wages I owed them. Why is the media interested in those two boys, and who told you they were here?" Beck said.

Nik sidestepped the question and asked, "Do you know where they're going, by chance?"

"Said they planned to do some gambling and then head to their hunt camp. 'Magine they're on the way to the camp now, if they're not already there."

"They mention what they've been up to lately?"

"Oh, they joked about blowing things up, shooting things. Just bullshitting."

"That wasn't bullshit, Mr. Beck," Nik said.

"Jud," Beck said.

"They're suspected of bombing a technology office park in Washington and killing a state trooper and a store clerk in Indiana, Jud. Last count, seven people were killed in the explosion."

"Nah," Beck said. "I don't see that."

"'Fraid it's true, Jud," Nik said. "FBI, Homeland Security, state authorities. They're all looking for them."

"Well, if they did something like that, and I ain't saying they did, then someone put 'em up to it," Beck said.

"Why do you say that?" Nik asked.

"'Cause I've known those two boys for a long time. One's

worth half a man, two ain't worth nothing. No way they plan and pull off something like that by themselves."

Nik asked Beck if he knew the location of the hunting camp. He did and gave Nik directions. Nik thanked him and left.

On the way out of town, Nik stopped by the *Pellston Herald*, the local community newspaper, to speak to its editor, seventy-one-year-old Alice Worden. Worden had been covering news and events in Pellston for five decades and knew everyone. She provided Nik background information on Cooley, Beck, and what little she knew about Nukowski. She also mentioned the Three Percenters, the anti-government organization the trio were loosely associated with.

Like small-town newspapers everywhere, the *Herald* filled its pages with the comings and goings of local citizens, and Worden told Nik she was certain it had run items about Cooley's military deployment over the years. She promised she'd dig through the archives to see what she could find and send it to him.

When Nik asked why she thought the two men were attracted to the Three Percenters, Worden said, "That's easy. Ever since the near depression in 2008, the farm economy here has struggled. It was only getting back on its feet when it got walloped again by tariffs and trade tensions with China. Milk prices are down by seventy-five percent from a year ago, and it seems there's a farmer filing for bankruptcy about every week now around here. It put us right back in the toilet. It's got people angry."

Nik could relate. He was an eyewitness to the destruction of the newspaper industry at the hands of giant internet companies. Last report he read, 45 percent of all newspaper jobs had disappeared since 2006. He knew he was lucky to have landed a position with *Newshound* in its early years when it was a fledgling online media start-up, but that didn't do much good for the thousands of journalists who had been thrown out of work.

"I could see how that could make people desperate," Nik said.

"Not to mention dangerous," she added.

CHAPTER 36

January 5/6, Upper Peninsula, Michigan

Hawk had visited the hunt camp once before, at the peak of summer, when the trees were leafed out, wildflowers in bloom, and the roads crowded with vacationers driving campers and RVs. The place looked different in the middle of winter, stark, like a deserted frontier outpost. Other than a fresh set of tire tracks in the lane leading to the camp, there was little sign of life, and the falling snow muffled any sound.

He parked his vehicle behind an abandoned Toyota Camry that was stuck in a snowdrift about twenty-five yards from the camp's main structure—a double-wide trailer perched on cinder blocks, its tin skirting hanging loose and rattling in the wind. He removed a duffle from the back seat and followed two sets of footprints from the Camry to the front of the trailer, dry snow squawking underfoot with each step.

There had been a self-imposed communications blackout between him and the pair ever since Cooley and Nukowski set out for Washington, DC, and he was anxious to find out if they held him responsible for the mistimed explosion. He worried, for good reason, they might have concluded they had been double-crossed. Hawk hadn't settled on a final plan on how to eliminate the duo. He had some ideas, but he wanted to leave his options open, see how things unfolded. He was prepared for a firefight, but he wanted to avoid that if at all possible. You could never predict how those would turn out.

He was thinking about how he'd be received by the pair when the door of the trailer blew open, Nukowski looming in the frame, his stringy mullet pasted to his head, a bottle of Jack Daniel's in one hand swinging at his side, a cannon-size Smith and Wesson .500 Magnum in the other, pointed squarely at the center of Hawk's forehead. Not the greeting he had hoped for.

Hawk squinted up at him and said, "If you're gonna shoot me, make it quick. It's colder than a witch's tit out here."

A reptilian grin spread across Nukowski's face, and he roared with laughter. "Come on in, you old fuckin' bandit. We've been waitin' on you."

It wasn't much warmer in the trailer than it was outside. Cooley was bent over a potbellied woodstove in the middle of the room, trying to coax a fire to life.

"Wood's wet and won't take," Cooley groused. "Hey, Hawk. Glad you made it. How were the roads?"

"Douse it with that can of kerosene we got," Nukowski said.

"Hey, Cooley," Hawk responded. "Roads were passable."

The trailer was sparsely furnished—an oak dining table covered in nicks, cigarette burns, and water stains sat planted between the kitchen and main living room. A worn and ripped rust-colored couch was pushed up against a wall, and two chairs with lumpy cushions crowded around the woodstove. Down the narrow hallway that led to the bathroom and the back end of the trailer, Hawk glimpsed stained mattresses scattered on bedroom floors. Tacked to the walls were outdated calendars of voluptuous young women in skimpy outfits, a Confederate flag, and pelts of dead animals. The place smelled like spoiled milk.

Nukowski sprawled on the couch while Hawk sank into one of the chairs. "Take your coat off and stay awhile," Nukowski said.

"If Cooley ever gets a fire going, I'll think about it," Hawk said, tugging up the zipper of his puffy down jacket. "I like what you've done with the place." He leaned forward and accepted the bottle of Jack that Nukowski extended his way.

"Could stand a woman's touch," Nukowski allowed, "but then it wouldn't be a hunt camp, would it?"

"We had a couple of female friends who would have spruced it up a bit, but they rubbed Nuky the wrong way," Cooley said sadly, his back to the pair.

"That so?" Hawk said. "I see you boys got yourself some publicity. Have to admit, didn't see that coming."

"Yeah, well, we never figured that fucking bomb would go off twelve hours before it was set to, either," Nukowski said. "How you suppose that happened?"

Cooley managed to get a small fire started in the stove, but it wasn't drawing properly, and the room began to fill with smoke. Hawk got out of his chair and pushed open a window. The snow was coming down harder now. It would be dark in a couple hours. He wanted to be back on the road before then.

"No doubt about it. That was a bit of bad luck, all right," Hawk said. "I chalk it up to operator error. That help the fire, Cooley?"

"It does, thanks. That bomb going off when it weren't supposed to wasn't my fault," Cooley protested, fanning the flames and banking the embers.

"Well, we'll never know, now, will we," Nukowski said.

Hawk thought he read something in Nukowski's voice. Suspicion? Or was it his own paranoia? Either way, he needed to be on guard. "No, I suspect we never will," Hawk said. He took another pull from the bottle and then asked, "What's the story with the cop and store worker?"

"Shit happens," Nukowski said, quoting the dead clerk. "Collateral damage. You and Cooley been to war. You should know all about that."

"They ID you?"

"They ID'd the van, s'all, but they'll never find it."

"Your buddy said he was going to chop it," Cooley clarified, "but we never actually seen him do it."

"Wait, there're others out there who know about your escapades besides me?" Hawk said. "Why do I feel like I'm not getting the full story here?"

Cooley grabbed the whiskey off the table and nearly emptied the bottle. "Yeah, bar full of people also saw us leave with those two girls Nuky shot."

"Stay in your lane, Cooley," Nukowski rumbled and eyed Hawk.

"Weren't no need to kill 'em," Cooley said plaintively.

"They're strippers, drifters, whores. No one's out looking for them," Nukowski claimed.

"Don't call them whores. They didn't charge us nothing," Cooley said.

The room fell quiet, the only sound the wind whistling through the drafty trailer.

Cooley broke the silence. "Need more wood," he said and got up and trudged out into the snow, slamming the door behind him as he exited.

When he had left, Nukowski said, "He was smitten, s'all. I predict he'll get over it."

"No doubt he will," Hawk said, "one way or the other."

Hawk reached inside the duffle sitting at his feet that he had carried with him into the trailer. He saw Nukowski watching him and slowly withdrew his hands, holding up a bottle of Pappy Van Winkle, an expensive and highly sought-after Kentucky bourbon; three crystal tumblers; and a fistful of Cuban cigars. "Whadja think? I was going to come out blazing?" Hawk said.

"Never can tell about you black-ops fucks," Nukowski said.

Hawk chuckled and then proclaimed, "Enough of that monkey piss. Let's drink some of the good stuff and discuss the future."

"Aw, hell yeah," Nukowski said. "Now you're talkin'." He edged off the couch to accept the glass Hawk proffered.

Nik was grateful he had taken the agent's advice and rented the biggest four-wheel-drive SUV the company had on the lot. He had not driven in a snowstorm like this since his college days in Ann Arbor, and the drifting and blowing snow made it nearly impossible to get a fix on the road's centerline. For long stretches, he fought to remain alert and not allow the pinwheeling snow squalls bursting against the windshield to lull him into a trance.

The navigation app on his phone estimated it would take just under six hours to reach the hunt camp. Dilworth had texted Nik that the GPS tracking device showed the Camry had been sitting parked for several hours, and he sent him an address and directions, which roughly matched the map Jud Beck had scratched out for him.

Five hours and forty-five minutes later, Nik's SUV skidded to a stop at the entrance to the camp. A sign tacked up nearby warned trespassers they would be shot first and then prosecuted.

Parked on the road in the predawn, Nik was having second thoughts about his plan, if he could even call it a plan. He really hadn't stopped to think about the consequences of his actions, but reality was setting in, and one outcome, perhaps the most likely, was he could wind up dead. In the moment, he had let the thrill of the chase overtake his better judgment. He wasn't the first, and certainly wouldn't be the last, reporter to leap before looking.

Turn around now, Nik, he told himself, *and let the authorities handle this. No story is worth getting killed over.*

It wasn't yet six a.m., and as he sat in the comfort of the vehicle, the heater on high, seat warmers toasty, he started to nod off. He cracked open the front windows to let in some fresh air and revive his brain and take time to reconsider what he was about to do. That's when the smell hit him.

Nik powered down the windows all the way and stuck his head out, flared his nostrils, and inhaled deeply, but he wasn't able to detect the odor again. Then the wind shifted and the vehicle's cabin filled with a wispy smoke that carried a scent of kerosene and wet cinders.

Nik reached down to the floorboard and locked the vehicle's gearshift into four-wheel drive and plowed through the snow toward the camp. Silvery birch trees and evergreen boughs, heavy with snow, crowded the narrow lane on both sides and obscured his view. When he rounded a slight bend, he saw the smoldering husk of what appeared to be a trailer home, blackened concrete piers and a cast-iron stove the only parts of the structure still remaining. A car sat off to one side buried under a half foot of ash-speckled snow. He figured it must be the Camry.

Nik drove to the perimeter of the camp, parked, and stepped out of his vehicle. He had only gone a couple of paces when he saw the two charred bodies lying facedown in the debris near the stove. He quickly checked his cell phone signal— two bars—and dialed 911.

CHAPTER 37

**Suspects in Trident Explosion
Found Dead in N. Michigan Camp**

By Nik Byron
Newshound *Deputy Editor*

The bodies of two men suspected of
setting off a bomb in the Trident Office
Park in southeast Washington and
killing a state trooper and store clerk
in Indiana were found early this morning in a burned-out trailer home in a
remote hunting camp in Michigan's
Upper Peninsula.

Law enforcement authorities are
still attempting to piece together how
the two men died, but one official,
who asked not to be identified, told
Newshound that "by all appearances, it
looks to be a murder-suicide."

The men were identified as Rodney

Nukowski, 33, and Lawrence Cooley, 34, both of the Pellston, Michigan, area.

Nukowski and Cooley, a military veteran who did two tours of duty in Afghanistan as an ordnance expert, were known by Pellston authorities to be associated with the Three Percenters, a loose-knit militia that advocates resistance to many federal and state regulations and, in some instances, favors the outright overthrow of the government.

A search of an apartment the pair rented in Pellston turned up more than two dozen assault rifles, small arms, bomb-making material, anti-government pamphlets, and detailed maps and drawings of the Trident Office Park, where a bomb exploded in mid-December, killing seven and injuring a score of others.

Authorities in Washington have speculated the men targeted Trident Office Park because it is home to several technology companies that conduct top-secret research for the federal government and its military and intelligence arms. The office park has been the site of protests in the past by anti-government and privacy advocates.

According to the northern Michigan medical examiner's preliminary report, Cooley and Nukowski were shot once each in the head with a small-caliber revolver at point-blank range. A .38-caliber handgun was found clutched in Nukowski's burnt hand, law enforcement officials said.

"Our best guess is Nukowski shot Cooley first before turning the gun on himself," a spokesperson said. "We speculate they believed authorities were closing in on them, and, instead of being captured, they took their own lives."

Fire officials said a wood-burning stove in the main living area caused the blaze that destroyed the trailer home. A can of kerosene was found near the stove and likely helped fuel the late-night fire. The area is sparsely populated, particularly in the winter-time, and investigators said it wasn't surprising the fire went unnoticed and unreported.

Alice Worden, the longtime editor of the *Pellston Herald*, said Cooley joined the US Army shortly after grad-uating from the local high school. She said Nukowski was not from Pellston but had moved to the area several years ago.

Jud Beck, a Pellston resident and business owner who knew both men and had visited with them recently, greeted the news of the pair's death and crime spree with skepticism.

"By God, you will never convince me those two boys blew up an office park in Washington, DC, shot a police officer and store clerk in Indiana, and then killed themselves," Beck said.

Worden, the Pellston editor, said Cooley's military experience seemed to have soured him on his government.

"He was very gung ho when he left to join the service, but when he returned, he had changed and said he no longer trusted his government after the things he had seen in Afghanistan. He never talked about what he saw exactly, but only said it was bad."

Members of Cooley's immediate family declined to comment and issued a one-sentence statement asking that their privacy be respected. Nukowski's next of kin could not be located.

No suicide note has been found, and authorities were at a loss to explain why the pair would drive all the way to a remote hunting camp to kill themselves. Based on interviews, it appears the pair had visited Pellston and a casino in northern Michigan before making their way to the camp.

CHAPTER 38

January 7, Three Rivers, Michigan

Hawk's plans didn't call for a side trip to Three Rivers, but that's where he found himself after he learned about Nukowski's friend who had furnished the pair with the stolen Camry. Each time Cooley left the trailer for another load of wood, Hawk followed him out to help carry and stack the wood inside. He took the opportunity to grill Cooley on details about what had transpired after the Trident explosion.

"Seems the only person we came in contact with that Nuky didn't kill was his buddy Dilworth," Cooley said, "and even then, it was touch-and-go."

That task now fell to Hawk. Even though he thought there was only a very slight chance that Nukowski had mentioned Hawk's name to Dilworth and that Dilworth could connect him to the crime spree, he couldn't afford to take that risk.

Standing in a copse of wintered-over birch trees, shin deep in snow, on the edge of Dilworth's property in the early morning, a clear line of sight to the house and its surroundings,

Hawk dialed in the Nightforce Optics sniper scope mounted on his Austrian-built Steyr SSG 69 bolt-action rifle.

The maximum firing range for the SSG is four thousand yards; its sweet spot eight hundred yards, give or take. Hawk calculated he was two hundred and fifty yards from the house, and, at that distance, it would be like shooting fish in a barrel. The morning air was crisp and still, the snowstorm having blown itself out, perfect conditions for a long-range shot.

Hawk had been in position for about a half hour when he saw a light and then movement in a second-story window. He lifted the scope to his right eye, and the crosshairs zeroed in on the image of a dark-haired woman carrying something in her arms. Cooley hadn't mentioned a female, but no matter. She could be dealt with easily enough, but he needed to hold fire until he confirmed that Dilworth, the primary target, was on-site. He could wait. If Dilworth was there, he'd show himself soon enough.

Hawk leaned back against a tree, sending snow cascading down on his head. He slung the rifle over his right shoulder and scanned the property with a pair of Zeiss binoculars he had strung around his neck. He was wide awake now, having squeezed in three hours of sleep at a roadside rest stop after he left the hunt camp.

Despite his trepidation, the showdown at the camp had turned out better than he anticipated.

On the third and final trip to the woodshed with Cooley, the pair returned to the trailer to find Nukowski passed out on the couch, the Smith and Wesson revolver resting on his chest in his cradled arms. The Rohypnol Hawk had used to spike Nukowski's bourbon had accomplished its job.

"Well, looky, looky. Nuky can't hold his liquy," Cooley said mockingly, stomping the snow off his boots before stepping inside, arms piled high with split wood. He swung his head back toward Hawk with a stupid grin spreading across his face, and that's when Hawk shot him once through the right ear-hole with a .38-caliber snub nose he produced from an inside pocket of his down coat.

Cooley crumpled, sending the logs skittering across the floor, his body slamming into the stove, knocking the door open and the stovepipe free. Hot embers escaped and settled on the chairs, couch, and table.

The gunshot and commotion jarred Nukowski from his drug-induced stupor, and he bolted to his feet, the gun clutched in his right hand.

Reflexively, he raised it and fired once, catching Hawk in the left side. Nukowski then froze—the booze and drugs seizing his mind, Hawk reasoned—and stood lifeless for a moment, zombielike, mouth agape, trying to process the scene unfolding in front of his eyes.

It was just long enough for Hawk to take two quick strides over Cooley's lifeless body and shoot Nukowski once in his open mouth, a part of his skull calving off as the slug exited the back of his head. Nukowski slumped forward, his body resting near Cooley's.

Hawk unzipped his jacket to examine the damage. Nukowski's bullet had grazed him midway up on the left side, between his fifth and sixth rib, tearing at the Kevlar vest but not inflicting any serious damage. He'd have a beauty of a welt, but nothing more. Hawk wasn't at all convinced the vest would have impeded, let alone stopped, a direct hit from Nukowski's Smith and Wesson cannon.

He had to work quickly. The chairs and couch were already on fire. He bent down and pried the Smith and Wesson from Nukowski's fingers and, in its place, wrapped the .38 revolver that he had used to shoot the pair. By the time he exited the trailer, the fire had poked through the roof, and the kerosene-fueled flames licked at the inside walls as they raced down the hallway toward the bedrooms.

Hawk could still detect a faint odor of kerosene and smoke in his hair and on his clothes as he lifted the binoculars to glass Dilworth's house a second time. He panned right and then left. There was Dilworth, standing in the upstairs window, gazing out, a coffee cup in one hand. Hawk let the binoculars fall to his chest, snapped the rifle up to his right shoulder, adjusted the scope, and just as he was sighting the crosshairs, he felt a presence and saw a blur out of the corner of his eye.

A large dog exploded from the underbrush and sank its teeth into Hawk's right thigh even before he could turn his head, the gun firing wildly off the mark as he writhed in pain.

The German shepherd ripped at the muscle of Hawk's thigh and, had it not been for the deep snow and the dog's bandaged leg, probably would have been tearing at his throat. Hawk fought an urge to scream as he tried to bring his elbow down on the dog's massive head, but the rifle sling and binocular strap got entangled, and he was only able to deliver a glancing blow.

A dark bloom spread across Hawk's pant leg as blood poured from his wounds, and he feared the dog's teeth had punctured his femoral artery. The shepherd snarled, shook its head violently, and momentarily released its grip to get a better bite, and when it did, Hawk reached down and unsheathed a bayonet strapped to his left leg. He slashed the dog across its shoulder and brought the butt of the knife handle down hard with a backhand on the snout with a loud crack. The dog yelped and slipped from Hawk's leg onto the snow.

Hawk lifted the knife over his head, set to plunge the blade into the animal's neck, when he heard a shout. "Pontiac," a man's voice blared through the woods. Judging by the sound, the man was maybe fifty yards south and moving his way. He assumed it was Dilworth, and he assumed he was armed.

Hawk was bleeding badly. He could stay and fight, but there was no guarantee he would survive in his condition.

He unclasped his belt and fashioned a tourniquet around his leg, unslung his rifle, tucked the stock under his armpit like a crutch, and hobbled off as quickly as he could manage back toward the roadway, leaving the dazed and wounded German shepherd behind.

CHAPTER 39

January 8, Detroit

Nik was sitting at the United Airlines gate at Detroit Metro Airport waiting to board his early-morning flight back to Washington, DC, when he got a call from Alice Worden, the editor of the *Pellston Herald.*

Worden told Nik she had found several articles that mentioned Cooley in the newspaper's archives, and after several attempts, she had finally managed to digitize the microfiche files and wanted Nik's email address to send them to him.

"There are a handful of stories and a picture or two. Hope that helps," Worden said and, before hanging up, thanked Nik for tipping her off about finding Cooley's and Nukowski's bodies in the burned-out hunt camp.

Nik's flight was boarding in fifteen minutes, and he kept refreshing his email folders, hoping the files would arrive before he got on the plane. He knew from experience that many United flights didn't offer Wi-Fi on board, and he was anxious to see what Worden's search had produced.

The gate attendant started the boarding process, and Nik

had just taken his place in the queue when the files arrived in his inbox.

The first file was a story about Cooley's initial deployment overseas. The second was about a letter his parents had received from Cooley describing the Afghanistan landscape and the regiment he was attached to, the 75th Rangers. He said Afghanistan was unlike anything he had experienced or seen growing up in Michigan.

There were two pictures, one of Cooley in full dress uniform after he graduated from basic training and another of him wearing camouflage in a desert somewhere in the Middle East.

The last file contained a story about a talk Cooley had given to the Pellston chamber of commerce when he was home on leave over the holidays during his first tour of duty. He described his day-to-day job as a demolition expert and his interactions with the Afghani people, whom he described as "fierce warriors."

When asked by a chamber member what citizens of Pellston could do to offer him support, Cooley said he liked to receive letters and emails from home and invited anyone who wanted to join a public Facebook page he had created, Rangers All The Way.

Nik tapped on the Facebook app on his smartphone and entered the name in the search box. Within seconds, he was surfing through Cooley's page.

There were pictures of Cooley on leave in foreign ports of call, Singapore, Bangkok, Sydney, often clutching a bottle of beer in one hand and a different girl in the other, smiling broadly, and several snapshots of a shirtless, lanky Cooley against mountainous backdrops in what Nik guessed was Afghanistan.

On the bottom of the app, there was a small TV icon with a Play button in the middle. Nik clicked on it, and up popped a series of YouTube videos. Most were of Cooley on R&R, but there was one that appeared to have been shot at a forward military base camp. The filmmaker was narrating the video in a low voice, describing what he was seeing to the viewer, which mostly consisted of desert-colored canvas tents, Humvees, and sandbag bunkers.

Then a voice, not the narrator's, could be heard. "Turn that goddamned thing off, Cooley, and get over here," a man barked. The camera swung toward the voice, and the screen filled with a group of men standing around a campfire laughing, dressed in battle fatigues, 75th Regiment insignias clearly visible on their uniforms. Except for one man, with a bushy mustache, dressed in native Afghan clothes, a Perahan turban wrapped around his head. Though his face was partially covered, Nik recognized him immediately.

Nik stepped out of line and dialed Mo.

"I found him," he said excitedly when Mo picked up.

"Who?"

"Colonel Mustard, or Calkins, or Brick, or whatever his name is."

"Where?"

"I'm not sure, but I'm emailing you a link to a YouTube video Cooley posted that shows his military outfit and includes a man in native dress that I'm certain is our guy. It shouldn't be that hard to find out who was serving in the 75th with Cooley. Once we get his fellow soldiers' names and contact information, we can send them the image. Someone's got to know who this guy is."

"I was just about to head over to the Pentagon to meet with a source. Email me the file and I'll see if he can help," Mo said.

"My plane's departing momentarily. I'll call you when I land," Nik said and stepped back in line. He studied the face of the man in the video and whispered to himself, "Where are you, Colonel Mustard?"

At that moment, Hawk was lying immobile in a snowdrift, blood seeping from his wounds, about fifty feet from his vehicle, which he had tucked away in a little turnout.

Hawk's first bit of good luck that morning came when a passing motorist swerved to avoid hitting a family of foxes that darted across the road in front of her car. The driver slowed to watch the fox and its kit scamper into the woods, and that's when she noticed what appeared to be a body in the snow. Hawk's second piece of good luck came when it turned out the woman was a triage nurse returning home after working the overnight shift at the local hospital's emergency room.

The nurse quickly stanched the bleeding and dressed Hawk's wounds. He told her he had been attacked by a wild dog, and she assured him the dog had not lanced his main artery.

"Believe me, if it had, you would have bled out by now. Good thing for you that you were wearing thick hunting pants or the dog's teeth might have severed it. What were you doing out in the woods this time of the morning, anyhow?" she asked.

He told the woman he had been out scouting possible spots to build a deer stand for hunting season.

"In this weather, this time of the year? I don't hunt, but I thought deer season was over," she said skeptically.

"It is, but I wanted to get a jump on next season," he said. To change the subject, he asked, "How can I ever repay you?"

She told him to make a donation to the children's wing at the hospital and then gave him directions to the facility to have his wound looked at and properly cared for by a physician. "That battlefield patch of mine won't hold long," she warned him.

"I'll be sure to make a generous donation as soon as I'm able," Hawk assured her, got into his vehicle, spun it around, and pointed it in the direction she indicated.

CHAPTER 40

January 8, Washington, DC

Nik's ex-wife, Maggie, joined the Badass Women's Book Club at Kramers shortly after relocating to Washington, DC. She didn't know many people when she arrived in the nation's capital and, as a once again single woman, thought it would be a good way to make new friends and get acquainted with the area, all the while indulging in her passion for reading. It was the one thing, maybe the only thing, she and Nik truly had in common.

What she hadn't counted on was how much she would fall in love with the bookstore's other offerings—the adjoining café and fully stocked bar. The combination of row upon row of books, chilled white wine, and the smell of frying bacon was not only ingenious but impossible to resist, and she wondered why other bookstores hadn't imitated the successful concept to fend off online booksellers, or if they had, she wasn't aware of it. She was particularly a big fan of the peanut butter waffles and stuffed French toast.

For those reasons, Maggie felt confident that Kramers was

the perfect setting for a meeting with Nik's current female companion, Samantha Whyte. Kramers offered a congenial atmosphere that would encourage girl talk, especially helpful since the topic was going to be Nik.

Maggie had heard a hesitation in Sam's voice when she'd called and proposed the get-together. She didn't know Sam, but she knew women and bet Sam would not pass on the chance to size up her one-time competition. Her instincts proved correct.

Maggie's call was fortuitously well timed. She learned Nik was somewhere in Michigan. Had he been available, she knew Sam would have consulted him about the invitation, and Nik likely would have discouraged the meeting. "What the hell, why not," Sam finally agreed, and the two made a date to meet the next morning at seven thirty at Kramers when the bookstore opened.

Kramers is located off Dupont Circle, and the area was beginning to stir to life as Maggie entered the bookshop precisely at seven thirty just as a young man was unlatching the front door. She took a chair tucked in one corner near a front window that overlooked the street outside and watched for Sam. She didn't have long to wait. Sam arrived a couple minutes later and asked the young man where she might find a copy of a recently released novel about a one-time female journalist turned private investigator. The author, Sam told the employee, was an old friend, a former reporter at the *Baltimore Sun*. The employee said, "Over there," and pointed to a wall of books.

Sam found her friend's book in the Thriller section, lifted it from the shelf, and tucked it under her arm. When she turned around to make her way toward the cashier, she bumped into Maggie, who was peering over her shoulder.

"I love that author," Maggie said. "I've been waiting for her next novel to come out." She removed a copy from the shelf and said, "Since we're the only two customers in the place, I'm going to guess you're Samantha."

"Maggie?"

"Correct," Maggie said and extended her hand. Sam shifted the book from under her arm and grasped the outreached hand.

"Nice to meet you," they said in concert, then both laughed.

———

Sam would later confide to friends that, based purely on first impressions, she and Maggie couldn't be more dissimilar. Maggie bordered on petite and wore her jet-black hair in a blunted bob cut. She had a slashing smile, a dewy complexion, and perfect posture. Her dress was professional and conservative, and several cuts above what one normally associated with government workers.

Her scarf, overcoat, and boots were Burberry, and her handbag Mark Cross, or a very good knockoff. On her head, she wore a Kyi Kyi beanie with a pom-pom that Sam told her looked adorable. Her overall appearance verged on impeccable.

Sam's working uniform, by contrast, consisted of J.Crew anything, Helly Hansen all-weather jackets, Filson backpack, and Red Wing boots. Her job as lead investigator and public relations liaison for the sheriff's department required she be out in the elements, mucking around crime scenes, and chasing down reporters.

The two made their way to the café in the back of the store and spent the next twenty minutes comparing notes on other authors they admired. Maggie extended an invitation to Sam to sit in on an upcoming Badass Women's Book Club meeting, but none too enthusiastically. Sam said she'd think about it but without any real conviction.

After they were served coffee and buttered croissants, the

discussion turned to Nik. Maggie asked how he and Sam met, where they met, and when they met. Sam said she and Nik had bumped into each other occasionally at the sheriff's office and county courthouse because of their jobs. "And one thing led to another," she related, keeping her answer as circumspect as possible.

Maggie volunteered that she and Nik probably should not have gotten married, but it had seemed like the sensible thing to do at the time. "It's what one did in the Midwest at a certain age," she confided. Maggie said she still cared deeply about Nik and that their lives, for better or worse, seemed destined to be intertwined forever.

Sam glanced at the clock on her cell phone as she answered an incoming text. It was already eight fifteen. She had told Sheriff Korum she would be at the office by eight forty-five for a meeting. "I've got to be going soon," Sam started to say when Maggie asked, "Have you heard of the OmniSoft story?" and wrapped both hands around her coffee cup and blew on it.

"Of course. It's the small technology company that's suing the federal government for stealing its software," Sam said.

"Allegedly," Maggie said.

"Sorry. Stand corrected," Sam said. "For *allegedly* stealing its software."

"I'm concerned that Nik is being led on a wild-goose chase," Maggie said in what Sam suspected was her most sincere voice, the corners of her mouth turning slightly down like a pair of parentheses, a squint forming on her brow.

"How so? Nik's a pretty seasoned reporter. Can't imagine what would be troubling you." Sam may have had her own doubts about the story, but if she did, she would keep those to herself.

"Oh, it doesn't have anything to do with Nik's abilities," Maggie said dismissively. "I know he's a good reporter. Gets out over the tips of his skis at times, but then, if he didn't, he wouldn't be Nik. But there are national security implications to the story that I don't think he fully appreciates. I can't go into details, unfortunately, but I thought since the two of us—you and me, that is—are in law enforcement, well, that together we might be able to persuade Nik to be more careful about what he writes and not be so trusting of some of his so-called sources."

Sam nodded. "I see. By any chance, did Nik mention what I did before I joined the sheriff's department?"

"Not that I recall," Maggie said. "Why, is it important?"

"Could be," Sam said and popped the last bite of croissant into her mouth and washed it down with a sip of coffee. "I've only been at the sheriff's department for two years. Before that, I was a reporter for nearly ten years, the last couple at the *Washington Post*."

"I'm sure I would have remembered that, had he told me," Maggie said. "Just like Nik to forget."

"So, you see," Sam said, standing and gathering her book and backpack, "I couldn't possibly betray Nik's trust."

"No one said anything about betraying anyone's trust," Maggie said coolly.

"That's true, you didn't ask that exactly," Sam said, "but nevertheless, that's what I'd be doing if I were to try to manipulate Nik or influence his reporting. I'm running late for a meeting I need to be at." Sam offered Maggie her hand and a quick *it was nice to meet you* nod of the head, turned, and walked away.

"Samantha," Maggie called out. Sam stopped and turned back toward Maggie, a quizzical look on her face.

"Yes?"

"Let me know what you think of the book," Maggie said, revealing the slashing smile again, but, this time, just a flicker, as quick as a firefly.

CHAPTER 41

January 8, Washington, DC

Nik's cell phone erupted with text and voice mail messages when his plane touched down at Ronald Reagan Washington National Airport in DC, and Signal, the encrypted app Cal Walker recommended that he download, was blinking like a beacon.

Nik wheeled his suitcase to a Green Beans coffee shop in the terminal, ordered a grande drip, no room for cream, and started plowing through the messages.

Mo had texted to tell him that he had a printout of all the names of servicemen and women in Cooley's outfit and was now tracking down contact information for them.

Keep me posted, Nik fired off in return.

Mo quickly replied. Several live in the DC area. Should be a piece of cake locating.

Nik didn't respond. He knew Mo had a tendency to be overly optimistic, and he'd wait for confirmation before breaking out the celebratory champagne.

There was a long, rambling text from King Kobe telling

Nik that he had fired his lawyer, had no intention of settling the lawsuits against him, and vowing to take his case all the way to the state supreme court if necessary. He said he was getting out of the cattle business and was starting a company to manufacture and market plant-based meats. Not for the first time, Nik regretted ever hearing the name King Kobe.

Mia texted and said she was in New York and had a solid lead on Mr. Liu and that she needed to talk to Nik as soon as his flight landed.

The first voice mail was from a blocked number with no caller ID. He recognized the voice immediately.

"Someone's been stalking me and Sara and tried to kill Pontiac, Byron. Pontiac's at the vet's, barely hanging on," Grant Dilworth growled. "Who the hell you been talking to? I knew I shouldn't have trusted you—fucking reporters. Don't ever set foot on my property again." There was a pause, then: "I'm going to get the son of a bitch who did this."

Before he departed Michigan, Nik had emailed Dilworth a link to his story about Nukowski's and Cooley's murder-suicide. He received a three-word reply: Not buying it.

Nik searched his memory, trying to recall if he had slipped up and mentioned Dilworth's name to anyone. He was certain he had not. Someone else had connected Dilworth to Cooley and Nukowski. Nik wasn't sure who that person was, but he recalled Jud Beck's assertion that there had to be a third party involved because the pair wasn't capable of masterminding the Trident attack themselves.

Nik sent Dilworth an email assuring him he had not divulged his name to anyone and repeated his telephone number, home address, and instructions on how to send him a message on Signal if he wanted to get in touch. Nik held out little hope he'd hear back from him. As a rule, Nik did not give out his home address, but he wanted to demonstrate to Dilworth that he had nothing to hide.

There was a short voice mail from Maggie. "Um, Nik, bumped into Samantha. She's lovely. I can see why you're attracted to her. We need to talk about OmniSoft. It's kinda important. Call me. It will be to our mutual benefit, I promise you. Bye."

He had no idea where or how Maggie had managed to run into Sam, but, knowing Maggie as he did, he was certain it wasn't just by happenstance.

The next message was from Nik's landlord, who never called unless Nik's rent was late, which it wasn't.

"Nik, happy new year. We slipped a note under your door yesterday, but in case you missed it, my mother-in-law is moving in with us, and we need to install her in your apartment. This is officially the ninety-day notice we're required by law to give you before terminating your lease and evicting you from the apartment. I hate that word, 'evict.' It sounds so harsh. Wish there were a nicer way of saying it. Anyway, you need to be out by April seventh, or thereabouts. Believe that's a Wednesday. Hope you're having a good day otherwise. So long."

"Unreal," Nik muttered.

Nik opened the encrypted app and read the message from Cal Walker: Nik, no longer feel safe here. Mr. L fears another attempt will be made on his life. Wounds are closing up nicely, but he's extremely paranoid. Can't say I blame him. Will be back in touch shortly after we're on safer ground. Don't trust anyone.

Nik messaged Walker back about Cooley and Nukowski in case he was living under a news blackout. Men who planted bomb at Trident dead. Murder-suicide?

Next, Nik dialed Mia.

"You back?" Mia asked when she picked up.

"Yeah, just landed. How's New York?"

"Cold, but fun. The *Dateline New York* podcast and singles events are really taking off. I always knew it would be a big hit here in"—and she paused a moment for effect—"the Big Apple. Anyway, we're set to launch our new app that will integrate with dating sites. It's exciting."

"That's great, but I'm not sure they still refer to it as the Big Apple," Nik said, feigning mild interest, having never actually listened to the popular podcast on single life in Washington his whole while in DC. "So, what's this about Mr. Liu?"

"Right," Mia said, "Mr. Liu. Pretty sure he's who he claims to be. I should have a picture of him in the next couple of hours or so. I'm at the airport and flying home in about an hour. Once I get it, I'll send it to you."

"Fantastic. So your friend at the UN was helpful," Nik said.

"Super helpful. She liked playing the part of investigative journalist, even if it was just for a day. She said the United States just assumes most of the Chinese delegation is made up of spies, in one form or the other, but even she was surprised by the response she got when she approached her China counterpart asking about whatever happened to Mr. Liu. She said the woman is normally pleasant, but she berated my friend for interfering in what she called China's internal affairs. Later, the Chinese colleague called my friend back to apologize for the outburst and claimed Mr. Liu had become very ill and it was hard on the whole staff. She said he had been sent back to China for an unspecified medical treatment."

"Good work, but don't push too hard," Nik said. "We don't want to tip our hand."

"Well, you haven't heard the strangest part yet," Mia said. "When the woman called my friend back to apologize, she told her Mr. Liu never worked for the Ministry of State Security."

"Why's that a surprise? Isn't that what we'd expect her to say?"

"It is."

"So?" Nik said, distracted by an incoming text from Sam, mentioning the meeting with Maggie.

"Because my friend never asked her about Mr. Liu's work with the ministry. The woman just volunteered that he never worked there. Why would she do that?"

CHAPTER 42

January 8, Washington, DC

Nik made a quick detour to his apartment before heading to the office. He was there just long enough to take a fast shower, brush his teeth, change his clothes, and pick up his mail, which included a certified letter from his landlord with the official eviction notice enclosed, just in case he hadn't seen the note that they slipped under his door and had ignored the voice mail.

As quirky as his apartment was, with the amputated staircase suspended over his bed, the place had its charm, and he'd miss it when he was gone. The idea of having to look for a new apartment made him tired, and he pushed the thought to the back of his mind.

He texted Sam about her bumping into Maggie but hadn't received a reply. He wasn't entirely surprised. Sam often said she was pulled into new investigations at the sheriff's office without notice, and sometimes it took her hours, and occasionally days, to respond if she got involved in a murder case. He'd wait to connect with Sam first before returning Maggie's call.

Nik texted Frank to tell him he was on his way to the office and should be there in a half hour. The traffic was light and he made it in just under fifteen minutes.

Nik strolled into *Newshound*'s office with his head down, reading a text message on his phone, a large cup of coffee in one hand, his satchel hanging from his shoulder, and when he looked up, he was staring directly at the soles of Dick Whetstone's shoes, the editor having planted himself in Nik's chair, his feet propped up on his desk.

"Well, well. If it isn't the Galloping fuckin' Gourmet returning from God knows where on his quest to capture the Unabomber," Whetstone said scornfully, "or maybe I should call you the Conspiracy Chaser."

"You're a little behind the times, Dick. The Unabomber was in the nineties, but I'm not surprised. News has never been your strong suit. Would you mind removing your shoes from my desk?" Nik said.

Whetstone's feet hit the floor with a thud, and he swiveled the chair and stood. "It would seem you're the one who lacks news judgment, my friend. I've scoured the other local media and can't find any recent coverage of the Trident bombing. Seems you got this phantom story all to yourself. Congratulations, scoop."

"The two guys who investigators believe blew up the office park killed themselves," Nik began to explain.

"Yeah, yeah. I read that happy horseshit. No one cares about a couple dirtbag losers from bumfuck Michigan. Can't you get that through your head, Byron?"

"Guess we'll just have to agree to disagree," Nik said.

"Not for long, we won't. I need to see you in my office."

"Okay, but give me twenty minutes. I've got to knock out a quick story."

"You've got ten minutes, and when you come, bring your *Newshound* identification, office keys, company-issued computer, cell phone, and credit card, and any other property that doesn't personally belong to you," Whetstone said as he walked toward his office.

"Sure thing, Dick. Can't wait to hear all about the media conference," Nik said as Whetstone stormed off.

Trident Park, Indiana Victims Laid to Rest

By Nik Byron
Newshound *Deputy Editor*

Dorothy Pence had plans to attend her best friend's wedding this weekend. Instead, she paid her last respects to her former college roommate as she and three other Trident Office Park victims were laid to rest in Northern Virginia. All told, seven lives were lost in the blast that authorities now blame on two Midwestern men who themselves have now been killed.

Separately, funeral services were held in southeast Indiana for a state trooper and a store clerk who were allegedly gunned down by the same pair who blew up part of the Washington office park in December.

The Northern Virginia deceased were identified as Margaret Stanley,

44, Arlington, Va.; Scott Tompiks, 62, Alexandria, Va.; Bert Pope, 42, Tysons Corner, Va., and Terry Willows, 33, Falls Church, Va.

Willows was engaged to be married this weekend, according to her long-time friend Pence. "It's unbearably sad," Pence said. "I've never seen her so happy. She was looking forward to starting her new life with her fiancé, and then this happened."

Officials believe the bomb was planted by Lawrence Cooley and Rodney Nukowski, a couple of farm laborers from northwest Michigan. Both men were loosely affiliated with the Three Percenters, an anti-government group, and were subsequently killed in what authorities have described as a murder-suicide. It's still unknown exactly what motivated the two to bomb Trident, but the office park is home to several high-tech companies that carry out classified research for the US government's spy agencies and has been the target of anti-government protests in the past.

Cooley, a military veteran, and Nukowski are also blamed for the deaths of Indiana State Trooper Clinton Ward, 36, and store clerk Patsy Howard, 29. Ward and Howard were shot to death at a roadside truck stop shortly after the Trident bombing.

Ward and Howard were laid to rest in
separate ceremonies this weekend.
Ward was the first Indiana trooper
to be killed in the line of duty in four
years, a spokesperson for the state
police association said.

CHAPTER 43

January 8, Washington, DC

"Remember boozehounders' motto," Mo wrote in an all-staff email inviting everyone in the newsroom to join him, Frank, Mia, and Nik at the Third Edition that evening after work for drinks, "All the Booze That's Fit to Nip." Mo explained Mia was returning from New York and might arrive late to the party if her flight wasn't on time.

The rumors had spread fast about Nik's run-in and follow-up meeting with Whetstone in the editor's office, which included a company attorney, security guard, and an HR official. It wasn't the first time the two had butted heads publicly, and everyone was dying to hear how it had been resolved.

"Kinda reminded me of a Mafia lunch," Nik told Mo afterward. "A kiss on each cheek and a bullet to the head."

Nik said he had no sooner sat down than Whetstone launched into a preamble of all of Nik's acts of insubordination in the course of covering the Trident Park story while Whetstone was out of town at the media conference and on vacation.

"He gave chapter and verse on how I didn't answer his calls, blocked his text messages, had his emails routed automatically to my junk mail folders, and pursued the story against his direct orders not to do so. I have to admit, he did a good job of prosecuting his case. He nearly convinced me that I had crossed a line when he was done."

"So, did Li'l Dick actually fire you?" Mo asked in astonishment.

"Yup," Nik replied. "Really, can't say I entirely blame him, and that's coming from someone who doesn't even like the guy."

"What a prick. He can't do that," Mo protested.

"Oh, but he can and he did. When the previous owners sold their media operation to *Newshound*, they got the company to agree to keep old management in place for eighteen months, and they granted them the authority to hire and fire as they saw fit. It's in the contract, and they wouldn't have sold without that stipulation."

"What're ya going to tell folks?" Mo said now as he looked around at the largish *Newshound* crowd that had gathered at the Third Edition. There were reporters and editors from nearly every department on hand, most of whom Nik knew, some he didn't.

"You'll have to wait and see," Nik said and jumped up on a table and called out, "People, I got an announcement to make."

Other than a few bottles slamming down on tabletops or ice rattling around in glasses, the group fell mostly silent, shifting their attention to Nik, who was now straddling two wobbly tables and looking a little uneasy.

"First things first," he announced. "Drinks are on me."

A roar went up.

"Until seven p.m. Then you're on your own." It was six forty-five.

A load moan and a few boos.

"I just wanted you to hear it from me before you get an

email in your inbox when you arrive at work tomorrow morning. As of midnight tonight, I will no longer be *Newshound*'s deputy editor."

A murmur rolled through the crowd.

Nik raised his hands, palms out, to quiet the crowd and continued, "I know what you're thinking—*I didn't know* Newshound *had a deputy editor.* Well, it did, and it was me. Tomorrow, Whetstone's going to name my successor. I've been sworn to secrecy, but I'll give you a hint: he's a bodybuilder." And he looked directly at Mo, who had a stunned expression on his face. In their meeting, Whetstone conceded that, as much as he didn't like Nik, the staff seemed to admire him, and, to preserve newsroom harmony, such as it was, he decided to give Patrick Morgan the deputy editor title.

There was a round of clapping and a few huzzahs, and then someone shouted, "What are you going to do, Nik?"

"I've already got a couple things in the works. Can't talk about them right now, but I should have something to share in a day or two," Nik replied. Truthfully, he had no idea what he was going to do, or where he'd be living come April.

"What's going to happen to the Trident story?" someone else asked.

"Good question, but a better question is: Who's going to get stuck with the King Kobe story? I don't know where Trident goes from here. My guess is it gets deep-sixed. You got ten minutes before seven o'clock. I'd advise you to drink up," he said, and when he hopped down off the tables, he saw Sam standing in the back of the crowd, a pool cue in one hand and a bottle of beer in the other, a wan smile on her lips, a ball cap with the sheriff's emblem on its bill tugged down on her head.

"Mo texted me," she said when Nik approached. She tilted the pool cue forward and pointed the tip at him. "How's your game?"

"Rusty."

"Perfect."

"Whaddya got in mind?"

"Eight ball. Best two out of three, winner take all."

"I didn't know you shot pool," Nik said.

"I've been known to play every now and then. Rack 'em. I'll break."

Other than to rack, Nik never left his barstool. Sam sank the eight ball on the break in the first game and ran the table in the second. He didn't complain. Sam's long legs and exquisitely rounded ass were built to hang out over the green turf of a pool table.

"So, what do I owe you?" he asked after she sank the last ball.

"You'll find out soon enough," Sam said.

Nik settled the bar tab, and thirty minutes later, they were sprawled out on Sam's couch, a knot of bare torsos, legs, and arms, with Little Eva's song, "The Loco-Motion," silently running through his head. "Gotta swing your hips now," he softly hummed.

CHAPTER 44

January 9, Washington, DC

Nik woke the next morning utterly at a loss about what to do with his day, forget the rest of his life. He lay in bed, propped up on pillows, a cup of coffee resting on his chest, the *Washington Post* open to the sports section, Sam busying herself getting ready for work.

"Maybe I could become a PI," Nik suggested.

"You, a private investigator? I don't see it," Sam said.

"Why not? I know other reporters who have gone that route."

"Because you'd be bored stiff spying on cheating spouses, investigating fraudulent insurance claims, and running down perps who skip out on their alimony payments," Sam bellowed from the bathroom where she was drying her hair with what sounded like a jet engine.

"Well, I'm sure as hell not going into public relations. I'd rather drink battery acid. By the way, did I mention I also got word yesterday I'm getting evicted from my apartment? I have to be out early April," Nik said, scanning the *Post*'s emaciated employment section.

Sam stuck her head around the door. "What's next, you going to tell me your dog died, too?"

"Hey, that's it. That's what I'll do," Nik said, sounding up-beat. "I'll drive down to Charlottesville and get Gyp from the trainer."

"You know, you could always move in here while you look for a new place to live," Sam offered.

"That's very charitable," Nik replied. "How does tomorrow work for you?"

"I'm serious. You could move out of your apartment be-fore April, save some money, and figure out your next ca-reer move. I still have a number of good friends at the *Post*. I'm sure they'd love to talk to you. I could set it up if you'd like."

"Let me think about it," Nik said. "Not sure I want to go back to daily newspapers, but thanks for the offer. You never told me about your meeting with Maggie."

"Well, it's kinda moot now. She was trying to recruit me in her efforts to get you to slow-walk the OmniSoft story. Said there were really big national security issues involved and something about a wild-goose chase. When I told her I used to be a reporter and couldn't possibly take part in something like that, she sorta dropped it."

"That's Maggie. Always working an angle. What did you think of her?"

"She's okay, I guess. You never said she was raven-haired."

"Never noticed," Nik said.

Sam peered around the corner and wrinkled her brow.

"Ah, what I meant to say is that it never occurred to me to mention it."

"Un-huh."

"Why don't you take the day off and go with me to pick up Gyp? We can watch the trainer work with him and then grab lunch afterward."

"Would love nothing better, but it's just not possible. Too much going on at work. What do you think of this top?" Sam asked and popped out of the bathroom to model a light-purple mohair sweater over a white blouse, her strawberry-blonde hair done up in a French twist.

Nik rolled onto his side. "I don't have my glasses on. Come closer." When she did, he grabbed her arm and pulled her back in bed on top of him. First the sweater, then the shirt and jeans came off, and the intricately sculpted French twist unfurled like a kite's tail as they spent the next fifteen minutes rolling in the sack.

―――――

Nik left the dog trainer's kennels in the late afternoon and rode east out of Charlottesville on Interstate 66 back toward Washington, Gyp sitting obediently in the passenger's seat, his copper-colored coat glistening in the bright sunshine. Nik was amazed at the transformation that had taken place with the high-strung dog. He didn't chew, he didn't howl, he didn't bolt. He listened. He wasn't convinced it was the same dog.

"Gyp's biggest problem is boredom," the trainer informed Nik. "The more engaged you are with him, the more responsive he will be to handling."

"This is your lucky day, Gyp," Nik said to the dog, who had curled up on the seat and lifted his head up at the mention of his name. "I'm going to be at home a lot more now, which means more exercise for you and me both, and it will give me an opportunity to work on the training you've already received."

Gyp yawned, dropped his head back between his paws, and

closed his eyes. Nik began to suspect the trainer had drugged the animal.

Two hours outside of Charlottesville and one hour from DC, Nik's phone began to light up with text and voice mail messages. He had temporarily lost cell coverage on the drive back and alternated between listening to a John le Carré book on tape and *Game Dog*, a CD Gyp's trainer had given him before he left.

He decided to pull off at a rest stop to let Gyp stretch his legs and relieve himself. In the past when he had taken Gyp on car trips and stopped for a break, the dog would launch himself out of the vehicle and be at a dead run before Nik could even get the car door closed. He was ready for a repeat performance this time, but Gyp remained seated until Nik gave him a command releasing him, and then the dog dropped into the parking lot and calmly remained at Nik's side.

Nik snapped a leash on Gyp's collar and strolled over to the pet area, where he took a seat on a bench and began scrolling through his messages. It was now dusk, and except for a couple idling semitrucks some ways off, the rest stop was virtually empty. He dropped the leash and let Gyp wander around unaccompanied to sniff trees and explore, an act he would never have remotely considered in the past.

Word of Nik's firing had spread, and most of the messages were from former colleagues or sources offering words of encouragement and condolences. After skimming a handful of the text messages, he stopped reading and ignored the rest. They left him feeling like he had been diagnosed with a terminal disease.

He scanned his incoming voice mail messages. They were more of the same. He didn't bother listening to those, either. He opened his email folder, and that's when it hit him he was no longer a *Newshound* employee. With the exception of two emails from Mia, there were no work-related announcements.

His *Newshound* account had been suspended, and the rash of daily story assignments and updates that normally clogged his inbox were missing.

He opened the first email from Mia, and attached at the top was a large image of Mr. Liu's United Nations photo identification badge and a brief biography. Before being installed at the UN, Mr. Liu had served in the Chinese military, according to a handwritten note attached to the bio by Mia's UN contact. Mr. Liu appeared to be who he claimed to be, after all.

Nik wondered where Mr. Liu and Cal Walker were hiding out, and that reminded him he needed to send Walker a message on the encrypted app letting him know he had been fired from his job at *Newshound*. He'd pass along Mia's and Mo's contact information in case Walker wanted to try to convince either one of them to pursue the story. Though Nik suspected they'd had their fill of Trident and Cal Walker.

Nik wanted to get back on the road and to DC before it got too late. He whistled to Gyp, and the dog trotted back over and heeled by him. Once again, he was astonished at the dog's obedience, and he sat there a while longer in appreciation of Gyp's newfound skills, soaking it in, and congratulated himself, though he knew he really had nothing to do with it.

He absentmindedly clicked on Mia's second email.

Nik—Been trying to get in touch with you. Left you a text message and tried to leave you a voice mail, but your mailbox is full. You need to clean it out. Anyhow, I've got a great opportunity for you. I talked to *Newshound*'s CEO and he agrees. Please call me as soon as you can. I'm really excited about this and think you'd be great . . . as long as you keep an open mind.—Mia.

Nik scrolled down through the rest of his text messages,

and, indeed, there was one from Mia, repeating nearly word for word what she'd written in the email. There also was one from Rusty Mitchell, *Newshound*'s CEO and founder. Nik, love Mia's idea. Hope you do it. Keep an open mind.

Neither message mentioned just what this "great opportunity" entailed.

Look forward to hearing more, Nik replied halfheartedly to the pair.

Nik turned to Gyp, who was staring up at him loyally. "It's been my experience, Gyp, that when people tell you to keep an open mind, it's their way of saying you better grab this chance because it's the best deal you're likely to get."

CHAPTER 45

January 9, Washington, DC

Hawk swore he would protect me, the woman thought, *that I'd never be exposed, that my DIA cover would never be blown, otherwise why take the risk. He's been true to his word, too. Until now. Now it feels like the wheels are coming off. It certainly wasn't my idea, blowing up that crappy office park. Sure, I made the anonymous call to lure Walker there on a Sunday night, but only because Hawk said he was going to try to reason with him, get him to see the fortune that could be made if only he'd keep his trap shut and stop badgering the government with that silly lawsuit, and, well, if he wouldn't buy in, then Hawk would do what Hawk would do. But bombing the place, killing all those innocent people, that was never part of the plan. Hawk said plans changed and he had to call an audible. Call an audible, my ass. This ain't the movies.*

And then there was the story by that reporter from the online site, Newsdog, or something like that, about all the funerals for those poor office workers and that police officer and store clerk in Indiana, well, that was just plain awful, no way around it, and so unnecessary. Those two lowlifes from Michigan, not goin' to shed any tears over them, though that one boy, Cooley— think that's what Hawk called him—seemed decent enough and, according to Hawk, a patriot to boot. Lost count of how many people been killed already. Don't even want to think about the ones I don't know about.

Hawk's call was unnerving. Needs to convalesce, he said, and will it be okay if he stays here at my place for a few days. Hell no, it won't be okay, but really don't have much of a choice in the matter, if I stop to think about it. Attacked by a dog, he said, trying to tie up some loose ends. Yeah, tie up loose ends, I know what that's code for. Told him I don't want to know who the victims were this time. The list just seems to keep growing longer and longer. I know way too much already and none of it is any good.

Where's Walker, that's what I want to know, and what's Hawk doing about him? All this other stuff is a sideshow if Walker remains at large yapping about a government conspiracy. Haven't seen any more stories from that Newsdog *reporter about Walker. Don't know if that's a good thing or bad, and who calls their company* Newsdog *anyhow?*

I've held up my end of the bargain, and now it's time for Hawk to hold up his. If that means killing Walker, so be it. There, I finally said it. Didn't want to go there, but maybe there's no way around it. It's messy. If Walker persists with this lawsuit of his, he might eventually get his hands on key internal government documents. Flooded Walker with government records, but most of the stuff is chicken feed, just enough to throw him off the scent. Withheld the important evidence, but sooner or later, a judge might force us to disclose everything, and if that happens, the trail will lead right to my doorstep. It's a miracle Walker hasn't connected the dots by now. Maybe he isn't as smart as everyone claims.

Told the housekeepers to go up to the attic and haul out a rollaway bed and set it up in the study. Not crazy about setting up Hawk in there, necessarily, but couldn't think of any other place on the ground floor to put him that works, and he can't be expected to climb the stairs of a three-story Washington townhome with a leg wound. The more he exerts himself, the longer it will take for him to heal. Want him in and out as quickly as possible. Also, don't want him near my bedroom, sniffing around. We've been down that road once before, and it didn't pan out. He complained I was too rough on him. God, what a whiner. I barely touched him with the cattle prod.

It's my turn to host the Badass Women's Book Club this week. That ain't happening now, no way. Have to make up an excuse and cancel. Hate to do it. It's always a good time and allows me to socialize with other smart, professional women. So few opportunities these days. Really like that one new member in particular—Maggie. We hit it off after she found out I was an analyst with the Defense Intelligence Agency. It was a stroke of genius, inviting her on that ski trip to Colorado.

She doesn't know that I was the DIA analyst who first discovered Walker, saw POOF's potential, and convinced my bosses to invest in the little start-up company called OmniSoft and its untested software. Later, I'd plant the rumor that Walker had a drinking problem and that he was deep in debt. Insinuated Walker was a loose cannon, unreliable, and couldn't be trusted to keep POOF out of the hands of America's adversaries.

It wasn't particularly difficult to get my bosses to take the bait. Everyone could see Walker was teetering. Man was a complete mess. Still is, far as I'm concerned. All it took was a little shove, and the government stepped in and grabbed POOF. Once it did, stealing a copy and getting it in Hawk's hands to sell on the black market was easy-peasy. We've had a nice little business, me and Hawk, down through the years, stealing and selling government secrets. Minted money, we did. How else could I afford a Washington townhome, a ski condo in Vail, and the cutest cottage you ever saw on Martha's Vineyard? Of course, I tell everyone it was all made possible by generational wealth on my mother's side. As if.

I was more than happy to befriend Maggie, and she's proved to be a good, albeit unsuspecting, pipeline of gossip about Walker and the OmniSoft lawsuit. Not being a part of the US Attorney's office, I have no visibility into what the legal strategy or status was, and that's unsettling. After a couple of glasses of Chablis, Maggie's a chatterbox. She's way too smart to divulge any confidential info, I'll give her that, but every little bit helps. Hawk thinks so, too.

Nearly fell off the chairlift in Vail when Maggie mentioned she was once married to the Newsdog reporter who covered the OmniSoft story. That's when I got the idea to have Hawk tail the reporter and see if he would lead us to Walker. It was just a hunch, but it's paid off nicely.

For Maggie's sake, hope the reporter doesn't become just another loose end that needs to be tied off, but with Hawk, one never knows about these things. That's what I know.

CHAPTER 46

January 10, Washington, DC

Nik met Mia at a Starbucks in Adams Morgan a little past seven a.m. on a dull January morning, the ash-gray sky spitting ice pellets. The radio announcer said it was twenty-nine degrees, and the forecast called for snow, sleet, and rain. Washington natives claimed it was one of the harshest winters in recent memory. Nik took comfort in it. It matched his mood.

Mia was sitting by a gas fireplace in a leather armchair when Nik arrived, a twentysomething male with charcoal-colored hair, thick stubble, and olive skin at her side. Mia was bundled up in a calf-length Patagonia jacket, Ugg boots, and a scarf knotted at her neck. She introduced her companion to Nik as Teofilo, no last name. Nik had seen Teofilo once or twice in the newsroom but didn't know him and didn't know what he did.

"Teofilo is my producer," Mia explained. "I wanted you to meet him, and he can answer any questions you might have."

"Great, 'cause I got a couple," Nik said. "Like how 'bout next time we meet a little later in the day? I'd like to take advantage of my unemployment and catch up on my sleep."

"We'll work on it," Mia said.

"Next question's for Teofilo. What do you think of the coffee in this place?"

"Tastes like turpentine, but my family's originally from Cuba, so my standards are a little higher."

"Couldn't agree more. Stuff's swill. So tell me, Teofilo, what does a producer do, exactly?" Nik said.

"It's Teo, and I put together Mia's show, *Dateline Washington*, and help coordinate other *Dateline* podcasts for *Newshound* around the country. I book guests, suggest topics, recruit feedback, post to social media, help host events, write and edit scripts, record the show, promote the podcast, handle analytics, build audience. I might be leaving a few things out, but that's the gist."

"Teo makes the trains run on time, and I'd be lost without him. He's a rock star," Mia said.

"Wow," Nik said. "Impressive. If I ever run a railroad, I'll be sure to look him up. What's this got to do with the job prospect you mentioned? You can't possibly want me to talk about the singles scene in Washington, DC. That would take all of about a solid minute, minute and a half, tops."

"Don't sell yourself short," Mia said, "but no, I'm not here to talk to you about *Dateline*, but I do want to talk to you about podcasts."

Nik looked at Teo. "She serious?"

"Un-huh." Teo nodded and added, "But I'm not sold."

Nik responded, "Hmm. Sounds complicated."

Mia said, "It's not. It's pretty straightforward. Tell him, Teo."

"It's pretty complicated," Teo agreed with Nik.

Mia said, "Maybe just a little, but if I can master it, so can you."

Nik demurred, "Mia, I appreciate it, but I really don't think so."

Mia countered, "You haven't even heard the idea yet, Nik."

"I don't need to," Nik said. "Look, Teo, the expert here, doesn't think it's a good idea, and it sounds like he knows a thing or two about podcasts."

Mia said, "He thinks you'd be a natural. Right, Teo?"

"Hard to say," Teo hedged. "You might do okay, depending."

Nik said, "That's a ringing endorsement if I ever heard one."

"You are an excellent reporter, Nik, and good reporting makes for strong podcasts," Teo said and stopped to sip on a metal straw that protruded from a polished gourd the size of a fist, "but I worry you would not think it serious journalism. Have you ever listened to *Dateline Washington*?"

Nik gave Mia an apologetic look. "I haven't. Sorry."

"How about any other podcast?" Teo said.

"A couple, but I never could understand what all the hoopla was about. Didn't click, at least, not for me."

"When was that?" Mia asked.

"I dunno. A couple years back."

"Lot's changed since then," Teo said. "Early on, there were just a handful of shows where hosts were merely reading news stories, like a radio broadcast. There are now more than half a million podcasts airing weekly. Those early trials didn't pan out, but we learned a great deal from their failures."

"Yeah, like what?" Nik asked, checking his phone for messages and trying not to sound bored by the whole discussion.

"That successful podcasts need to be conversational, exploratory, expansive. Good ones start with a narrative that introduces the story line for that episode or episodes. That's where old-fashioned, shoe-leather reporting plays a role. And, generally speaking, podcasts work better in pairs. Mia always has a guest or a secondary host on her podcasts, for example."

"We think the OmniSoft story would be a fantastic topic to explore," Mia interjected. "Could be the type of story that we might be able to build a whole season around."

That got Nik's attention. "Where does Li'l Dick Whetstone

fit into all this? Can't imagine he's supportive, since he just fired my ass."

"He doesn't," Mia said. "Podcasts are run out of corporate. He has zero input into the product and doesn't control the budget or talent."

"Talent?" Nik said skeptically.

"That's what we call the hosts," Mia said, sounding a little sheepish. "But you're free to call yourself whatever you like."

"How 'bout reporter?" Nik said. "Always liked the ring of that."

"Fine."

"Do you have a name for this podcast?" Nik asked.

Teo looked at Mia, then Nik. "We were thinking *The Front Page*."

"Hmm. Not bad. I like the sound of it."

"So, you on board?" Mia asked.

Nik hesitated, then nodded. "I guess so. Not like people are beating down my door with job offers."

"Great. I think you're going to do great. Don't you think so, too, Teo?"

Teo was noncommittal. "Perhaps." He sniffed. "We'll see."

"Any ideas on how'd you like to kick it off?" Mia asked.

"A couple, but I need to think about it."

"Okay, but you want to pull out all the stops for the first podcast if possible. Get people talking about it," Teo advised.

"What about a story on our Chinese friend?" Nik said to Mia.

"Fantastic idea. I could see an opening show that teases a whole season of podcasts. If you go that route, I can sit in the second chair since I'm up to speed on the story. I can also envision a spot for Mo down the road."

"Let me make a couple calls and do some more reporting. There're more questions I have for Mr. Liu, and I need to get an official response to his allegations from the Justice

Department. It's going to take me a few days to nail everything down."

"That's fine," Teo said. "And if you get a chance, go to Wondery and download a couple of their podcasts. I'd recommend *Dirty John* or *Dr. Death*. Give you an idea of the kind of style we're shooting for, longer term."

"Will do. By the way, what's that you're drinking?" Nik finally asked Teo after he took another long slurp from the metal straw.

"Yerba maté tea. It's from Argentina."

"Any good?"

"It's an acquired taste," Teo said with a shrug.

"Sorta like podcasts," Nik said.

"Sorta like podcasts," Teo agreed.

CHAPTER 47

January 13, Washington, DC

Nik, Mia, and Teo debated whether to launch *The Front Page* with just Liu Li's tale about POOF falling into the hands of the Chinese or wait until they had assembled all the pieces of the far-flung story to make a much bigger splash. Nik had messaged Cal Walker on the encrypted app the day before and arranged to conduct a more extensive interview with Mr. Liu using the burner phones. But there was still much to the story he didn't know. He was leaning toward holding off on the podcast until he could do more extensive reporting and gather more information.

Mia was in favor of rolling the story out episodically. "If you're waiting on perfect, Nik, we'll be here a very long time," she cautioned.

Teo came down somewhere in the middle.

"There's a good argument for holding off until all the stars align," Teo said, "but the downside to that strategy is then we only have one shot to get it right."

After several hours of batting it around, they still couldn't reach a consensus, so they did what they often did in similar types of situations and turned to Frank Rath, the veteran newsman, for his input. They found Frank standing outside *Newshound*'s offices in his overcoat, looking pale, smoking a Merit Ultra Light, and reading a paperback.

Frank's advice was short and to the point: "Either phone or get out of the booth," he said.

His message was clear, and Nik, with Teo's assistance, sat down to write the script for his first-ever podcast. He couldn't help but wonder if it would also be his last, if Mr. Liu's story didn't hold up.

Teo had been promoting the podcast for the past couple days on social media, and Mia plugged it extensively on her show, *Dateline Washington*, as did other *Newshound* podcasts across the country.

The Front Page debuted midweek with Nik as host and narrator. He strongly doubted anyone would listen to it, let alone pay it much attention. He could not have been more wrong.

———————

PRODUCER'S INTRODUCTION: This is the inaugural podcast of *The Front Page*, an enterprise-reporting program. The podcast is narrated by reporter Nik Byron, who is joined by Mia Landry, creator and host of *Newshound*'s popular podcast *Dateline Washington*. Now for Part One.

The Crown Jewels

On a brisk New York weekend morning, an unassuming member of China's United Nations delegation was enjoying a leisurely walk back to his apartment after a light breakfast when he was approached by a stranger, a dark-haired woman, with an intriguing proposition: Would China be interested in acquiring one of the United States's most guarded and promising surveillance technologies?

The woman, who quickly disappeared into the crowd after delivering the message, could not have chosen a better target to approach. The man, Liu Li, was not only a UN delegate, he was also secretly a member of China's Ministry of State Security, the country's sprawling and all-powerful intelligence apparatus. In other words, he was a spy, working undercover as an interpreter for his country at the United Nations.

Her timing couldn't have been any better, either.

China's spymasters had been suffering a crisis of confidence ever since Edward Snowden, an American whistleblower, had leaked sensitive National Security Agency cables while he was employed by the CIA. The leaked classified diplomatic cables revealed a breathtakingly audacious spying enterprise the CIA had launched against US allies. While foreign diplomats and heads of state protested the security breach and claimed the US had violated their trust, the Chinese hierarchy saw the matter in an entirely different light.

The disclosures exposed just how superior US advanced spy technologies were compared to China's. Snowden's leaked documents confirmed what many already suspected but could never prove: that the US possessed new capabilities that allowed them to crack even the most hardened and sophisticated encryption systems.

The incident set off alarm bells across world capitals, but nowhere more so than in Beijing.

The country's leaders instructed the Ministry of State Security and the People's Liberation Army to join forces to close the technology gap by any means possible and to do it quickly. The PLA and State Security have a long history of working together to steal US military technologies, and they quickly spun up a bold, long-range plan not only to close the gap but to leapfrog the US, as well, in the all-important and evolving field of quantum computing.

What the Chinese plan didn't envision was the stroke of good fortune Liu Li would have on that blustery autumn day. Seemingly out of nowhere, someone was offering to sell China the newest generation of US spy technology that the unidentified woman described as "the crown jewels of the US intelligence community."

US officials referred to the "crown jewels" by another name. They know it as POOF, the name given to it by its creator, Cal Walker, who has filed a multimillion-dollar lawsuit against the federal government, alleging it illegally seized the software and forced his company into bankruptcy.

POOF, short for Phantom Omniscient Ocular Functionality, was initially developed by Walker after 9/11 to be an encryption-cracking, data-mining, and software surveillance program all rolled into one. When fully operational, POOF is capable of casting a net over an individual's digital activities to capture their every move, transaction, and interaction in real time, and it was originally developed to track terrorists.

Starting with the thinnest piece of digital information, such as an email alias or IP address, POOF is capable of building and mapping comprehensive databases on targeted individuals, their families, and associates with exacting precision and invisibility.

Over the course of many months, the Chinese became convinced the technology they were being offered was genuine, and eventually purchased the stolen software through a third-party intermediary, the North Koreans.

At first, Liu Li was enthusiastic about the technology that had dropped into his country's lap, but over time, he became disillusioned when he realized party leaders intended to use the powerful software not only to spy on other countries but to couple it with other programs to spy on and oppress its own citizens. Eventually, he says, China planned to offer the software to rogue governments to help suppress their populations as well.

China, Liu Li claimed, intended to marry POOF with artificial intelligence and facial-recognition software to build, quote, "a digital Great Wall" to imprison individuals where they lived.

Liu Li fled China to the United States to warn other countries of what his government intended.

When contacted about Liu Li, the Chinese government labeled him a mentally unstable traitor and denied any knowledge of POOF.

The US Department of Justice, which is involved in a lengthy legal battle with Cal Walker over the POOF software program, said it has never heard of Liu Li and denied that a leaked copy of the software program has been offered for sale on the black market.

"The whole story is preposterous, and if this Liu Li actually exists, he should present himself to the US attorney general's office in Washington, DC, for questioning," a spokesperson told *The Front Page* podcast.

Hi, Nik.

Hi, Mia.

Nik, that's an incredible story. Where is Liu Li now, and will he talk with US officials?

He's in hiding, Mia, in the US. One attempt has already been made on his life, and he fears for his safety.

Have you been able to confirm there was an actual assassination attempt? Forgive me, but that sounds a little dramatic, Nik.

I was sitting across from him when someone tried to blow his brains out. It *was* dramatic.

So, where does the story go from here, Nik?

In Part Two, we attempt to root out and identify a shadowy character who we believe is at the heart of the POOF story. We've been able to piece together clues about this person—we believe he has ties to paramilitary groups and is connected to one of the men suspected of blowing up the Trident Office Park, where OmniSoft was located. We have a partial description and have tracked down military personnel we believe he served with overseas.

That all sounds fascinating, Nik. We will take a short break for a word from our sponsors, and when we return, we will join Nik for Part Two of "The Crown Jewels."

CHAPTER 48

January 18, Washington, DC

Before last week, Nik had no concept of how much work went into producing podcasts. "Enunciate," Teo barked into Nik's headset repeatedly. "Project," he demanded. "Slow down," he ordered. They did nine takes over the course of four-plus hours before Teo was finally satisfied with the second episode of *The Front Page.* It'd been nearly a week since "The Crown Jewels" had aired, and, given the strong and favorable reaction to the program, Mia was anxious to rush out the next episode.

The process left Nik mentally and emotionally drained, and he escaped the cramped, stuffy little studio where they recorded the show as soon as it was finished, but a host of demands pursued him as he fled out the door: Mia and Teo wanted to immediately begin work scripting the third episode; Sam texted to suggest drinks and dinner later that evening with a newly married couple she wanted to introduce Nik to; Maggie was demanding that he get in contact with her about the shock wave his podcast had unleashed inside the Justice Department; and Cal Walker sent him a message on the encrypted app asking for an urgent meeting. I'll be in True Face, Walker's message said.

True Face???? Nik replied.

Spy speak for not in disguise, came the answer.

For the first time in weeks, the sun was shining and the temperature was hovering around fifty degrees. Nik wanted nothing more than to take Gyp for a run in Rock Creek Park and decompress.

Nik dodged Mia and Teo; returned Maggie's call when he guessed she was at her yoga class with Spence and unable to answer her phone; texted Sam and counterproposed drinks, no dinner; and messaged Walker to meet him at the stone bridge over Rock Creek at five p.m. when the park was certain to be all but deserted. He then raced home to change into running gear and collect Gyp for some much-needed exercise for the both of them.

———

Rock Creek Park is a 2,100-acre oasis in the northwest quadrant of DC, and Nik, like many transplant Washingtonians, was drawn to its open spaces, extensive running and biking trails, eighteen-hole golf course, and the forested swaths that bisected the park and made visitors feel like they were in the remote outdoors and not smack-dab in the middle of an urban metropolis.

Nik had purchased an expensive pair of Danner trail-running shoes and loved nothing more than to explore the park off the beaten path with Gyp. He was privately embarrassed more than once when he got turned around and lost in the dense woods. Lucky for him, Gyp had a natural sense of direction and would eventually lead the pair back to well-maintained trails and civilization.

Nik arrived at the park just before four p.m., the sky

already darkening. He'd have to get moving if he wanted to meet Walker on time. The stone bridge was on the other side of the park, and if he kept to the trails, it was about a five-mile trek, according to the navigation app on his watch.

Nik figured he could cover the five miles in about an hour, with time to spare, if he were in shape, but he wasn't. He hadn't exercised for more than a month and was carrying a few extra pounds that he'd put on over the holidays. If he cut across country, he could shave a mile to a mile and a half, maybe a little more, off that distance.

Nik was still nursing a sore ankle from the spill he had taken on Walker's boat and knew it would be safer, especially with night approaching, to stick to the trails. He looked to Gyp for guidance. The dog responded by tugging at the leash, panting faster, and striding toward the woods, a look of sheer joy on his face.

"Okay, off-trail it is, but take it easy," Nik said and lashed the dog's lead around his waist, then commanded Gyp to heel. Nik activated the navigation app on his watch to make sure he didn't get lost and set off at a moderate pace. He left his phone in his vehicle because he found it a pain to run with, and, besides, he didn't want to be pestered by calls or text messages, especially from Teo or Maggie.

Nik didn't see another soul the whole time and crested the hill above the stone bridge a couple of minutes before five. As he made his way down the slope, he could see a lone figure at the far end of the bridge, his back to him, peering down into the water. Every once in a while, the man would lift his head and survey the path leading to the bridge as if he were waiting for someone.

Getting down the hill quickly proved tricky. The slope was steep, and the recent snow and rain made the going slow. Nik picked his way around exposed roots and downed trees, and it took him and Gyp almost ten minutes to descend.

When he finally reached the bottom, Nik could make out the Washington Redskins sock hat, scarf, and peacoat Walker wore. The man had remained pretty much in the same spot on the bridge, staring down into the creek that rambled below.

"Cal," Nik called out when he stepped onto the bridge.

The man swiveled his head in the direction of the voice and, after hesitating for a moment, took a tentative step toward Nik, who detected something awkward in Walker's movement that he had not noticed before. He seemed to favor his right side and appeared to have a pronounced limp.

"You okay, Cal?" Nik asked as he approached, and then looked down at Gyp and commanded the dog to sit. When he looked back up, he was staring into a pair of yellow eyes and a thick tuft of mustard-colored bristles.

CHAPTER 49

January 18, Washington, DC

Jesus, Mother Mary, Joseph, the woman thought, *this can't be happening. Maggie was beside herself when I called to tell her I'd be late for book club. "Whole Justice Department in an uproar," she said. "Heads will roll." I pumped her for details, but she clammed up. Told me to listen to a podcast called* The Front Page. *Said it would explain everything. Well, what do I know about podcasts, so I made Hawk pull it up on his computer. For a moment there, he thought I was in his bedroom for some other mischief. I set him straight on that score pronto. I couldn't believe what I was hearing. The whole world now thinks the Chinese have got their hands on top-secret US technology. Sure, they denied it, but who's gonna believe the Chinese? No way to sugarcoat it. This is bad.*

I mean, what are the odds that, of all the spies in China, we pick one with a conscience? That's just terrible luck, plain and simple. After they're done trying to cover their asses, government investigators are gonna start knocking on doors, looking for the person who stole the technology and sold it to the Chinese. *There goes everything—ski condo, beach cottage, townhome. Talk about poof. Got some funds stashed offshore as insurance. I could get by, but, Jesus, who wants to live like that? Not me.*

Hawk's got a plan. Says it'll work. It better, all I have to say. Need to shut up Walker, Liu, and that Newsdog *reporter— sorry, Maggie—once and for all. Won't solve all our problems, but it buys us time to think things through. Get our heads straight. Never seen Hawk so worried. That reporter's got him rattled. And motivated. Just maybe I'll give him a little more incentive. Put on those Louboutin stilettos with the red soles and that skirt that barely covers my ass. Give him a peek at the Brazilian wax job. Dangle it in front of him. Make him cross-eyed with lust. Couldn't hurt.*

And besides, a girl has needs, too.

CHAPTER 50

January 18, Washington, DC

Mo hit pay dirt on the next-to-last name on his call list. Dallas Armstrong worked for a defense contractor in San Diego and had been stationed in Afghanistan with the 75th Regiment for one tour of duty. He immediately recognized the face and the luxuriant mustache of the man Mo emailed him.

"Name's not Calkins, though," Armstrong told Mo over the phone. "It's Hawkins, with an *H*. Everybody called him Hawk. I didn't have a lot of interaction with him. To be honest, I tried to keep my distance."

"Why's that?" Mo asked.

"He's bad news. Lots of stories, rumors, gossip, really, about him killing civilians, torturing prisoners, running black sites. Our guys were there because we took an oath to defend our country and the Constitution and had a duty to fulfill. Not Hawk or guys like him. He was there because he enjoyed it. It was never clear to me who he was working with, or for. Could have been the CIA, could have been a private security firm."

"You believe those stories about him?" Mo asked.

"I believe about half of 'em, and even then, that's bad enough. Worse thing I heard is that he sliced off the tongues of young Afghani boys, no more than twelve or thirteen years old, who were reportedly spying for the Taliban. I know the story is partially true, because I met some of those poor bastards. All they could do was make gurgling noises. It's none of my business, mister, but if I were you, I'd steer clear of him."

"Cut off their tongues, Jesus. That's barbaric," Mo said. "Anybody you know who was close to him that I might talk to?"

"There was one guy, an explosives expert named Cooley. They were thick as thieves, always talking about blowing shit up and throwing in together when they got back to the States. You might want to try to track him down. He was from the Midwest somewhere, Minnesota or Michigan, one of those northern states, I think."

"Lawrence Cooley?" Mo said.

"Well, ah, yeah, Larry Cooley, what we called him."

"Thanks, we know about Cooley," Mo said. "It was a YouTube video he posted that put us on Hawkins's trail in the first place. We didn't know how close they were. That's helpful."

"You already talk to Cooley, then?" Armstrong said.

"Nope. Too late. He's not talking to anyone."

"Why, he flee the country?" Armstrong asked.

"He's dead. Murder-suicide. Allegedly."

"You don't say? You think Hawkins might have had something to do with it?" Armstrong said.

"Possibly," Mo said. "I certainly wouldn't rule it out. Cooley was wanted by authorities in the bombing of Trident Office Park here. Calkins—I mean, Hawkins—was seen at the office park shortly after the explosion."

"Well, good luck getting to the bottom of it, but keep my name out of it," Armstrong said. "I don't want that psychopath coming for me."

"Promise," Mo said, then texted a quick message to

Nik, telling him about the link between Cooley and Colonel Mustard. But his name's not Calkins. It's Hawkins. That's why we couldn't track him down. They call him Hawk, and apparently he's one murderous son of a bitch. You need to be careful.

Nik's phone, safely tucked away in his vehicle's console, buzzed forlornly with the incoming message.

CHAPTER 51

January 18, Washington, DC

"Colonel Mustard," Nik stammered.

"What?" the man said and stepped toward Nik like a peg-legged pirate, one hand in the pocket of the peacoat; in the other, a bayonet, its blade glistening in the bridge lights. Before Nik could register what was happening, the man pulled a Taser from his coat pocket and fired it into Gyp's shoulder. The dog let out a yip, his legs caving in as his body slammed into the bridge deck.

Nik lunged for the man's knife hand, but the soles of his shoes were muddy from the hillside, and he slipped to one knee. The man clubbed Nik hard on the side of his head with the handle of the bayonet. Blood streamed from Nik's ear, and he went down on all fours.

The man drove a knee into Nik's right kidney, grabbed a fistful of hair, and violently slammed his head on the bridge's cobblestone deck. Nik's kidney felt like it was on fire, and a lightning bolt of pain shot through his head and neck, his eyes welling with tears.

"Now you fuckin' listen to me, shit for brains," the man hissed into Nik's good ear. "You pick up that fuckin' mongrel of yours and climb down under the bridge. You fuck with me again, and I'll run this blade right through your gizzard and cut the nuts off your dog. We clear on that?"

Nik nodded and slowly hoisted himself to his feet.

"Now get fuckin' moving," the man ordered and shoved Nik in the back.

Nik wobbled over to Gyp, bent down, and scooped up the dog, his eyes half open, vacant, his tongue lolling out the side of his mouth. He scrambled down the bank, and when he reached the bottom, he found Cal Walker lying under the bridge in a heap, face swollen and bruised, hands zip-tied in front of him, mouth covered with duct tape.

"He ain't dead," the man said and kicked Walker in the ribs, causing him to emit a low moan. "Tough nut, though, I'll give 'im that. Had to beat him nearly half to death before he told me where he stashed Liu. Need to keep him around just in case he's lying."

The man sheathed the knife and unholstered a 9 mm semiautomatic Glock from a rig under his coat. He placed the barrel of the gun against Nik's forehead, released the safety, and pulled back the slide to chamber a round.

"Now it's your turn, paperboy. I want to know who knows about me and when your next story is going to air and what's it going to say. You tell me the truth, and maybe you and that mutt of yours might live to see tomorrow, but if I think you're lyin' for one second, I'll cut both of your throats, no questions asked. We understand each other?"

Nik nodded again and glanced over the man's shoulder at Walker, whose eyes were filled with fear and who was shaking his head vigorously, side to side.

"Good," the man said, and fingered the safety back on. "Now, get on with it."

"There isn't a next story," Nik said. "Not yet. That was hype. We don't know your identity. All we know is that you were at Trident the night of the explosion, obviously, since I saw you there, but that's it. How, or if, you're tied into the bombing, the Chinese, and OmniSoft, that's all a complete mystery to us."

Nik stopped and spit out a mouthful of blood along with what felt like a part of a tooth.

"Nukowski and Cooley, we know about them, but they're dead. We assume the three of you crossed paths at some point in the past, but, there again, we don't know where, when, or how."

That last part was a lie, and Nik looked up at the man to gauge his reaction. There wasn't any, so he continued. "I'm the only reporter assigned to the story. No one else, quite frankly, gives a rat's ass, and my boss fired me for pursuing it. The podcast was a desperate attempt to keep the story alive, and I doubt more than ten people listened to it. Honestly, I don't think you have anything to worry about."

Nik stole a look at Walker again, whose chin was now pinned to his chest. He couldn't tell if he was resting, passed out, or dead.

"He tell you where Liu is?" the man asked and gestured toward Walker.

"No. I know he was on Cal's boat over on the Eastern Shore, but I think you probably already know that, since you tailed me over there."

"Spotted me, did you? Must be slipping," he said.

"I didn't. Cal did. How did you know we were meeting here tonight in the park? I left my car five miles back and ran cross-country. You didn't follow me, and you were here before I arrived."

"Easy," he said and produced an electronic device from his pocket. "Ever see one of these?" he said, holding it up.

Nik shook his head no.

"It's a StingRay, and it mimics a cell tower to trick mobile devices into giving location and identity information. Placed one by your apartment, and it captured both your mobile and burner phone info. I then used Walker's software to compile a database of all your digital activity and devices. Once I had that, it was easy to hack into the encrypted app the two of you used to communicate. Walker's technology works as advertised."

"In normal circumstances, I'd think that ironic," Nik said. "You don't plan to let me go, do you?"

"Nope. Figured that out, did ya?"

"Didn't think so. At least spare the dog," Nik pleaded. "He can't possibly do you any harm."

"Sorry, but no can do. Can't have any loose ends. Way too many in this op already, but guess that's what I get for relying on a couple losers like Cooley and Nukowski. Learnt my lesson."

"So," Nik said, "Cooley and Nukowski, that was your handiwork, up there in northern Michigan in that burnt-out trailer?"

"Yup, but shoulda never went down that way. They were supposed to get killed in the Trident explosion along with Walker. Best-laid plans and all that. Had them convinced we were on an anti-government jihad. Dopes."

"Well, there are a few other things you should probably know, then," Nik said, frantically trying to think of some way to stall the inevitable and drag out the conversation.

"I don't think so," the man cut him off, "and, besides, I need to get going. I got two dates to keep tonight—one with Liu and the other with a red-hot female friend just itching to get her hands on my junk."

"Just curious," Nik asked casually, "who stole POOF from the government and gave you a copy?"

"Guess it won't hurt to tell you, seeing how you ain't going anywheres," he said. "My female friend. She's the one who first came across the mad scientist here," he said and nodded toward Walker, "and got the idea to have the feds invest in his little company. Later, she convinced her overlords that Walker was a security risk and couldn't be trusted with guarding the software. Pretty ingenious, no? Now, no more questions."

The man walked over and slapped the unconscious Walker across the face. "We need to go, Professor," he said when Walker stirred. "On your feet." And he yanked him up with a jerk.

The streetlights from above bathed the ground in a gauzy haze, and Nik watched as the man reached into his coat pocket and extracted a metal tube that he screwed into the end of the gun barrel. He pointed the Glock at Gyp's head and thumbed off the safety.

"No," Nik pleaded. "Please, shoot me first. I can't bear to watch you kill my dog."

"Fine. Have it your way." He shrugged and swung the barrel of the gun toward Nik.

Nik dipped his head, and images of Sam flooded his thoughts. How he wished he had lingered longer in bed with her that morning, inhaling her essence and absorbing her spirit. They had made arrangements for him to begin moving into her bungalow over the weekend. Now, she'd be faced with the death of yet another lover. What a nightmare.

Nik squeezed his eyes shut and waited, with labored breath, for the gunshot that would end his life, but instead of a bang, he heard the faintest whoosh of air, followed by a primordial scream.

"*Fuuuuccck!*" the man cried. "*My fucking hand!*"

Nik's eyes snapped open. He was staring into a bloody, dripping stump, all that remained of Colonel Mustard's gun hand.

Nik recoiled, horrified, and then heard a second shot whistle past his ear that clipped the man's cheek and severed the tip of his nose, spinning him around and loosing a gusher of blood.

The third shot caught the man in the lower back, lancing his spine, dropping him to his knees in a prayerful position.

The final, and fatal, shot hit him in the back of the neck and exited his Adam's apple, the arrow's shaft impaled half in, half out, the fixed broadhead with four razor-sharp blades covered in a gelatinous hash of blood, skin, sinew, and windpipe, his yellow eyes, like two butterscotch candies, frozen open, manic.

Nik dropped his head between his legs, retched, and passed out.

CHAPTER 52

January 18, Washington, DC

Grant Dilworth's mood had steadily darkened after Nukowski's unannounced night visit and went into free fall when he heard the early-morning gunshot outside his home and discovered Pontiac, his German shepherd, sliced open, beaten, and unconscious in the snow.

He brooded, waiting for an assault, never knowing when or where it might come. He blamed Nukowski for his troubles, though he couldn't also help faulting Sara, who had led that reporter right to their doorstep.

For a man who bent stainless steel for a living and stalked grizzly bears in remote parts of Alaska, Dilworth felt powerless and fearful. Tired of the waiting, he told Sara he would not sit idly by any longer.

Dilworth stuffed his camouflage outfit, night-vision scope, Scorpyd Aculeus crossbow, MTech hunting knife, a small GPS tracking device, and a change of clothes into a duffle and piled everything into Sara's Subaru for the nine-hour trip to Washington, DC, figuring his massive Ford F350 pickup, which he used to haul his stainless-steel sculptures, would draw too much attention in the nation's capital.

He thought about packing a gun but decided against it. It was too risky, and he had no way of silencing gunfire, and the Scorpyd, while not the most powerful bow in his collection, was deadly accurate and could hurtle an arrow through the air at the blinding speed of 460 feet per second. And for close-in work, there was always the knife, and, admittedly, he wasn't a very good shot with a handgun anyhow.

Dilworth reached DC just before nightfall and made his way to the address the reporter had attached in an email. He spent a cold, mostly sleepless night outside Nik's dark apartment but had not seen any sign of the reporter.

He was about to abandon his stakeout in the afternoon, grab something to eat, and check into a motel when he saw Nik, driving a Land Cruiser, glide past him on the street, searching for a place to park. He watched the vehicle in his rearview mirror as it circled the block and decided he'd approach the reporter when he was entering the front door to his apartment, his back to the street. Dilworth hoped threats would work to get what he wanted, but he needed information, and he was prepared to do whatever it required to get it.

Dilworth was still looking in the mirror when a dark-blue sedan inched down the street with a man behind the wheel. Something about him caught Dilworth's eye.

After Dilworth had found Pontiac's lifeless body in the snow and rushed the dog to the veterinarian's office, he had returned to the woods to search the site for clues. It was clear there had been a vicious mauling, and whomever the German shepherd had attacked had lost a great deal of blood. Dilworth traced the trail and boot prints to the roadside, where they disappeared.

Given the amount of spilled blood he found on the ground and in the snow, Dilworth felt certain the victim had needed to seek medical attention, and the only place a person could get it was at the regional hospital. He drove straight there.

Dilworth had donated several of his sculptures to the hospital for its annual fundraiser over the years and was on good terms with the hospital's administrator. He told the administrator he thought Pontiac had attacked someone who had wandered onto his property, and he wanted to find the person to apologize and offer to help pay for any medical bills. Within minutes, Dilworth was reading the hospital report and talking to the emergency room doctor who'd sutured the wounds.

Turned out the man had given the hospital a fake name and address and paid in cash, but the doctor provided Dilworth with a detailed physical description. "About six one, fit, yellow hair, and a mustache as thick as a cat's tail," the doctor said, "and he's limping, badly. Probably will be for a while, maybe forever. Your dog did a real number on his leg."

The man in the dark sedan had a large, bushy mustache, and Dilworth swung the Subaru around and fell in behind him. He followed the car to a leafy neighborhood in DC and watched as the man gimped up a flight of stone stairs, one tread at a time, to a three-story townhome. After the man entered the front door, Dilworth slid out of his car and planted the GPS unit under the back tire wall of the sedan and activated the device, convinced he had found Pontiac's assailant and the man who had waited outside his home in the early morning to ambush him.

Later that day, Dilworth tracked the sedan into Rock Creek Park and witnessed the mustached man confront another man on a stone bridge and shove him down the embankment. Dilworth couldn't see what was happening, but he could hear cries coming from under the bridge.

Dilworth, dressed in camo, had taken up a position in the woods that surrounded the bridge when he saw the reporter stumbling down the hillside with a dog.

Dilworth was about forty-five yards from the bridge with an unobstructed shooting lane and just the slightest of breezes, four Grim Reaper broadhead carbon arrows affixed to the body of the Scorpyd bow, rear-mounted scope dialed in for a forty-two-yard shot to account for the downslope of the terrain.

He saw Nik step onto the bridge and approach the mustached man, who was now dressed in the peacoat and hat the other man had been wearing. He heard a scuffle break out, but the stone arches blocked his view of the bridge deck, and after a few minutes, the reporter reappeared, trundling down the bank, dog in his arms, the overhead lights illuminating the ground beneath the bridge.

Dilworth armed the bow with one of the Grim Reapers and drew back the string, the cables and pulleys locking the pull in place. He could maintain that position indefinitely without the slightest discomfort.

Dilworth saw the man lay the barrel of a revolver against Nik's forehead but determined he wouldn't fire the weapon and risk drawing attention. Dilworth leaned against a tree stump and waited, and it was only when he saw the man screw a silencer onto the end of the gun, point it at the dog, and then swing it away and level it at the reporter's head that he made the split-second decision to release the arrow.

The second arrow was on its way by the time the man's scream reached Dilworth's ears.

CHAPTER 53

January 19, Washington, DC

The painkillers the nurse had administered were starting to wear off, and Nik began to stir from a deep, thick slumber. Several figures stood at the foot of the bed talking, but he couldn't make out their faces and didn't recognize the voices. To his right, a window, blinds partially drawn, let in small pools of light that hurt his eyes when he looked directly at them. As he slowly regained consciousness, his head started to throb, and when he ran his tongue inside his mouth, he could feel holes where teeth once were.

"Nik," a soft voice said, and he rolled his head away from the window toward the sound, white pain stabbing at his neck and radiating down his spine, arms, and legs.

He closed his eyes and passed out.

———

When Nik woke again, it was dark outside and the only light in his room came from a monitor next to his bed that cast a bluish glow. He pushed on his elbows and propped himself upright and looked around. The effort exhausted him. Sam was in a chair to his left, asleep, her head resting on a rolled-up coat.

He picked up a mirror from a bedside table and held it up to his face. His left eye was partially closed, the whole left side of his face covered in deep-purple bruises, his forehead bandaged, and it felt like his nose was stuffed with cotton balls. He pulled a tissue from a box on the table and blew hard, and when he did, he heard an odd crunching noise, like someone cracking open a walnut, and his left cheek bulged out like a bullfrog's.

"Don't do that," Sam said and sat bolt upright in her chair. "Doctors said you shattered your cheekbone and fractured your eye socket. There's no bone structure holding in your sinuses, so when you blow your nose, your cheek bulges. It's really disgusting."

Nik looked at Sam through clouded vision. "Have to admit, though, I'm a sight for sore eyes," he slurred and sank into the bed and fell back asleep.

———

Two DC detectives were stationed on either side of Nik's bed when he was wheeled back into his room from the X-ray lab. Doctors told him one of the blows he suffered had fractured his skull and they were worried about the potential of swelling in the brain. So far, the tests were negative, but they recommended he remain in the hospital for a few more days for further observation just to be on the safe side.

The senior detective was Yvette Jenks, a veteran of the DC police force and a former marine. She was wearing a lavender pantsuit and a frown. Her partner was Jason Goetz, a recently minted detective who had started his career as a secondary school teacher in DC's inner city. He flashed Nik a toothy smile. After quick introductions, Jenks led off the questioning.

"We got a body down in the morgue full of holes like a pincushion, Mr. Byron. Normally, we'd be lookin' for a gun or knife, sometimes both, but that's not the case here. The murder weapon appears to be a crossbow. A crossbow, you believe that. I've been on the force for twenty-odd years and have seen people killed with all manner of weapons—lawn mower, nail gun, hay bale hook, and, even once, a high-heel shoe, but never no crossbow. There's a Robin Hood running 'round in the woods in Rock Creek Park shootin' people, and I want to know if you know who it is."

"Never saw the shooter, Detective Jenks," Nik said. "I passed out."

"That's not what I asked, is it? I asked if you know him or her, as the case may be."

"I don't know if it's a man or a woman, and no, I don't know who it is."

"You got any guesses?"

Nik shook his head no.

"You better not be messin' with me, Mr. Byron. You think you're hurtin' now, I'll land on you like a ton of bricks if I find out you're lyin'," Jenks threatened.

Detective Goetz cut in. "I believe what Detective Jenks is trying to convey to you, Nik, is that it would be in your best interest to cooperate. You and Mr. Walker are the only witnesses, and Walker claims he was unconscious most of the time, and, judging from his injuries, we tend to believe him. The shooter removed the arrows, so we don't have any physical evidence to trace."

"Kinda strange, don't you think, that William Tell was hiding in the woods just when you needed help," Jenks said. "Whatcha do, whistle?"

"I'm just grateful he or she was there," Nik said.

"I bet you are," she said. "I am not at all convinced it was a mere coincidence, and I think you know more than you're saying. We're done here for now, but we'll be back," Detective Jenks promised and gave a nod of the head to Goetz, who withdrew his wallet and handed Nik a business card with his cell phone number, email address, and Twitter handle on it.

"You can reach me twenty-four seven, Nik, if anything else should occur to you," Goetz said and thanked Nik for his time and wished him a speedy recovery.

After the detectives left, a parade of visitors streamed through Nik's hospital room. Sam dropped off several paperbacks, an iPad with a handful of downloaded movies, and a large vase overflowing with colorful flowers to brighten the drab surroundings.

"I'll be back after work," she said and kissed him on the cheek. "Don't go anywhere."

"Bring PJs and we can have a sleepover. And cards. To play gin," Nik said. "And speaking of gin, I could use a drink."

"I'll see what I can do, but these Georgetown Hospital nurses are pretty strict," Sam said before dashing out.

Nik was sitting up in bed reading one of the paperbacks when Mo pushed Frank into the room in a wheelchair, followed by Mia.

"What now?" Nik said.

Frank revealed to Nik for the first time that his kidneys were failing and he was in the hospital for preliminary testing for a possible transplant.

"I been trying to tell you that you needed to talk to Frank," Mo said.

"I'm sorry, Frank," Nik said. "What did the doctors say?"

"Said it shouldn't be a problem if we can find a donor."

"And guess who's a match?" Mia said.

Nik looked puzzled.

"Mo."

"Get outta here," Nik said.

"Yup, and I plan to do it, too," Mo said. "Doctors tell me you only need one kidney, and they assured me the operation won't hinder the performance of my johnson. If they're wrong about that, I swear to God I'll order a lead sandwich from Café Smith and Wesson."

"Don't joke about things like that," Mia scolded.

"Who's joking?" Mo replied.

Mia told Nik to expect a visit from Teo. "We're sitting on the hottest story in DC, and we need to get that next podcast episode produced, like, really fast."

"He knows where to find me," Nik said.

A burly nurse came in and shooed the trio out of the room and ordered Nik to get some sleep. He napped, restlessly, for about an hour and then strolled down the hall to visit the convalescing Cal Walker.

Walker was in good spirits. He said he had just had a visit from the US attorney general, who told him the government was anxious to get the OmniSoft matter straightened out and offered a high seven-figure settlement, as well as the return of POOF, to Walker in exchange for his cooperation in dealing with the Chinese.

"What did you tell him?" Nik said.

"Told him I was a patriot and that I stand ready to assist in any way I can but I wouldn't consider anything less than an eight-figure settlement for all I've been through."

"Think they'll go for it?"

"Don't think they have a whole lotta choice. You see, like any self-respecting developer, I built a back door into POOF. Two, in fact. One I want the Chinese to find, the other they'll never find in a million years. With Mr. Liu's help, we can cause all sorts of mischief for them and anyone else who uses an unauthorized copy of the software once it's actually activated and up and running. It's now up to our government to decide just how much pain they want to inflict."

"Brilliant," Nik said, and got up to leave. "I need to start work on a script."

"Those two detectives dropped by," Walker said. "Asked me about the shooter."

"Yeah, what did you tell them?"

"Told them the truth. I got no idea who it was. What about you? What did you say? Who do you think it was?"

"No clue," Nik said.

"Oh, by the way," Walker said as Nik headed out the door, "your ex-wife, Maggie, she's been a big help in getting this thing worked out with the AG's office. Thought you'd like to know."

CHAPTER 54

January 19, Washington, DC

Uber driver's here. 'Bout time. Oh, he's cute. Can't go there, she told herself. *Need to focus. Hawk's gone dark. Put out the distress signal. Still nothing. Not like him, and he knew what was in store when he returned. Gave him a little taste of the poontang before he set off on his mission to Rock Creek Park. He was nearly delirious. No way he passes that up. Now there's a story on the news about a body being found in the park. Maybe Hawk's plan wasn't so good after all. One thing's for sure, I ain't waiting around for jackbooted thugs to kick in my front door. No, sir.*

Mind's made up. Time to evacuate, put plan B into effect. Hawk will either find me or he won't, if he's still alive, that is, and not in prison somewhere. If I'm being totally honest, he's better off dead than alive as far as my welfare's concerned. Told him to sell Walker's software to the Russians, or the Iranians, like we done in the past, and be done with it. But no. This time, he had to retail it. Make a big killing. Cut out the middleman, he said. Told him that was greedy. Risky, too, but the man wouldn't listen.

Well, I'm outta here. Maybe that Uber driver's got a friend. Whoever said two's company, three's a crowd, didn't know what the hell they were talking about. They certainly never spent any time in France, that's for damn sure.

CHAPTER 55

PRODUCER'S INTRODUCTION: *The Front Page* podcast is based on court documents, sworn testimony, social media posts, metadata, and interviews with US and Chinese diplomats and intelligence officials. It is narrated by reporter Nik Byron, who is joined in the podcast by Mia Landry, the host of *Newshound*'s popular *Dateline Washington* series.

In the Beginning

On a hot, muggy late-summer afternoon in 2012, a top analyst with the Defense Intelligence Agency made an unannounced visit to the offices of OmniSoft Corporation in southeast Washington, DC, to evaluate a potentially powerful new surveillance technology for the United States government's war on terrorism.

That analyst's seemingly innocuous visit would eventually lead to a multimillion-dollar investment in the company by the federal government and ultimately set in motion an elaborate scheme to wrestle control of the software from the company and its founder and sell it on the black market for millions of dollars to some of the same terrorist organizations and rogue operators the program was initially designed to thwart.

Before the scope of the criminal enterprise was fully exposed, nearly a dozen individuals would be killed, an office park bombed, millions of taxpayers' dollars squandered, a company left in ruins, careers damaged, and the software circulated worldwide to terrorist cells and police states seeking to suppress their citizenry.

At the heart of the story is a software program code-named POOF, which stands for Phantom Omniscient Ocular Functionality, and its creator, Cal Walker.

Until now, Walker's claims that the government subverted his company to gain control of POOF have largely gone unheeded, if for no other reason than Walker could never substantiate the allegations.

As it turns out, Walker's allegations—which appear now to be largely accurate, albeit at times overstated and misdirected—represented only one piece of what would become a multidimensional, multinational conspiracy.

Unbeknownst to both Walker and the US government, a third party was operating behind the scenes to steal POOF's code and sell it to the highest bidder on the black market.

Our investigation reveals that the third party consisted of at least two key individuals—a female analyst who originally evaluated POOF for the Defense Intelligence Agency, the military's top spy operation, and a shadowy, quasi-military accomplice who used several aliases and had underworld contacts from his time as an international soldier of fortune.

The man has been identified as Lewis Hawkins, a West Point dropout, who was killed in Rock Creek Park recently during a failed attempt to abduct Walker.

Based on our reporting and government sources, we believe his female accomplice is Candice Smothers, a DIA counterterrorism analyst who held the nation's highest security designation. Smothers is believed to have fled the country, and her whereabouts are currently unknown.

Hi, Nik.

Hi, Mia.

I'm riveted by this story, Nik, as I'm sure are listeners of *The Front Page*. But it's very complicated, with a lot of moving parts. What's the best way to tell a story like this?

That's a great question. To fully comprehend and appreciate the complexity of the OmniSoft story, we need to travel back in time to September 11, 2001, otherwise known as 9/11.

In the beginning . . .

CHAPTER 56

March 1, Rehoboth Beach, Delaware

Nik and Sam rented a two-story, four-bedroom faded-peach-colored clapboard house in Rehoboth Beach, Delaware, half a block from the Atlantic Ocean, in the off-season and spent almost every free moment they could taking quiet walks on the nearly deserted beach in nice weather or along the boardwalk when it was stormy. They often invited friends for clambakes, steamed crabs, and cold beer on the weekends, but just as many nights, it was just the two of them and Gyp.

Nik's injuries took longer to heal than doctors had anticipated, and Rehoboth, only a three-hour drive from Washington, was the perfect place to convalesce, with its sea air and unhurried pace. While his medical team did an expert job repairing his broken bones, fractured skull, and chipped and missing teeth, Nik's kidney was badly bruised and slow to recover. His parents; brother, Alec; and sister, Hanna, rotated in and out of DC, to keep his spirits up.

Gyp, on the other hand, bounced back almost overnight from the Taser shock. The only noticeable aftereffect appeared to be that the dog's memory bank was wiped clean, and he reverted to his old habits of chewing through seat belts, bolting out the front door, and digging in the yard as if he had never attended several very expensive weeks of obedience training. Nik was resigned to the fact that Maggie, his ex, was right. The dog was incorrigible.

Nik was packing up the Land Cruiser for the 120-mile trip back to DC after a weekend at the beach when his cell phone buzzed. It was Rusty Mitchell, *Newshound*'s founder. Other than a get-well card and a bottle of bourbon, Nik had not heard from Mitchell when he was hospitalized, and he thought it odd he'd be calling on a Sunday evening.

"How you getting along?" Mitchell asked.

"Mending. Not as quickly as I'd like, but the doctors are optimistic I'll be good as new. You calling to tell me you fired Whetstone?" Nik said.

"Sorry, can't do that, Nik," Mitchell said, "but I am calling with some news."

"Good news, I hope."

"I think so, and think you'll agree when you hear it."

"The suspense is killing me," Nik said.

"Are you in DC now?" Mitchell asked.

"Nope, but I'm heading back there shortly. I'm at the beach, Rehoboth. It's in Delaware," Nik said, and decided it might be a longer call than normal with Mitchell and sat down on the tailgate.

"Then you'll be there tomorrow."

"Yeah, well, later tonight, actually. Why, something big happening tomorrow that I should know about?"

"We plan to file the S-1 paperwork with the Securities and Exchange Commission in the morning for *Newshound*'s initial public offering. It's what I've been working on nonstop for the past several months. Finally got all the details ironed out this weekend. *Newshound*'s going public."

"That's great news," Nik said. "Congratulations."

"You remember those stock options the company granted you a while back?"

"Yeah, kinda. Haven't thought a lot about them."

"Still have them, don't you?"

"I do. Somewhere," Nik said, and wondered where he had put the paperwork when he moved in with Sam.

"Our underwriters are pricing the offering between twenty-two and twenty-seven dollars a share."

Nik did the quick math in his head. Not believing the results, he opened the calculator app on his cell phone to double-check his figures. "Holy shit, I'm rich."

Mitchell, whose net worth was north of half a billion dollars, chuckled. "I wouldn't go that far, but, yeah, you're going to make out all right."

"Well, I don't know what to say," Nik said.

"'Thank you' always works."

"Yes, of course, thank you."

"You're welcome. You need to promise me you won't breathe a word about the filing to anyone until tomorrow. Understood?"

"Perfectly."

"Have a good evening, Nik," Mitchell said and hung up.

Nik sat on the tailgate, looking up at the sky and listening to the sounds of the ocean's waves as they crashed onto the nearby shore, and decided the first thing he'd do with his new-found wealth was purchase a stainless-steel sculpture from an artist he knew in Michigan.

He figured it was the least he could do for the man who was responsible for saving his life.

ACKNOWLEDGMENTS

I could not have completed one novel, let alone a series, without the encouragement, prodding, and support from a number of individuals along the way: Huntley Paton, a truly gifted writer who one day the world will discover; Philipp Harper, a sounding board for all things; Mark Caputo, an unwavering ally; the dedicated staff at Girl Friday Books; and last, but certainly not least, my life partner, Jennifer, who spent countless hours patiently listening and offering improvements to my day's efforts.

ABOUT THE AUTHOR

Mark Pawlosky is an award-winning reporter, editor, and media executive, as well as the author of four novels featuring *Newshound* reporter Nik Byron. A former reporter for the *Wall Street Journal*, editorial director for American City Business Journals (ACBJ), and editor in chief of CNBC.com/msn, Pawlosky oversaw financial news channels in the US, London, Munich, Paris, Tokyo, and Hong Kong. He successfully helped launch several news operations nationwide, including MSNBC, ACBJ, and *Biz Magazine*. A graduate of the Missouri School of Journalism at the University of Missouri, Pawlosky now lives on an island in the Pacific Northwest with his family.